THE HATMAKERS

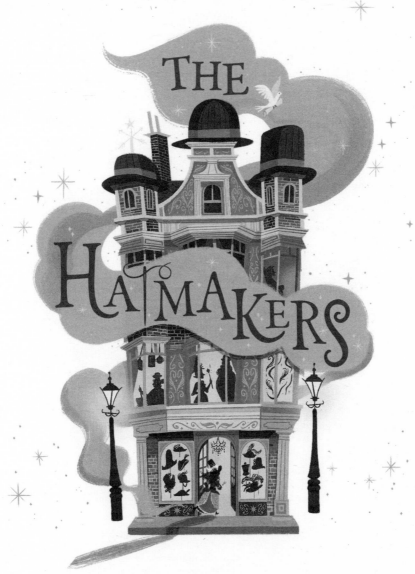

THE HATMAKERS

TAMZIN MERCHANT

Illustrated by PAOLA ESCOBAR

PUFFIN

PUFFIN BOOKS

UK | USA | Canada | Ireland | Australia
India | New Zealand | South Africa

Puffin Books is part of the Penguin Random House group of companies
whose addresses can be found at global.penguinrandomhouse.com.

www.penguin.co.uk
www.puffin.co.uk
www.ladybird.co.uk

First published 2021
001

Text copyright © Tamzin Merchant, 2021
Illustrations copyright © Paola Escobar 2021

The moral right of the author and illustrator has been asserted

Set in 13.3/18 pt Bembo Book MT Std
Typeset by Jouve (UK), Milton Keynes
Printed and bound in Great Britain by Clays Ltd, Elcograf S.p.A.

The authorized representative in the EEA is Penguin Random House Ireland,
Morrison Chambers, 32 Nassau Street, Dublin D02 YH68

A CIP catalogue record for this book is available from the British Library

HARDBACK ISBN: 978–0–241–42630–2
INTERNATIONAL PAPERBACK ISBN: 978–0–241–49197–3

All correspondence to:
Puffin Books
Penguin Random House Children's
One Embassy Gardens, 8 Viaduct Gardens, London SW11 7BW

For my family

List of illustrations

1   Hatmaker House   3   Glovemaker House

2   Bootmaker Mansion   4   Cloakmaker Hall

5 Watchmaker Lodge   7 The Guildhall

6 The Palace   8 Theatre Royal

CHAPTER 1

It was a wild and lightning-struck night. The kind of night that changes everything.

Jagged forks of light ripped across the sky and thunder rolled in tidal waves over the rooftops and spires of London. With the rain lashing down and the clouds crashing above, it felt like the whole city was under the sea.

But Cordelia Hatmaker was not afraid. In her candle-lit room at the very top of Hatmaker House, she was pretending to be aboard the *Jolly Bonnet*. The ship was being tossed by massive waves as she staggered across the deck (really her hearthrug), fighting a howling wind.

BOOM.

'Batten down those hatches, Fortescue!' she yelled. 'I've got to lash myself to the wheel!'

A tin soldier stared blankly from the mantel.

'Aye, aye, Cap'n!' Cordelia squeaked, out of the corner of her mouth.

BOOM.

'Enemy fire!' Cordelia cried, seizing the back of her wooden chair and heaving. Under her hands it became a great ship's wheel.

BOOM.

A violent gust of wind blew the window open. The candle sputtered out and Cordelia was plunged into darkness.

BOOM, BOOM, BOOM.

Echoing up the five storeys of Hatmaker House came the sound of somebody pounding on the front door.

Cordelia scrambled down the ladder from her bedroom and galloped along the top corridor. Aunt Ariadne emerged from her chamber, wrapped in a plum-coloured velvet dressing gown. Uncle Tiberius appeared, grizzle-headed from sleep.

'Father!' Cordelia cried, skidding past them. 'My father's home!'

BOOM, BOOM, BOOM.

Cordelia raced down the spiral staircase that twisted through the middle of Hatmaker House. She hurtled past Great-aunt Petronella, snoozing in front of the flickering lilac fire in her Alchemy Parlour. She rushed past the tall doors of the Hatmaking Workshop and, deciding that sliding down the corkscrew bannister would be quickest, in three heartbeats she reached the bottom floor.

Her bare feet slapped the cold tiles of the hallway. She shook her head to chase away the dizziness and ran (in not quite a straight line because she was still a little giddy) across the wide hall to the door.

White light flared across the sky as she turned the hefty key in the lock. A tall figure loomed through the pebbly window.

Thunder clapped overhead as she pulled open the heavy oak door.

A crack of lightning split the sky in two.

A man stood on the front step of Hatmaker House. He was drenched, ragged and gasping in the wind.

It was not her father.

CHAPTER 2

Cordelia stumbled backwards as the man lurched through the door, bringing the rain and the unruly wind into the house with him. His rich brocade cloak smelled of sea spray and salt.

'Lord Witloof!' It was Aunt Ariadne, carrying a lantern down the stairs. 'What on *earth* has happened?'

Lord Witloof was dripping a puddle of rainwater on to the hall floor.

'Alas, not *earth*, Madam Hatmaker, but sea!' Lord Witloof wheezed. 'Something has happened at *sea*!'

Cordelia felt as though a Siberian Ice Spider was crawling down her neck.

'Please, my Lord, tell us what has occurred,' said Uncle Tiberius.

'Has something happened to the *Jolly Bonnet*?' Cook appeared in the kitchen doorway, her hair in rag-rolls and a wooden spoon in her hand.

'Where is my father? Captain Hatmaker?' Cordelia's voice was thin and quivery with fear.

Lord Witloof took the black tricorn hat off his head and tipped out a large volume of water from its brim.

'The *Jolly Bonnet*,' he pronounced, 'has been sunk. She crashed on to those ghastly rocks that guard the entrance to Rivermouth.'

The wind howled through the house.

'But my father? Where is he?' Cordelia asked.

The Ice Spider was spinning a freezing web around her insides.

Lord Witloof looked down at his boots.

'I was there. Waiting at the top of the lighthouse to see that the ship was guided safely through the strait,' he muttered, gripping his hat, knuckles white. 'The palace has been most anxious for Captain Hatmaker to return with the final ingredient for the king's new hat. But tonight . . .'

Lord Witloof stopped, eyes filled with horror.

'The sails came into view through the storm,' he went on, face grey. 'I was close enough to hear the crew's cries on the wind, saw Captain Hatmaker himself at the wheel . . . but before the ship could pass the rocks to reach the safe haven of

Rivermouth, a terrible wave crested from the black ocean and cast the *Jolly Bonnet* upon them. The ship was matchsticks in a matter of moments.'

Cordelia was shaking her head. Then she realized her whole self was shaking.

'All went down with the ship,' Lord Witloof whispered. 'None survived.'

'But . . . no,' Cordelia said. 'My father is the best swimmer I know. He can swim through storms and whirlpools. He can't have sunk!'

Lord Witloof looked seasick and sad.

'Captain Hatmaker is lost at sea,' he said. 'I am sorry.'

Cordelia's grief and fury, stronger than her shaking legs, carried her back up the stairs. Aunt Ariadne's voice was a ragged flag fluttering behind her. A treacherous tide of tears swelled in her eyes as she felt her way along the top corridor. She wrenched open the door at the end and the achingly familiar smell of her father broke over her.

It was the smell of spices he brought back from his adventures, and cedar and woodsmoke and sea air. Cordelia launched herself on to his empty bed and buried herself in the scratchy wool blankets.

She lay with her face pressed into the pillow, feeling as

though the saddest song she had ever heard was trying to burst out of her. It howled through her stomach and into her chest and wound round her heart and up into her throat, where she could feel it juddering with despair.

'Cordelia?' whispered Aunt Ariadne, tiptoeing into the room.

The thunder rumbled overhead. It sounded like ships crashing on rocks.

'My poor Cordelia.'

Cordelia lay with her whole body tense, determined not to let the sad song out of her mouth. A warm hand rested on her back. Eventually her aunt said, 'This will help you sleep, my love.'

She stroked Cordelia's hair aside and Cordelia felt the velvet of a Moonbloom Nightcap being pulled gently on to her head.

The nightcap worked a dark-purple kind of magic and she was asleep in the space of a single sigh. Tentacles beckoned her from the deep and she called to her father, but her voice was lost among the shapes of waves. All night long the words *lost at sea, lost at sea, lost at sea* whispered to her in storm-tossed dreams, and an albatross keened and curled in a strange sky.

In the morning, she woke with an idea.

What is lost can be found.

CHAPTER 3

Cordelia pulled on her father's jacket. Its gold buttons glinted in just the same way hope does. She pushed up the sleeves and padded out of the room.

Hatmaker House was quiet. Through the window, the sky was a clean blue and the raindrops that speckled the windows glowed in the rays of pale-yellow sunlight.

The Library smelled of beeswax and polished wood and Turkish carpet. Thousands of books stood shoulder to shoulder on the shelves. Ancient grimoires, guides to new sciences, and tomes full of eldritch secrets all jostled for space. Some were taller than Cordelia's knees, with ridged leather spines; others were smaller than the palm of her hand and bound in jewel-coloured silk. They were all the kind of book whose pages whispered when she turned them.

It was so early that the Quest Pigeons still dozed in

their aviary beside the window, heads tucked under their wings.

'*Coo, coo,*' Cordelia hooted in a low voice. Several bright black eyes blinked at her, as she filled their tray with new seeds and poured fresh water into their dish.

She looked at one bird in particular.

'Agatha,' she said. 'My father is lost at sea and you're the only one who can find him.'

Agatha flurried her wings importantly and cooed.

Cordelia's father, Captain Prospero Hatmaker, had hatched Agatha himself, keeping her (as an egg) warm in his armpit. One day she pecked her way out of her shell to find herself cupped in his gentle hand, and decided he was the perfect mother.

When a Quest Pigeon is hatched this way, they will always fly to their mother, wherever they are in the world, to bring a message home. So Cordelia took a tiny scroll of paper from the top drawer of the desk and wrote:

> *Father, they say you are lost at sea. If you are lost you can be found. Please find yourself at sea as soon as you can*

There was hardly any room left on the scroll so she crammed in:

> *and please come home. Love Dilly*

9

She kissed the paper – carefully so she would not smudge the ink – and waved it in the air to dry. Then she rolled the scroll up tight and sealed it in a minuscule glass bottle with a cork and red wax.

She lifted Agatha gently out of the aviary and tied the bottle to the bird's leg. She could feel Agatha's little heart pattering triple time.

'To Prospero, to Prospero!' Cordelia whispered, like a spell.

She threw the window wide and Agatha took flight. Cordelia leaned out, watching until the bird was a pale speck above the new-washed houses of London.

'Cordilly?'

Uncle Tiberius was standing in the doorway, rubbing his sleep-creased face. He looked like a bear who had been woken from hibernation too early.

'Are you all right, little one?' he asked, his rumbly voice gentle.

'Yes, Uncle,' Cordelia answered. 'I've just sent a message to Father.'

Uncle Tiberius's shoulders sagged.

'Oh, Cordelia, my sweet girl,' he said.

'You see,' Cordelia explained, 'if he's *lost* at sea, that means he can be *found*. So I've sent Agatha to find him.'

'Little Hatmaker,' Uncle Tiberius said heavily, 'when a Quest Pigeon's mother is . . . gone . . . the poor confused pigeon just flies away . . . and is never seen again.'

Uncle Tiberius's eyes suddenly glistened and he blew his nose on a green silk hanky.

'Don't cry, Uncle!' Cordelia said, climbing on to a chair to pat his shaking shoulder. 'Agatha will find Father. He isn't *gone* – he's just *lost*, which is very different.'

Uncle Tiberius wiped his eyes.

'Now, let's look lively!' Cordelia grinned. 'We have to finish making the Concentration Hat for the king. They'll be expecting us at the palace!'

Usually on a palace delivery day, Hatmaker House was humming with a mixture of jollity and chaos. But the Hatmakers, except for Cordelia, were red-eyed, black-clad and slow that morning. Cook put extra honey on Cordelia's porridge and a heavy kiss on the top of her head.

Jones, the Hatmakers' coachman, leaned in through the kitchen window, clutching a cup of tea. He wore his smart blue uniform, an ink-black tricorn and a sombre expression.

Pale-faced at the head of the breakfast table, Aunt Ariadne bit a dry corner of toast. She adjusted a sprig of rue on her black Mourning Hat and said, 'I am sorry we must go to the palace today, Cordelia, my brave girl. Being Hatmakers to the Crown has its burdens, and duty beckons.'

'And we can't be outdone by the blasted Bootmakers. Or

those finicky Glovemakers, for that matter,' Uncle Tiberius growled, stirring his porridge moodily.

'Nor the Watchmakers or the Cloakmakers!' Cordelia added.

'Twitchers and posers,' Uncle Tiberius muttered.

'And anyway,' Cordelia finished, 'Father would want us to go.'

Aunt Ariadne's mouth went a little wonky. 'We must finish the hat as best we can, even though it will be without the special ingredient Prospero was bringing home.'

'What was the ingredient?' Cordelia asked.

'An ear feather from the Athenian Owl of the Platonic Forests,' replied Uncle Tiberius. 'Wisest bird in the world: it goes to great lengths to avoid human company. It would have kept the king closely focused on his work and keen to remain undisturbed.'

'Run along and help Great-aunt Petronella with her fire, my Cordelia,' Aunt Ariadne said, in a peculiar wobbling voice.

'Give it some vim, child!' Great-aunt Petronella croaked.

Cordelia pumped the wheezy bellows so hard that the lilac fire leaped into life, licking violet tongues of flame up the sooty chimney. The Alchemy Parlour danced with purplish shadows as the fire threw flickering light over the brass instruments. Great-aunt Petronella placed her cool hands on Cordelia's cheeks.

'You are a strong girl,' the ancient lady said with a kind of fierce caw.

Cordelia thought the grown-ups were being rather silly, all dressed in layers of black and telling her she was brave and strong.

'I know you think Father has drowned. I did too, last night,' she said to her great-aunt. 'But actually, when I woke up, I realized he's just *lost*. It's very different, you know. And he once survived twelve days on a leaky raft floating on the ocean. He can survive anything.'

Prospero Hatmaker had, indeed, survived twelve days drifting at sea on a shard of broken hull. And so had Cordelia. It was her favourite story.

'You were born on the ocean, littlest Hatmaker,' Cordelia's father would tell her. 'Your mother and I went on many ingredient-seeking adventures together. One day, we realized we had a third Hatmaker on our journey with us: you! You arrived in the world one very starry night, a little way off the coast of Morocco. The whole crew threw a party and your mother and I were overjoyed. We didn't have a crib on the ship, so we made a hatbox into a cradle and you slept very happily. It was the hatbox that saved you . . .

'Many weeks later, a terrible storm broke over us out of a blue sky. The mast was struck by lightning and our ship caught fire. I was at the wheel, trying to steer us out of the storm, when I saw your mother run down into the belly of the ship. She emerged through fire and smoke with the hatbox in her arms.

'Just then, with a calamitous screech, the ship ripped in two; fire had torn it right down to the keel. The world seemed to split in half and your mother hurled the hatbox across the chasm, across the churning water. I dived for you. The hatbox landed on the crest of a wave as I threw myself into the ocean. When I surfaced, half of the ship was gone. I dragged myself on to the wrecked remains. By a miracle, you were alive, though very wet and wriggling in your hatbox.

'All night, I searched for survivors. But I saw by the light of the rising sun that your mother was gone. The crew were gone. You and I were the only ones left, stranded on a half-sunk ship and surrounded by miles and miles of empty ocean.

'After twelve days, we were picked up by a passing Portuguese caravel and eventually I arrived back in London with you – the greatest treasure I've ever brought home.'

Her father always wore a seashell hanging from a chain round his neck. A tiny painting was inside, no bigger than Cordelia's eye. It was a portrait of her mother. Cordelia could stare at the painting for hours, at her smooth skin, her halo of dark hair, and her kind, smiling eyes. It held her spellbound.

'You look just like her, littlest Hatmaker,' her father always said, his eyes full of love. 'Her beauty and cleverness were her gifts to you.'

Cordelia would smile at her father when he said this, and reply, 'What are *your* gifts to me, Father?'

He would grin back and say, 'The gifts of a Hatmaker. Wildness in your wits and magic in your fingertips!'

'You are a brave girl, as well as strong.' The croaky voice of Great-aunt Petronella broke into Cordelia's thoughts.

Cordelia blinked. Her great-aunt was gazing at her with pride and sadness.

'He's not dead,' Cordelia told her firmly. 'He'll come back. I've sent Agatha.'

Her great-aunt gave her a kiss on the forehead and a Sunsugar toffee from her tin.

'Cordelia! I need you in the workshop!' Aunt Ariadne called up the stairs.

CHAPTER 4

For as long as Cordelia could remember, she had been helping her family with their craft. Before she could walk, she had crawled between the oak benches in the workshop, carrying ribbons and lace in her mouth. If they arrived a little damp, her uncle would patiently dry them by the fire before stitching them on to his creations.

When she began to walk, she staggered across the Trimming Room with feathers for hats held carefully aloft. She toddled through plumes of steam from her aunt's hat blocks and tottered around eddies of crystal light swirling in the Alchemy Parlour.

The first words she learned were written in spiky runes, from the whispering books in the Library. She made friends with the lush plants that burst from the glasshouse perched on the roof, became acquainted with the stars through her great-aunt's stargazing telescope, and gave all the Quest Pigeons names.

She wrapped the Moon Cactus in a woolly scarf when there was snow on the ground and cooled the Vesuvian Stone with a fan in summer, to stop it oozing lava on to her great-aunt's table. She knew the brushes that were brusque unless you talked to them politely, and she was the only one who could coax the Timor Fern to unfurl a new frond, by whispering kind things to it.

Hatmakers had lived in this house for more generations than anyone could quite remember. Magic from the ingredients, brought home from adventures all around the world, had seeped into the grain of the wood and into the time-worn stones. The wrinkled glass of the old windows, the walls and even the chimney pots bristled and shivered with their own eccentric magic.

Some of the magic was rather exasperating. For example, if you trod on the workshop hearthrug in the wrong place, it would deliberately trip you up. One of the floorboards was very ticklish and tended to wriggle if you walked over it. Uncle Tiberius often got impatient with the cupboard where invisible things were kept. The door of the cupboard had slowly faded – from being inconspicuous, it had become obscure, then completely invisible. But when her uncle could not find it, Cordelia knew just how to squint at the wall to glimpse the handle.

Useful around the house as Cordelia was, she was not actually allowed to make any hats herself.

'Ingredients are unpredictable,' her aunt often warned her. 'They can be exceedingly harmful if used in the wrong way. And some ingredients should never be used at all.'

These forbidden ingredients were locked away in the Menacing Cabinet, an iron cupboard in the workshop. Cordelia was always sent out of the room when it was opened. She was very curious about the treacherous treasures it contained, but had never managed to glimpse any of them. Anything gathered during a ingredient-seeking expedition that was deemed too perilous to use was locked away behind its iron walls, and the key to the Menacing Cabinet was always on Aunt Ariadne's belt.

The Hatmakers' motto was inscribed in Latin across the doors of the cabinet:

NOLI NOCERE

It meant 'Do no harm', which was the most important principle in Hatmaking.

Cordelia once heard Prospero and Uncle Tiberius weighing a single whisker from a Sabre Tiger. She'd had her ear pressed to the keyhole of the Hat-weighing Room when she heard her uncle sigh: 'It's far heavier than my strongest measure of Menace, Prospero! It will have to go in the Menacing Cabinet.'

For as long as Cordelia could remember, she had
been helping her family with their craft.

So the Menacing Cabinet had been opened and the whisker locked away.

Cordelia had even heard whispers that the cabinet contained a Croakstone, but she didn't dare ask about *that*.

She had, however, tried to bargain with her aunt on several occasions about Hatmaking in general.

'I wouldn't make a *bad* hat!' she reasoned, making her eyes as big and sincere as she could. 'I'd make a really *nice* hat. A very safe one.'

'You're not old enough, Cordelia,' her aunt always answered. 'You still have a lot to learn before you can even *think* about making your first hat.'

But Cordelia *did* think about making her first hat. She longed to wrap a bright skein of felt round a hat block, cover it with ribbons and feathers and gems and twisting twigs, lace it with pearls and stud it with buttons and shells and flowers and –

'It's absolutely out of the question,' was always her aunt's final word on the matter.

That was never an exciting thing to hear.

Aunt Ariadne had a gold hatpin, decorated with an emerald as big as a gooseberry. She would stick it in her hair with a purposeful jab before rolling up her sleeves to start on a new hat. The hatpin contained the power to make her aunt a brilliant and enchanting Hatmaker.

Uncle Tiberius had a sleek silver hatpin that he kept tucked into his breast pocket. Great-aunt Petronella's was always stuck through her bun, its red stone gleaming. Prospero's hatpin was whittled from the branch of a Fleetwood tree and he wore it in his captain's hat.

Every birthday Cordelia hoped to be given one of her own: a hatpin that would make her a Hatmaker. Having a hatpin would finally allow her to begin the work her fingers itched to do. But she knew that, like all Hatmakers before her, she would only be allowed to make her first hat on her sixteenth birthday.

It felt like several lifetimes away.

As a very special treat, on her eleventh birthday, she had been allowed to brush the freshly blocked hats with a stiff badger-hair brush to make them shine.

'On your twelfth, littlest Hatmaker, you will begin learning about the powerful ingredients we use to trim hats. We'll begin with feathers,' Prospero had promised. 'Feathers have so much magic and personality in them.'

Today, with a few months still to wait before her twelfth birthday, Cordelia ran into the workshop to find her uncle bending over the sage-green hat on the hat block, sewing a garland of rosemary on to the wide velvet brim.

'Rosemary for remembrance,' he murmured.

Her aunt and uncle had laid aside their black Mourning Hats while they worked. Both of them now had frilly bonnets on, tied with big canary-yellow bows under their chins.

'I know we look rather silly,' Aunt Ariadne said when she saw Cordelia's eyes widen, 'but we cannot allow our own sadness to creep into the king's hat. It would ruin all our hard work. So we're wearing Blithe Bonnets while we finish it, to keep our spirits up.'

She offered Cordelia a bonnet, but Cordelia did not take it.

'I don't need it, thank you, Aunt,' Cordelia said.

Aunt Ariadne turned away, her face hidden by the blowsy frills of the bonnet.

Cordelia knew that her aunt was trying very hard to be positive. A Hatmaker's state of mind was vitally important while making a hat. Aunt Ariadne had told her more than once: 'It is most important to keep good intentions flowing from your mind to your hands to the hat.'

If a Hatmaker was sad or angry or careless or fidgety, for example, their state of mind would be transferred to the hat, and then to the wearer of the hat once it was on their head. Uncle Tiberius once told her about a Hatmaker who had been moonishly in love with his sweetheart while making a Gravitas Hat for a politician. The Hatmaker's love suffused the Gravitas Hat with a blossoming adoration, which, when the politician put it on, gave him an overwhelming sense of love for the Leader of the Opposition. (Cordelia suspected that Uncle Tiberius himself was the maker of that particular hat, though he had never admitted it.)

'Spider silk,' Aunt Ariadne pronounced, turning back to Cordelia and holding up a silver skein of delicate web. 'Spun by a Brown Study Spider and collected yesterday before moonrise. Come, Cordelia, I need your help with it. Remember to concentrate.'

Cordelia held her hands out wide while Aunt Ariadne carefully wound the fine spider silk round them. Soon a shining bridge of silver was swagged between her hands.

'Now twist it round,' Aunt Ariadne instructed.

Cordelia turned her hands, making the threads twist together to form a slender silken rope. Aunt Ariadne snipped it and knotted it neatly at both ends.

'Next, we shall sew this to the hat, starting here, just above the left eye . . .' Aunt Ariadne pinned the spider-silk rope on to the hat. 'And twist it clockwise round the crown to the very tip . . .'

Cordelia watched in admiration as her aunt skilfully wound the gleaming rope round the hat.

'And it should help to encourage the king's concentration, which is what this hat has been commissioned for.'

Cordelia nodded. Her aunt turned to her.

'Can you tell me why I chose silk from a Brown Study Spider?'

Cordelia thought for a moment before answering. 'You

chose spider silk because spiders work hard to make their webs, and this hat is to help the king to work hard . . . and a *Brown Study* Spider likes paper and silence, and the king needs paper and silence to concentrate.'

'Excellent.' Aunt Ariadne smiled. 'We should finish it off with a fresh flower from the St Aegis Vine. Will you fetch one?'

Cordelia ducked under the drying lines, which were hung with freshly dyed silks, and dashed up the stairs to the glasshouse. As she passed the Alchemy Parlour, a cloud of sky-blue smoke billowed out of the door.

'Splendid!' she heard Great-aunt Petronella crow. 'The Fathom Glass droplet is nearly ready!'

Cordelia swerved into the dark parlour to see her great-aunt holding a shimmering droplet in a pair of iron tongs. It looked like liquid sunlight. A hot smell peppered the air. Alchemy, to Cordelia, seemed a strange mixture of poetry and science.

'Ah, child – fetch me the jar from the windowsill,' Great-aunt Petronella croaked. 'Careful, it's full of Thunder Rain.'

Cordelia pushed open the window and carefully picked up the jar that stood on the sill. It was brimful of storm-grey rainwater, which sloshed a little as she carried it across the room. A rumble of thunder rolled up from the jar and a tiny crack of lightning flashed across the water.

'It's good and fresh,' Great-aunt Petronella said with a smile as Cordelia set it down on the table.

Her great-aunt plunged the glowing droplet into the water. A huge plume of steam burst like a nimbus cloud into the room. In the air around them, tiny zig-zags of lightning crackled and zapped.

When Great-aunt Petronella came back into view through the rising cloud of steam, Cordelia saw that the glass droplet she held in the tongs was now crystal-clear and shining.

'This Fathom Glass will help the king to focus on what matters,' her great-aunt explained.

'How did it change like that?' Cordelia asked.

'Storm water is the best strengthener. Sometimes surviving a storm is the making of a person.'

Cordelia's breath caught in her throat. Great-aunt Petronella fixed her eyes on Cordelia. They were like two crystals glinting in the ancient folds of her face.

'What does one need to survive a storm? Good heart and good judgement,' she said steadily. 'Prospero has both.'

'Do you think –' Cordelia began.

The old lady held up one paper-pale hand for silence.

'The Glassmakers in Venice know all about storms,' she said. 'They have huge casks full of storm water. They collect different waters from different sorts of storms. And the collecting casks are big enough to bathe an elephant. Those Venetians are the masters of glass.'

'Have you been there and seen them?' Cordelia asked, round-eyed.

'Ah – a long time ago –' her great-aunt began, but she was interrupted by a shout from below.

'Cordelia! Where's that flower?'

'Coming, Aunt!' Cordelia called back, skidding out of the Alchemy Parlour and dashing up to the glasshouse.

A few minutes later, the newly made Fathom Glass droplet had been sewn on to the tip of the hat, where it hung like a fat bead of clear water. A pale-yellow blossom from the St Aegis Vine gleamed on the brim and the hat was taken to the Hat-weighing Room.

A large set of wooden scales stood in the middle of the room and hundreds of brass weights were ranked on shelves around the walls.

Uncle Tiberius selected a weight the size of an apple.

'Concentration,' he said, putting it on the scales. 'To the power of ten Engrossments.'

Aunt Ariadne carefully placed the hat on the other side of the scales. Slowly, the wooden contraption tilted like a see-saw and the hat sank down until it was level with the weight on the scales.

'Bravo!' Uncle Tiberius boomed. 'Concentration aplenty!'

'Try Sobriety,' Aunt Ariadne suggested.

'What's Sobriety?' Cordelia whispered, as Uncle Tiberius reached for a weight the size of a cannonball to test against the hat.

'It's an extra-special sort of Sensible,' her aunt whispered back.

The hat was slightly lighter than the measure of Sobriety so Uncle Tiberius tried a smaller weight. Against this one, the hat sank.

Aunt Ariadne nodded. 'It will do.'

Finally, Uncle Tiberius placed a tiny weight, no bigger than a ladybird, on the scales.

The hat and the tiny weight were perfectly balanced.

'What's that one?' Cordelia asked.

'Joy,' Uncle Tiberius murmured. 'In a small measure. Just to take the edge off all the work.'

The Hatmakers surveyed their creation. It was an elegant hat, pale grey-green and twisted about with silver and rosemary. Cordelia imagined the king wanting to spend all day and all night diligently working in his study once he had put it on.

Her uncle sniffed.

'It would have been better with the ear feather from the Athenian Owl,' he croaked, his voice cracked with sadness.

'Come now, Tiber,' Aunt Ariadne coaxed.

Usually after a new hat had been weighed, it was put in the hat hoist and winched down to the Hatmakers' shop on the ground floor.

This hat, however, was destined for the king.

Nestled in fine silks in a handsome grey hatbox tied with a navy-blue ribbon, the Concentration Hat was conveyed to the Hatmakers' carriage.

Jones had the carriage ready at the front door. He sat up in the driver's seat, holding the reins of two gleaming horses, who tossed their heads and whinnied, eager to set off.

Aunt Ariadne and Cordelia climbed in. Uncle Tiberius followed, holding the hatbox carefully. Great-aunt Petronella waved them off from her window.

Jones clicked the horses into a quick trot. The hatbox joggled on Uncle Tiberius's lap all the way from Wimpole Street to the palace.

There was silence inside the carriage. Aunt Ariadne sniffed occasionally and held Cordelia's hand tight in her black gloves. Uncle Tiberius frowned down at the hatbox. Both Aunt and Uncle had removed their bright Blithe Bonnets and donned their sombre Mourning Hats once again. The black hats filled the carriage with shadows. It was a quiet journey.

The palace, however, was in uproar.

Frilly red footmen with black velvet berets and skinny white-stockinged legs (they did look rather silly, Cordelia thought) chased around the vast courtyard. They were trying to catch hundreds of letters and papers that were looping and floating in the breeze.

The Hatmakers' carriage pulled up in the middle of the

mayhem. A dignified footman opened the door and the Hatmakers all climbed out.

'This way,' the footman said, directing them through the golden palace doors. His noble attempt to ignore the chaos unfolding around him was undermined when he was hit in the face by a flying sheet of paper.

Cordelia just had time to read a line of spidery writing that said:

His Majesty the king does hereby commission the Ironfire Cannon Factory to make 10,000 ...

Before she could continue, a panicked young servant, velvet cap half-covering his eyes, lunged for the paper and sent the footman reeling.

The Hatmakers knew the way to the king's chambers and they set off through the maze of corridors, Uncle Tiberius carrying the hatbox importantly before him. Grand ladies, maids and white-wigged courtiers alike turned to stare as the Hatmakers passed. Cordelia glowed with pride, marching along beside the hatbox destined for the king.

A maid carrying an armful of laundry gasped, 'Blimey! The *Hatmakers*!'

Cordelia grinned at her and the maid dropped her laundry in surprise.

When they arrived at the doors to the king's chambers,

there were four soldiers in silver and black uniforms standing guard. They seemed to be doing their best to ignore the strange bleating noises coming from inside the room. Oddly, there was one pale-blue boot lying on its side at their feet.

'Ah! Hatmakers!' one guard cried. 'We have been expecting you!'

He pushed open the doors and the Hatmakers entered the king's chamber.

King George was on his throne. But that was the only normal thing about the scene they saw before them.

The king was wearing nothing but lacy bloomers, shiny snakeskin shoes and an unbuttoned scarlet jacket. And he was not *sitting* on his throne. He was *standing* on it on one leg, baaing like a lost sheep. He had a velvet glove draped over an ear, a radish up one nostril and the other blue boot balanced on his head.

CHAPTER 5

'Your Majesty,' Aunt Ariadne uttered, bowing deeply.
Cordelia and Uncle Tiberius bowed too.

The king's chamber was in turmoil. Papers and clothes littered the floor, a peacock flapped on a footstool and the curtains blew at the open windows. The king's curly white wig was perched, lopsided, on a statue of a Greek goddess.

Princess Georgina stood tense beside her father's throne, dressed in a beautiful gown of pale-pink silk. She was holding a shimmery purple cloak in clenched fists and seemed to be trying not to cry.

Lord Witloof stood on the king's other side. He looked even more tired than he had at the Hatmakers' door last night. But he was there, dutifully prepared to catch His Majesty if he lost his balance and fell.

'Ah, my hat people!' the king declared. 'A spoon is a spoon until it is holey, and then 'tis a fork to eat jam roly-poly.'

Uncle Tiberius inclined his head gravely. 'Indeed, Your Majesty.'

'Write that down, Perkins,' the king said to the peacock, plucking the radish from his nose and munching it.

Cordelia giggled and Aunt Ariadne poked her in the ribs.

The king looked keenly at Cordelia. 'A child's laughter is the best medicine,' he said, waving the radish leaves. 'Excepting, of course, in cases of excessive hiccups. Then one must be sat upon by a springer spaniel until it stops.'

Cordelia nodded politely.

'Clap this madman in irons!' King George bellowed, leaping down from the throne, crunching a silver fobwatch underfoot as he landed. Then he kicked up a great pile of papers and sniggered as they fell around him like autumn leaves.

'Majesty, I beg you, do not kick those papers,' Lord Witloof implored. 'They are important documents to ensure we keep peace with France!'

'Shall we try again, my lord?' the princess suggested, shaking the purple cloak.

Lord Witloof nodded.

'I shall ready the documents,' he whispered, shuffling the papers back into order as the king became distracted by his own reflection in a golden plate. Lord Witloof piled the

32

papers on to the desk by the window and dipped a swan's-feather quill in the inkpot.

'Will you please be bait again?' the princess asked him.

Lord Witloof sighed, before holding the quill up over his head like a cockatoo's crest.

'Come and get me, Your Majesty,' he cooed.

The king stopped pulling faces into the shiny plate and crept towards the lord like a cat stalking a sparrow. When he paused to pretend to wash his whiskers, the princess threw the cloak over his shoulders.

For a moment King George stood rigid and tall, suddenly regal. The cloak flowed around his shoulders and Lord Witloof swept him towards the desk.

'Sign here, Your Majesty! Just *GR*, that will do,' Lord Witloof said, in a jovial, encouraging sort of voice.

The king took the quill, gazing down at the papers.

Nobody breathed as he raised it, twirled it once in his hand – and suddenly tickled Lord Witloof's nose with it.

'*Nah-CHOOO!*' Lord Witloof sneezed.

Cackling with furious glee, the king swept the entire pile of papers out of the open window and smashed the inkpot for good measure.

The princess sobbed.

'Enough of that guff!' the king cried, jumping up. 'Watch my polka!'

His Majesty twirled round and round his disordered room,

flinging the purple cloak out behind him like a pair of thistledown wings.

Lord Witloof stared despairingly out of the window at the papers drifting down to the ground.

'It is well past the time those papers were meant to be delivered,' he sighed, fishing in his jacket. He pulled out a glass pocket watch with a blue butterfly on its face and groaned. 'Lord above, *horribly* late! And His Majesty's behaviour is getting worse! He began by just being a little flighty – playing with his food, doing silly voices and such. But it's so bad now that he can't concentrate even for a minute! It's all farting and dancing and refusing to put on his trousers!'

Cordelia could see how difficult it must be to have an excessively silly king running amok in the palace, though she did think he danced an excellent polka. The king tried to whirl his daughter into the dance, but she pulled her hands away.

Her father is lost too, in a different way from mine, Cordelia thought.

'Everything he's tried only works for a moment or two!' the princess burst out. 'The Watchmakers' Logic Watch only worked for two seconds, and now it's smashed to bits; the Bootmakers' Pondersome Boots didn't even reach his feet; the Heavy-handed Gloves from the Glovemakers wouldn't stop him fidgeting even for a minute. And the Cl– Oh, no!'

The king had thrown the cloak off the state balcony and

was gazing in wonder as it swam down through the air like a strange purple jellyfish.

'You are our last chance, Hatmakers! If this hat does not cure my father of his baffling behaviour, I don't know what else is to be done!'

'We have actually called for the king's doctor,' Lord Witloof told them. 'To see if he can shed any light on this. Please fetch him, Probert.' He signalled to a footman, who hurried out.

'Dear me,' Uncle Tiberius murmured. 'A *doctor*. How modern.'

Moments later the footman returned, followed by a tall man wearing a serious frown to match his serious moustache.

'Ah, Doctor Leech, do come in,' Lord Witloof said.

'Good morning, Your Highness.' The doctor nodded gravely. 'Lord Witloof.'

He raised one eyebrow at the Hatmakers before setting his black bag down on the desk.

'I was just telling the Hatmakers how it is vitally important that the king ceases this silliness,' Lord Witloof continued soberly. 'France is threatening war. And if His Majesty cannot concentrate long enough to sign these papers, the whole kingdom will be in danger. It is a most distressing situation.'

Aunt Ariadne opened the hatbox and lifted out the Concentration Hat. Doctor Leech looked down his nose at it.

'I am sorry to tell Your Highness and Your Excellency,' Aunt Ariadne said, 'that this hat is incomplete.'

Princess Georgina looked crestfallen.

'As Lord Witloof may have told you, Your Highness, my brother, Prospero Hatmaker, has been lost at sea along with the family ship,' Uncle Tiberius began. But he stopped suddenly and flourished his green silk handkerchief in front of his face. Princess Georgina's hands flew to her mouth and Lord Witloof looked wretched.

The king pranced gaily past them, riding his sceptre like a hobby horse.

'He was bringing back a rare feather, from the Athenian Owl, which we are sure would have helped His Majesty . . .' Aunt Ariadne explained.

The doctor cleared his throat, but Cordelia thought it sounded as though he was smothering a scornful laugh. Aunt Ariadne's voice tailed off and a sorrowful silence held the room, punctuated by the clip-clopping the king was making for his pretend horse.

'Prospero Hatmaker was a good man,' Lord Witloof declared. 'We were at Cambridge together, though he was several years below me, of course, studying Alchemic Theory and Practice. He won the Dee Prize in his first year for decocting Spiritus Sancti, if I recall. England has lost a fine adventurer and an excellent Hatmaker.'

We shall see about that! Cordelia's thought blazed, fire-bright.

Uncle Tiberius sniffed then said firmly, 'We must be-hat the king, and, in the absence of the Athenian Owl feather, trust that we have done enough.'

'Of course,' Aunt Ariadne added delicately, 'in the oldest customs of the Makers of the Royal Garb, the clothes are most powerful when all of them are worn together . . .'

She glanced around at the scattered clothes.

Lord Witloof sighed. 'Indeed, but it is difficult enough to persuade him to put on *one* thing, Madam Hatmaker.'

All heads turned to the king, who had abandoned the sceptre and was dangling upside down from a long velvet curtain. It was decidedly difficult (though not unheard of) to put a hat on an upside-down head.

'Your Majesty, please come down from there,' Lord Witloof wheedled. 'You are the Commander of the King's Army and the Grand Admiral of the Royal Navy, but you can sensibly be neither with your feet up over your head.'

'Majesty, here is a very fine hat for you to try,' Aunt Ariadne said in a sing-song voice.

The king looked sideways at the hat. Lord Witloof took a step forward and the king shrieked and tried to scramble up the curtains.

'He'll fall!' cried the princess.

The king howled, clinging to the brass curtain pole. The princess, Lord Witloof and the Hatmakers all beseeched His Majesty to come down. The doctor watched with folded arms.

Poor king, Cordelia thought. *It must be very difficult to always have to be sensible. It must be awful for people to take you terribly seriously at all times. And it must be so lonely to have nobody to dance with.*

So, without really thinking about it, she began to dance.

She held out her skirts and romped in a circle, whistling a shanty her father had taught her. She leaped into the air and threw her arms above her head and wiggled her fingers.

The king was enthralled. He gazed at the dancing girl, eyes filled with wonder. Slowly, he slid down from the curtains, and Aunt Ariadne gently motioned for everybody to step aside.

The king inched towards Cordelia, joining in with her song.

She tapped her toe; he tapped his toe.

She twirled; he twirled.

She stood on her tiptoes and floated her arms out by her sides and so did he, and –

'There!' breathed Aunt Ariadne, placing the hat on the king's head.

The king changed.

Cordelia was almost nose to nose with him when it happened: the Concentration Hat was working its magic.

CHAPTER 6

The frenzied expression melted from the king's face. Cordelia was surprised to see a look of desolate sorrow sweep into his eyes.

'Oh,' she said very quietly.

'Yes,' answered the king. He sighed the sigh of a sensible, sad man.

'Why?' Cordelia whispered.

'I will tell you,' replied the king. 'But first I must take off my shoes!'

He began hopping up and down on one foot, tugging at his tightly buckled shoe.

'Oh dear,' Lord Witloof groaned.

'The hat has failed,' Doctor Leech said, stepping forward.

'No! It's working!' Cordelia objected.

The doctor ignored her. He took the king's wrists, but the king resisted, reaching for his shoes.

'Could we at least *try* to dress him in all the clothes at once?' Aunt Ariadne suggested, picking up a Heavy-handed Glove.

'We should try,' Lord Witloof agreed, as Cordelia retrieved a blue Pondersome Boot. 'We must leave no stone unturned.'

There was a scuffle between the doctor and the king, and the beautiful green-and-silver hat fell off the royal head and was trodden upon. The spider silk tangled around the king's foot and the smell of crushed rosemary wafted through the room.

'*No!*' Uncle Tiberius wailed.

'We are wasting time with these fripperies!' the doctor snapped, kicking the ruined hat away. 'Now is the time for science, not old-fashioned superstitious nonsense.'

'*Non*sense!' Uncle Tiberius burst out indignantly, but Aunt Ariadne laid a hand on his arm and he fell silent.

The doctor stuck his finger in the king's ear and pronounced, 'It is as I thought. His brain is too hot. He should be sent on a trip to the seaside. Sea air will blow the excessive heat away.'

Lord Witloof crinkled his forehead. 'Is there no immediate cure?' he asked. 'I do not think the king should be away from the palace . . .'

The doctor shook his head firmly. Princess Georgina gave a sob, and the lord placed a comforting hand on her arm, saying, 'Let us trust the doctor, Your Highness. A holiday at the seaside will clear his head. He'll be good as new soon.'

The king was now blowing raspberries at Doctor Leech.

'I shall take His Majesty to his bedchamber,' the doctor announced. 'And prepare him to travel tonight.'

The doctor led the king out of the room, enduring the very rude raspberry noises. Princess Georgina forlornly watched him go.

Uncle Tiberius and Aunt Ariadne were silent. But Cordelia could not stop herself.

'He only wanted to take off his shoes!' she cried.

'A king is never seen without his shoes,' Lord Witloof said seriously. 'It is considered most undignified.'

He turned with great ceremony to the princess.

'Your Highness, Princess Georgina,' Lord Witloof intoned. 'As the king's only heir, it is your solemn duty to assume the duties of your father, while he is absent.'

The princess stood, bewildered, amid the chaos her father had left.

'Do not fear, Your Highness,' he continued. 'As Lord Privy Councillor, I shall be with you every step of the way.'

He bowed low, his nose almost touching his knee. The princess gave him a grateful smile.

Cordelia suddenly had an idea. 'Does that mean *you're* the Grand Admiral of the Navy now, Your Highness?'

The princess paused, looking uncertainly at Lord Witloof, who nodded.

'Yes,' the princess said. 'I suppose I am.'

Cordelia felt a surge of hope break like a wave in her chest.

'Please can you send a ship to look for my father?' she asked. 'He's lost at sea, and he'd be found so much more quickly if the fastest ship in the Navy was sent –'

Before the princess could respond, Lord Witloof shook his head.

'I'm afraid that will be impossible, my dear Miss Hatmaker,' he said gravely. 'No ship can be spared while France threatens war. They must all wait in the English Channel in case of an attack.'

'But –' Cordelia started to argue.

Princess Georgina got there first. 'Surely one boat –' the princess began, but Lord Witloof cut across her.

'No boats can be spared, I am afraid!' he said fretfully. 'Not even the post boat. War could erupt at any moment and every vessel is needed to defend our shores. The king would agree with me, Your Highness, if he was not being so silly.'

The princess blushed. Cordelia swallowed a protest as Lord Witloof smiled down at her in an understanding sort of way.

'Even if your dear father somehow survived the wreck,' he

said, 'the currents around the Rivermouth rocks are treachery itself.'

When the Hatmakers sat down for supper that night, Prospero's absence solidified around them, like snow hardening to ice.

Aunt Ariadne stared silently at the tablecloth while Uncle Tiberius muttered darkly about doctors. Great-aunt Petronella fidgeted. Cordelia kept twisting in her seat to look out of the window. Around the shoulders of neighbouring buildings, fog was settling in a thick cloak.

Would Agatha rest overnight, or try to find her way home in the dark with the message from Father?

Though none of the Hatmakers desired even one bite of food, Cook had other plans. Every meal she made was a symphony of deliciousness. 'Food is a kind of magic, just like Hatmaking,' she'd once whispered to Cordelia, sprinkling a pinch of pepper over a dish. 'Food can heal all manner of maladies.'

Cook would stir up herby stews to soothe hurt feelings, bake honey cakes to mend broken hearts, make crinkle-crusted pies for courage, and melting-cheese pastries to bolster tired souls. Her cucumber soup could cool a hot temper and her bread-and-butter pudding inspired kindness in even the grumpiest person. Her roast potatoes seemed to help with everything.

Tonight she brought a huge plate, laden with roast potatoes, to the table. Their golden hot scent made everyone look up.

'Here we are,' Cook clucked, dishing up a small mound of potatoes on each plate. 'Start with these and we'll see how we go.'

Through a clever combination of temptation and praise, Cook coaxed each Hatmaker to finish their dinner. Then she brought out a caramel custard and a jug of cream. Half an hour later, she ushered the Hatmakers up to bed.

'Sleep well, my love,' Cook said, kissing Cordelia on the head. 'Things will feel a little bit better in the morning.'

Cordelia smiled drowsily at Cook, thinking, *I won't sleep! I'll stay wide awake until Agatha gets back.*

But somehow, when she clambered under the blankets, her limbs grew heavier and heavier as sleep called her down into the deep.

When Cordelia woke, the fog had cleared in the morning sun, but there was still no sign of Agatha. In the Library she filled up the Quest Pigeons' seed tray, frowning.

The birds cooed, blinking at her. One tendril of doubt clung like a cobweb around Cordelia's brain, but she shook it – hard – out of her mind.

'Agatha will be back very soon, with Father's exact

location,' she said, as she tickled Margaret's tawny wing. 'He'll have drawn me a star-map to show where he is. I'll be head of the rescue expedition.'

'MAAAAAAK-ING!'

A sudden, terrible squawking erupted outside. Cordelia fumbled with the latch of the window and stuck her head out into the morning air.

On the street below stood a small figure. It was human but there was a lot of flapping going on, rather as though it was a large brown bird. It wore a ragged assortment of clothes topped with a too-big cloth cap. And it was holding a newspaper in each hand and waving them in the faces of passers-by.

'MAAAAAAK-ING!' the figure shouted, making a passing gentleman in a blue waistcoat jump, but a coachman took a copy and flipped a coin to the flapping figure.

'MAAAAAA–'

'HELLO!' shouted Cordelia.

The figure looked up: she saw a grubby face with big eyes and a bigger smile. It was a boy about Cordelia's age. He brandished a newspaper at her and shouted, 'MAAAAAAK–'

'Why,' interrupted Cordelia, 'are you shouting so loudly this early in the morning?'

'Sellin' papers!' said the boy.

'Could you do it a bit more quietly?' asked Cordelia.

'Don't sell 'em so easy if I'm quiet,' said the boy. 'Gotta yell 'em the news so they buy the paper.'

'Out of interest, what is the news this morning?' Cordelia enquired.

'MAAAAAAK-ING!' the boy shouted at the top of his lungs, frightening a milkman and a pigeon in one go. The Hatmakers' horses whinnied in their stable and the donkey from across the way brayed.

Cordelia covered her ears.

'What *is* Maaaaaak-ing, in plain English?' she asked.

He coughed and said, 'Mad king.'

'Wait there, please – I'm coming down!' Cordelia said to the boy.

CHAPTER 7

Cordelia poured two cups of Honeymilk tea from the copper kettle hanging over the kitchen fire. She carried the steaming cups out on to the street and handed one to the boy.

He took it gratefully and emptied it with a single gulp.

'Blimey!' he said. His eyes flicked to Cordelia's full cup so she handed it to him as well.

'Try sipping it,' she suggested. But the boy had already swigged all the tea.

'MAAAAAAK-ING!' he bellowed, making her flinch.

A lady snatched a paper from the boy, tossed him a copper coin and stalked away, frowning. Cordelia frowned too when she glanced at the printed black letters.

~ THE DAILY SLAPP ~
ANTICS IN HIS PANTS FROM
HIS MAD-JESTY!

Under the headline was a collection of unkind comments about the king.

'How do they know he was only in his underpants?' Cordelia wondered.

'Oi!' said the boy. 'If ya wanna read it, ya gotta pay!'

Cordelia blushed, but he winked at her, pushing his cap up an inch to scratch his forehead.

'Wouldn't waste me money if I was you,' he said, grinning. 'Every time a grown-up buys a paper, all they do's frown at it. Why spend yer money on somefing makes ya miserable? I'd rather spend mine on a pet canary.'

'Do you have a pet canary?' Cordelia asked.

'No,' he said. 'But I'm savin' up for one.'

Cordelia felt she could definitely be friends with someone who wanted a pet canary. She held out her hand to the boy.

'Pleased to meet you. I'm Cordelia Hatmaker.'

'Cor,' said the boy. 'A real Hatmaker?'

'Cordelia,' Cordelia corrected. 'But you can call me Cor if you like.'

The boy rubbed his grubby hand on his grubby trouser leg. 'Sam Lightfinger,' he said, shaking her hand vigorously, brown eyes bright as a sparrow's.

'Nice to meet you, Sam.' Cordelia smiled.

'Miss Hatmaker! Come inside, please!'

It was Miss Starebottom, beckoning from the kitchen door. Miss Starebottom was Cordelia's governess. She carried a thin cane, which (Cordelia thought) made her look like a spindle-legged heron. She had a laugh to match: long and pointy. She was exactly what a governess was expected to be: plain and serious. But Cordelia also knew that she kept a secret supply of sweets in the pockets of her cloud-grey dresses.

When Cordelia first met Miss Starebottom, three years earlier, she had looked her new governess up and down and eyed her cane sideways.

'What's that for?' Cordelia had demanded.

Miss Starebottom studied her for a long moment.

'Pointing at things,' she eventually said.

'What kind of things?' Cordelia enquired.

'Algebra equations,' came the answer.

Cordelia wished she had not asked. But then Miss Starebottom had put her hand into her pocket and pulled out a bright, paper-wrapped sweet. The paper had crinkled when Cordelia unwrapped it and she decided, chewing the gooey caramel, that her new governess had potential.

Today the cane rapped importantly on the doorstep, so Cordelia said goodbye to Sam Lightfinger and ran inside with the empty cups.

'Don't run, Cordelia!' Miss Starebottom exclaimed.

Cordelia slowed to a stately walk.

'That's better,' Miss Starebottom said. 'Remember, we are trying to be *ladylike*.'

The governess closed the door behind Cordelia, so she did not see her roll her eyes. But when she caught sight of Cordelia's hands, Miss Starebottom gasped. 'Your hands are *filthy*, child! You must never shake hands with a ragamuffin! Wash at once. It's time for our morning walk.'

Cordelia's hands were, indeed, black and grimy. But she laughed as Cook passed her a bar of soap.

'He's not a ragamuffin, Miss Starebottom!' she said. 'He's a newspaper seller, see? This on my hands is only newsprint.'

The soap turned black and the water blacker. When her hands were clean enough, even for her governess, Cordelia pilfered two pieces of toast, spread thickly with honey, from the kitchen table. On her way out, she slipped a slice to Sam Lightfinger, who whispered, 'Cor – thanks, Cor!' as she and Miss Starebottom crossed the street.

By the time Cordelia and Miss Starebottom reached Hyde Park (promenading at a slow pace approved of by the governess), the toast was finished but the taste of honey lingered on Cordelia's lips. They walked to the Serpentine, a ribbon of lake glimmering in the greenery.

A small, round boy with an unfortunate haircut stood by the water's edge, holding a model boat under one arm.

'Goose!' Cordelia yelled, bounding over to him.

He grinned. 'Hello, Cordelia!'

'Good morning, Master Bootmaker,' Miss Starebottom said gravely.

'Good morning, Miss Starebottom.' The boy bowed politely.

Miss Starebottom surveyed the park to make sure there was nobody watching them. It was highly irregular for a Hatmaker and a Bootmaker to be on speaking terms. In fact, a Hatmaker had not been friends with a Bootmaker for several generations. Miss Starebottom (not to mention the children) would be in a considerable amount of trouble if either of their families found out about Goose and Cordelia's friendship. It would be almost as frowned-upon as a shoeless king.

Cordelia and Goose met secretly in Hyde Park several mornings a week. Miss Starebottom was also Goose's governess, although she had conveniently forgotten to tell the Hatmaker and Bootmaker families that she was educating both children. On Mondays, Wednesdays and Fridays Miss Starebottom taught Cordelia at Hatmaker House. On Tuesdays, Thursdays and Saturdays, she went three streets over to Bootmaker Mansion, to instruct Goose in arithmetic, drawing and letters. On Sundays she attended church and polished her pointy shoes.

Even though Miss Starebottom made them do algebra and walk everywhere much too slowly, Cordelia and Goose shared a kind of grudging affection for their governess. After all, she did have a pocketful of caramels. And she had introduced them to each other, when they had both, separately, been rather lonely children. Of course, Cordelia adored her family, and Cook and Jones and the Quest Pigeons, and the mice who lived behind the pantry skirting board at Hatmaker House. But there is nothing quite like having someone your own height to gallivant around with. Someone your own height always seems to see the world the same way you do.

But Miss Starebottom had not introduced Cordelia and Goose three years ago purely out of the goodness of her heart. In fact, this was another reason Cordelia and Goose secretly admired their governess. When the children met in the park, Miss Starebottom met a gentleman friend in the bushes. It was an arrangement that suited everybody involved.

'What's that you've got there?' Cordelia pointed at Goose's wooden boat as Miss Starebottom sloped away into the undergrowth.

'It's an exact replica of the *Polished Boot*,' Goose told Cordelia, his eyes shining. 'See, it's even got my brother Ignatius at the wheel!'

Goose held up the boat for Cordelia to see. Handkerchief-sized sails were hung between the spindles of masts, with thin string for the rigging. The hull and the balustrades were expertly carved, and at the tiny ship's wheel stood a whittled captain.

'It's brilliant!' Cordelia said.

Goose glowed with pride.

'Ignatius spent all voyage making it for me,' he said. 'He gave it to me when he got home.'

Cordelia paused.

'Did your brother's ship get through the storm safely?' she asked, a whirlpool twisting in her belly. 'And past the rocks that guard Rivermouth?'

'Ignatius said it was plain sailing,' Goose replied. 'And the lighthouse guided them round the Rivermouth rocks as usual.'

Cordelia blinked. Why had the lighthouse failed to guide the *Jolly Bonnet* and her crew past the rocks, too? It was a passage of water that every London sailor knew well. Her father had once told her: *When you line up the figurehead on the prow with the glowing lighthouse lantern, the boat slips through the water like a dream.* Captain Hatmaker had steered the ship past the jagged rocks a hundred times, using the lighthouse as his guide.

A frown creased Cordelia's face. Goose stopped tinkering with his model ship and said, 'Why d'you ask?'

Cordelia wanted to make the awful words sound as small

as possible but, whichever way she thought about saying it, they sounded huge.

'My father is lost at sea,' she blurted. 'The *Jolly Bonnet* was wrecked on the Rivermouth rocks.'

Goose seemed to sink a little.

'Cordelia,' he breathed, 'I'm so sor–'

'He's not dead,' Cordelia insisted loudly. 'He's just *lost*. He'll be found very soon.'

Goose nodded dumbly.

'Does it sail?' Cordelia asked, pointing at the model boat. She wanted him to stop looking at her with pity.

In answer, Goose knelt down and carefully placed the miniature galleon on the water. It bobbed and lilted on the lapping waves. He fiddled with the rigging and delicately turned the ship's wheel.

'I think, if we put the wind behind her and give her a push – YES!'

The little boat was skimming out into the middle of the lake, the wind filling its tiny white sails. Cordelia clapped and whooped and Goose danced on the spot with his hands in the air.

'Look at her go!'

'Just like the real ship on the ocean!'

The *Polished Boot* was out in the middle of the Serpentine now. A couple in a rowing boat stopped to let it pass. Cordelia and Goose watched it get smaller and smaller.

'Goose . . .' said Cordelia, a thought occurring to her.

'Yes?'

'How will your boat sail back?'

Goose looked as though he had swallowed a lemon.

They took off around the lake, Cordelia's hat ribbons flying out behind her and Goose's boots pounding the ground. Cordelia hoped Miss Starebottom was nowhere nearby, so she would not see her running at a most *unladylike* pace.

But, as they rounded the bend at the end of the lake, a much bigger problem than an annoyed governess presented itself.

Cordelia skidded to a stop and Goose collided with her a second later. Four children stood blocking the path: a pair of identical twin boys and a pair of identical twin girls. They grinned down at Cordelia and Goose with identical, malicious grins.

The Glovemaker children.

CHAPTER 8

'What do we have here?' one Glovemaker boy sneered. 'A Hatmaker and a Bootmaker in cahoots?'

Cordelia raised her chin defiantly (also so she could look the Glovemaker in the eye, because he was a head taller than her).

'It's none of your business!' she declared, hoping she sounded fiercer than she felt.

Behind her, Goose whimpered. The Glovemakers chuckled. One of the girls cracked her knuckles in her velvet gloves.

'Shouldn't you be out collecting severed heads for your hats, Hatmaker?' she jeered.

'And guts for your bootlaces, Bootmaker?' her twin added gleefully.

'What are you talking about?' said Cordelia.

'Pa says you Hatmakers use the heads of criminals to mould your hats on,' one of the boys said.

'He says you wait outside the Tower of London for the heads of traitors to fall off the spikes,' his twin continued. 'Then you put them in a bag and take them home.'

'That's not true!' Cordelia shouted.

She twisted on the spot, trying to keep all four Glovemakers in her sights at the same time. Goose was not helping. He was trembling so violently that Cordelia could hear his teeth chattering.

'The Bootmaker doesn't look brave enough to tie his *own* bootlaces, let alone pull the guts out of bodies to make new ones,' one of the girls taunted.

'What's the matter, Bootmaker?' one of the boys scoffed. 'Hatmaker got your tongue?'

His sisters giggled.

'She's going to put it on a hat!' one of them shrieked.

'Eurgh!'

'A Tongue Hat!'

All four Glovemakers waggled their tongues ghoulishly at Cordelia and Goose.

'Tongue Hat! Tongue Hat!'

Goose panicked and tried to push past the nearest Glovemaker, but the boy shoved him back into the middle of the circle.

'Scared someone'll scuff those shiny boots of yours?' he snarled, then stamped hard on Goose's toe. Goose yelped and clutched his foot.

'HEY!' Cordelia whirled round and one of the girls swatted at her hat, knocking it off her head. The other one stomped on it.

Cordelia snatched her crushed hat off the ground as the Glovemakers laughed. She scrunched up all her anger and disgust and fear and fury and funnelled it into her voice.

'Well, *I* heard,' she began, feeling for Goose's hand and squeezing it very hard, 'that the Glovemakers once made a pair of gloves for Queen Elizabeth ... THAT MADE HER SLAP HERSELF IN THE FACE CONTINUOUSLY FOR HALF AN HOUR IN FRONT OF THE SPANISH KING!'

The Glovemakers' faces went slack with surprise.

'RUN, GOOSE!'

Cordelia used the moment of shock to her advantage. She dived between the Glovemaker sisters, towing Goose behind her. Hatmaker and Bootmaker hurtled along the path, hand in hand, Glovemakers bellowing behind them.

Cordelia was fast, and fear spurred Goose on. They tore along the shore of the lake. But the Glovemakers were charging after them.

'Goose, we have to hide!'

'Where?' Goose wailed.

Cordelia yanked Goose off the path, into the middle of dozens of ducks settled on the bank. The birds took to the air, quacking angrily, and flew right into a party of sedate ladies strolling along the shore towards them.

'Perfect!'

Cordelia pulled Goose through the confusion of flapping parasols and flapping ducks and flapping ladies. They dived between the green curtains of a weeping willow leaning over the water. The leaves closed behind them, completely hiding them from view.

Goose fell to his knees in the shallows, red-faced and shaking. Cordelia sank down on a tree root sticking out of the water. She put a finger to her lips to warn Goose to be silent, but she needn't have worried: Goose looked as though he might never speak again.

They heard the ladies shriek as the Glovemakers shoved past them.

'Where are they?'

'We've lost them!'

To Cordelia's immense relief, the Glovemakers rushed away down the path. She made a tiny hole in the curtain of leaves and watched them storm out of sight beyond the bulrushes.

'They're gone,' she said, sighing.

Goose was goggling at his model boat, which was gently nudging his knee in the lapping shallows.

'Found it,' he murmured.

Cordelia grinned. 'There's the silver lining!'

Goose gave a wan smile.

'D'you think they're going to tell someone that we're friends?' he muttered.

Cordelia chewed her lip.

'If they do, they'll only tell their parents. And Hatmakers haven't spoken to Glovemakers for years anyway,' she reasoned.

'Same with the Bootmakers.'

'I think our secret's safe,' Cordelia concluded.

'But we should be careful,' Goose added.

They decided to stay hidden under the weeping willow for a little while, to make sure the Glovemakers did not come back again. As Cordelia counted the distant gongs of St Auspice's Church bell sounding the quarter-hour, she heard the slick sound of oars cutting water and Miss Starebottom's voice rang through the air, clear and close.

'Yes, Whitstable, but *when*?'

'I don't know, Delilah,' came the somewhat sulky reply. 'It takes some planning, hence the delay.'

Miss Starebottom was floating past, in a boat rowed by her mysterious gentleman friend.

'I am tired of waiting,' Miss Starebottom said with a sigh. 'I've been waiting *years*.'

Cordelia and Goose stared at each other, horrified to hear a private conversation between their governess and her sweetheart. Cordelia wanted to stick her fingers in her ears and sing a loud song, but she thought that might not help the situation.

'Well, *I* am ready, even if *you* are not –' they heard Miss

Starebottom say before her voice was lost beyond the sound of the lake kissing the shore.

Goose's face was pink and Cordelia's ears felt hot.

'Poor Miss Starebottom,' Cordelia whispered.

'She must have been waiting years for a proposal, Mother says,' Goose added.

Cordelia decided to be extra-good in her lessons later to try to make up for Miss Starebottom's disappointing romantic attachment.

'What does "hence" mean?' Goose asked, lifting his boat out of the water.

Cordelia shrugged. 'Better not ask Miss Starebottom,' she advised. 'But I think it's safe to come out now.'

Miss Starebottom was rather subdued for the rest of the day. Back at Hatmaker House, she wrote out fifty algebra problems for Cordelia to solve, and sat eating her sweets and humming a sad song while Cordelia worked. When Cordelia finished the algebra, Miss Starebottom did not even bother to look at it. Instead, she instructed Cordelia to walk up and down the corridor outside the Library, balancing a book on her head.

'But, Miss Starebottom,' Cordelia said, on her fifth lap of the corridor, 'wouldn't this book do me a lot more good if I was *reading* it? Not walking around with it on top of my head?'

'Unfortunately, Cordelia –' Miss Starebottom sniffed back a tear, tapping her cane moodily against her leg – 'a lady who cannot walk elegantly is not considered worth listening to.'

Cordelia felt that this was distinctly untrue, but she did not want to argue with her governess when she was feeling so low. Cordelia gave Miss Starebottom her handkerchief to wipe her eyes and tried her best to glide elegantly down the corridor. The book fell off her head more than once.

Cordelia was very glad when Miss Starebottom had finished for the day. In fact, Cordelia was *always* glad when these classes finished because that was when her Hatmaking lessons began.

It is impossible to describe what happened in a typical Hatmaking lesson because every Hatmaking lesson was completely different.

Once, Uncle Tiberius made Cordelia run different twists of thread through her fingers and think of a word to describe how each thread felt.

'The thread holds the creation together,' he told her, 'like the melody of a song holds the notes.'

Another time, Great-aunt Petronella stoked the fire in her Alchemy Parlour and threw different powders, leaves and twigs into the flames to show Cordelia how they turned the fire from golden to emerald green to brick red to sky blue to royal purple.

Aunt Ariadne gave her chalky and confusing instructions in arithmetic, measuring the angles between sections of her head with a pair of compasses before drawing hypotenuses and spiky triangles on the blackboard.

Her father showed her how to bow respectfully before picking a flower, how to flatter a peacock into dropping a plumy tail feather, and took her on a search for bits of fallen moonbeam on the rooftops of Mayfair.

'When ingredient-seeking, Dilly, never take more than you need,' her father told her. 'And always ask politely.'

All her Hatmaking lessons were fascinating. But Cordelia's favourite was the one her father had given her last year when he was home from a long ingredient-seeking voyage.

He'd scooped her up and carried her in a piggyback through London down to the quayside. The *Jolly Bonnet* was moored at a bustling dock. Sailors swung through the rigging like monkeys, whistling in code to each other and singing. The ship was being loaded with fresh supplies for the next quest. Prospero set her down on the deck and said, 'Now, my girl. The most important rule to follow when you seek hat ingredients is this: *keep wildness in your wits and magic in your fingertips.*'

Then he put his hand in his pocket and pulled out seven Sicilian Leaping Beans.

'Catch these beans, Cordelia, using your wits and your magic!' Prospero threw the wriggling beans into the air.

You might think that catching a handful of beans would be a doddle, but the Leaping Beans did not want to be caught. They sprang around the deck, hid behind barrels and vaulted into the sailors' hammocks. Cordelia darted after them but they skittered away from her.

After twenty minutes of grabbing at the Leaping Beans and catching none, Cordelia lay panting on the poop deck. Prospero was watching from the crow's nest at the top of the mast.

'Use your wild wits and your magic, Cordelia,' he called down.

A Leaping Bean was idling by the ship's wheel just out of her reach. A few sailors were hanging in the rigging, placing bets on Cordelia versus the bean.

Cordelia thought about what it must be like to be a Leaping Bean: they were boastful and curious and a little bit naughty. She let her mouth fall open and closed her eyes, then pretended to snore very gently.

The bean bounced closer. Cordelia kept her eyes shut and gave an extra-enticing snore. The bean leaped into her open mouth and she clamped her lips shut.

The sailors cheered as she spat the wriggling bean out into her hand. Then she did a victory leap into the air, which sent the remaining beans into a frenzy of competition. The free Leaping Beans each tried to leap higher than Cordelia. She hopped across the deck and launched herself into an empty hammock. All the beans followed her, jumping as high as they could. They leaped into the hammock as she rolled out of it, swirling the canvas round them and catching them all at once. She could hear them pattering huffily against the cloth, trying to leap free.

Prospero shimmied down the mast, a huge grin lighting his face.

'That's my girl!' he exclaimed. 'When my father set loose the Leaping Beans for me, it took me twice as long as you to catch them!'

Cordelia shone with pride.

'You see, littlest Hatmaker,' Prospero said, scooping the Leaping Beans back into his hand and into a small glass jar. 'You used your wild wits and your magic.'

'What *is* my magic?' Cordelia asked.

'Everybody has their own unique magic, littlest Hatmaker,' Prospero explained, handing her the jar of beans. 'But it's up to you to discover what it is. You've got to adventure into your own heart and head and belly to find out just what your own special magic is made of.'

Prospero led Cordelia into his captain's cabin. It was bursting with life: there were exotic plants growing in barrels, butterflies flitting among them. A parakeet screeched from his perch on the telescope and Singing Shells jingled in the window. Alongside the fine brass instruments needed to navigate the seas, there were books in unknown languages open on the desk and sprawling maps unrolled on the floor.

Cordelia spied a wooden box of wax-stoppered bottles. 'What are those, Father?'

'Ah! They're special inks!' He took a tiny bottle from the box to show her. 'One is invisible, but becomes visible when exposed to the heat of a candle flame. One can only be seen by starlight. One only appears on a Tuesday. They're all good for sending secret messages.'

Cordelia felt the glass jar of beans in her pocket humming. She pulled it out, studying the beans as they bounced around. 'How do they work?' she asked.

'Magic, Dilly. Magic is in everything natural in the world. Magic lives in the wind, in the rivers, in the earth, in the sunlight. It's in flowers and trees and rocks and it's born in all creatures. But most people have forgotten about it or — even worse than forgetting — they think it's old-fashioned.'

'But how could anyone forget?'

Prospero sat down on the floor and pulled Cordelia to him. 'Some people are never taught,' he said. 'And some people spend their lives trying very hard to be sensible.'

Cordelia shook her head. 'I've never really seen the point in being sensible,' she admitted.

Prospero laughed and rumpled Cordelia's hair. 'What was once known as the Age of Magic is now called the Dark Ages by people who think they know best,' he continued. 'And now, as more and more machines are being made, and more and more children are being put to work in dismal factories, they are calling this the Age of Enlightenment.'

'Why are they calling it that?'

'I think to convince themselves that things are better this way,' Prospero said.

Cordelia frowned. 'But things aren't better,' she said. 'Not if people are forgetting about magic.'

'Our hats help,' he told her. 'They connect people with the magic contained in the treasures I collect. They connect people with their own inner magic, even when they don't know it.'

'Has the magic in some people gone?' Cordelia whispered.

'It's never really *gone*,' Prospero assured her. 'Forgotten magic is like a flower in winter. It disappears down into the depths of the person, and anyone looking could be forgiven for thinking it had gone away completely. But it hasn't gone – it just has to be woken up again.'

'How do you know all this?' she breathed. 'Have you always known it?'

Her father smiled and shook his head. 'I studied alchemy out of books for years, until one fine morning, when the sunshine outside was thick and gold, and I could see dust from the laboratory floating in the air, I realized I was looking in the wrong place for the answers I sought. You see, alchemists conduct experiments to turn earth into pure gold.

But I realized that it cannot be done, at least not in the way the books say. The true alchemist must turn their *soul* to gold. To do this, the experiment we must participate in is the great experiment of life.

'So that fine morning I stepped out of my laboratory, into the golden sunlight, and instantly felt richer than a king. I knew that I belonged to nature and nature belonged to me. I saw a single daisy growing in the grass and in that moment I understood that one flower has more magic in it than all the man-made riches in a prince's palace. That is how my great adventures began, of discovering the wild magic of the world, and discovering it in myself.'

Cordelia's eyes shone.

'And you made maps of everywhere you went?' she asked, gazing around at the vast and intricate maps spread across the cabin. 'So I can go too, one day?'

Prospero grinned.

'Some are maps *of* places, some are maps *to* places. Some are maps of cities, or states, or states of mind. Some are just *parts* of maps.'

'Parts of maps?'

'Yes. Anything can be part of a map. These seven freckles on your nose, for example,' he said, touching each freckle gently with the tip of his finger, 'they could be part of a map.'

Cordelia stared into the mirror, remembering. She traced the seven freckles sprinkled like a constellation of stars across her nose and cheeks, lightly touching each freckle with a fingertip, as her father had done that day on the ship.

'Cordelia!'

It was her aunt. Time for today's Hatmaking lesson.

However, when she reached the Hatmaking Workshop, she found Aunt Ariadne putting on her Wise Bonnet. Uncle Tiberius had his Logic Top Hat perched on his head.

'There will be no Hatmaking lesson today, Cordelia,' said her aunt. 'The princess has summoned us most urgently to the palace. We need you to look after the shop while we are gone!'

CHAPTER 9

The Hatmakers' shop had sparkling windows that looked out on to Wimpole Street.

Hats of every description were displayed in them. Today there was a sky-blue bonnet with a feather from a Moonwing bird, a bright red beret studded with Love Beetle wings, a sleek purple top hat with its brim dipped in Silverglass, and a yellow silk turban with a Saturn Cactus flower sewn on to the ribbon.

The shop's shelves were stacked with hats of every colour and design. There was a wide wooden countertop and a glass case containing the hats with the most potent magical ingredients. Behind the counter, a hatch opened on to the hat hoist. The hoist was operated by a pulley system that brought hats from the Hat-weighing Room down to the shop floor.

Cordelia polished the mirror that gleamed on the wall so

that customers could see the full effect of a hat they were trying on. An Impression Measurer was screwed to the wall: a brass ruler inscribed with words like *Noble*, *Beautiful*, *Splendid* and *Statuesque*, with a little pointer that went up and down, to measure the effect of the hat.

She arranged herself behind the counter, standing on a stool so she looked taller and more in charge. She had never been responsible for the shop before.

She practised greeting customers in a gracious voice: 'Good afternoon, madam . . . Good after*noon*, sir.'

The brass bell above the shop door dinged and a young man strode in.

'I need a hat, my good lady, to win a duel!'

Cordelia was surprised. Firstly, she had never been called a 'lady' before; and, secondly, the man was carrying a set of duelling pistols. He banged the box on to the counter, making Cordelia flinch.

'Um . . . G-good after*noon*, sir,' she stammered.

'My opponent is a good shot, but I must be a better one!' the young man declared.

He was really no more than a boy. Cordelia looked sceptically at his moustache, which seemed more like peach fuzz than the bushy moustache of a hardened duellist.

'Might I enquire what your quarrel is with your opponent?' Cordelia asked. 'Simply so I can find you the most ferocious hat for the job.'

'He has insulted my lady love!' the boy cried, cheeks pink with anger. 'I demand satisfaction of him!'

Cordelia nodded. *Remember the Hatmaker motto, Cordelia,* her aunt's voice warned her. *Noli nocere*: Do no harm.

Very aware of his zealous gaze following her, Cordelia hopped off her stool, selected a hat for the boy and carried it to the counter.

'What does it do?' the boy asked sharply.

Cordelia held up the hat. It was the bright red beret. Pink Love Beetle wings glimmered all over it.

'This hat makes the wearer most ferocious. These little pink . . . scales . . . are Chinese dragon scales,' Cordelia lied, pointing at the Love Beetle wings. (In truth, Love Beetles were very agreeable little insects that lived among the petals of sweet Bulgarian roses.)

'Why are they pink?'

'Because they're from a baby dragon. They're red when they're fully grown, the dragons, but they're pink when they're young,' Cordelia invented.

'A baby dragon?' the boy said acidly. 'How is a *baby* dragon dangerous?'

'They haven't got control of their flame-breathing yet,' Cordelia explained. 'Makes them far more dangerous. One hiccup and you're on fire.'

The boy seemed pleased with this. He emptied his little

velvet pouch of silver and gold coins while Cordelia wrapped his hat in soft paper and placed it in a hatbox.

'Don't put it on until right before your duel,' she warned. 'Otherwise you might rampage around London fighting people, and I don't want that on my conscience.'

The boy nodded, seized the hatbox and his duelling pistols and raced out of the shop, the brass bell clanging behind him.

After the boy came an old lady who wanted a bonnet to make her look young. Then a young lady who wanted a thinking cap to make her seem wise. As Cordelia was helping a portly gentleman with a nut-brown bicorn, another young man barged into the shop.

'Shop girl!' he snapped at Cordelia. 'I need a hat post-haste.'

Cordelia was not sure what 'post-haste' meant, but the lad was pacing up and down in quite a state of agitation.

'Do excuse me, sir,' Cordelia said to the portly gentleman, who was testing the bicorn against the Impression Measurer, which read, *Cutting a Dashing Figure!*

'I need a hat to help me win a duel!' the flustered lad said, pretending to point a duelling pistol at his reflection.

Cordelia fought to keep her eyebrows down at their usual level.

'And may I enquire as to your quarrel –'

'He has taken umbrage at my pet name for his lady love!' he interrupted. 'Just because I said she sounds like a mountain goat with a head-cold and decided to call her Sniffy Goat Gruff.'

Cordelia fought to keep her mouth at the usual level. She wanted to laugh. She nodded slowly, which gave her time to arrange her face into a dignified expression.

'So you shall need a hat to keep you cool-headed and icy-hearted,' she said with authority.

'That sounds just the ticket!'

She fetched a pale cap with a silver ribbon and a feather from a Common White Dove. It was finished with a single crystal from the Peace Mountain.

'This hat will give you frosty resolve and a steely soul,' Cordelia announced. 'The ribbon is woven from Steelheart fibres and the feather is from a Tufted Maniac.'

'What's a Tufted Maniac?' the lad asked with round eyes.

'The most merciless bird in the world,' Cordelia replied. 'And this crystal was stolen from the Tomb of a Villainous Prince.'

She knew it wasn't good to lie, but she thought on balance it was better to fib than to have the two young men firing pistols at each other.

'You must only put this hat on your head once your opponent is in sight,' she advised. 'Otherwise it could make you so cold-hearted that you catch pneumonia.'

The lad nodded, threw a fistful of coins on to the counter, grabbed the hat and rushed out of the shop.

Cordelia sank on to the stool. Surely nothing could be more exciting than averting a duel?

She was wrong.

CHAPTER 10

In a swirl of capes, a flurry of floppy hair and a cloud of musky perfume, a man whirled into the shop. Cordelia jumped up as he flung himself on to the carpet, moaning.

'To be . . . *or not to be!*'

'Are you all right, sir?' Cordelia asked, afraid that the man rolling on the floor was gripped with pain.

'Alas! Poor Yorick! I knew him, Horatio,' he wept into the carpet.

'Can I get you anything, sir? Or would you like something for Horatio?'

The man turned to stare at Cordelia.

'GET THEE TO A NUNNERY!' he roared at her, leaping to his feet.

'*WHY SHOULD I?*' she roared back, so shocked by him that she couldn't help shouting her reply.

Then the man swept his hair out of his face, leaned wretchedly against the counter and muttered, 'Miss Hatmaker, I need your help! I perform my Hamlet tonight at Drury Lane and I have an awful case of stage fright!'

Now Cordelia understood: this man was an actor. He could not help how ridiculous he seemed, rolling around on the floor and clutching himself. That was simply how actors behaved! She smiled encouragingly at the desolate expression on his face and his bottom lip wobbled.

'Help me, Miss Hatmaker!' he rasped, falling to his knees. 'Princess Georgina will attend tonight's performance and I fear I shall make an ignoble fool of myself!'

'Princess Georgina?' Cordelia repeated.

'Aye! That nymph of rare beauty and virtue!' the actor began. 'She is an exquisite damsel of peerless distinction –'

He continued gushing lyrically about the princess, but Cordelia was not really listening.

If I could get to the theatre and see the princess, she thought, *I could persuade her to lend me a boat so I can go and rescue Father. She was about to say yes to me at the palace, but that lord stopped her. I'm sure if I was allowed to explain things properly, she would lend me a boat in an instant. I can set sail on the tide tonight!*

'Not to mention, of course, that she is extremely rich,' the actor finished.

Cordelia smiled.

'If I find you the perfect hat, will you do me a very important favour?' Cordelia asked.

'Name it, O Maker of Hats!' he cried.

'Will you give me a ticket to your play tonight?'

'Indeed I shall, fair Hatmaker!' the actor declared, but then his expression crumbled. '*Tonight!* So soon! I fear the stage and all its dreadful boards!'

Cordelia patted him on the head. 'Don't you worry, sir. I'll find you the best hat we have.'

She gazed up at the shelves, at the hundreds of hats in every colour and style.

'How about this nice Aplomb Beret?' she suggested. 'In a very impressive shade of purple?'

But the actor waved his hands impatiently. 'No, no, no! I must have a hat as unique as I am! It must be made for my head, and my head alone!'

Cordelia paused. She must have had a thousand Hatmaking lessons, but, of course, she was strictly forbidden to make a hat by herself.

She chewed her lip. The actor looked at her expectantly.

'Listen,' she said. 'If I make you a hat from *scratch*, I'll have to block it and sew it together, and it wouldn't be ready for two days at least.'

'But I must have it right away!' The actor turned pale. 'The play is tonight!'

'So let me choose one of these hats for you, sir. I'm sure I can find you a marvellous one, just right for chasing away stage fright.'

She waved her arm around the shop, at the hundreds of beautiful hats waiting for the right person.

'All right,' he agreed meekly. 'But . . . maybe we could add an extra feather to it or something? If it doesn't have enough decoration.'

Cordelia nodded. 'Very well! That's what we'll do!'

She climbed the ladder and started taking hats down from the shelves. She handed the actor tricorns and bicorns, felt stovepipes and straw cloches, armfuls of bonnets, velvet turbans and linen nightcaps and even a gleaming helmet. After trying on and discarding about fifty hats, he eventually chose a tricorn in a thrilling shade of turquoise.

'Excellent decision, sir,' Cordelia congratulated him, climbing down the ladder. Uncle Tiberius always said it was best to tell the customer that they were making wise and insightful choices.

She read the paper label pinned to the inside of the hat.

'This hat is trimmed with Warble Ribbon and decorated with a Singing Sapphire,' she told the actor. 'And it has these —' She pointed at the three fat brassy buttons on each point of the three-cornered hat.

'Yes!' the actor enthused. 'Buttons of gold.'

Cordelia did not tell him they were called Braggart Buttons.

She thought the hat was very generously decorated already,

but the man clapped his hands and cried, 'A feather, O Seraph! I must have a feather!'

Aunt Ariadne's face swam before Cordelia's eyes. *You are not allowed to Hat-make, Cordelia. End of story.*

But there was something much more important at stake than breaking Aunt Ariadne's rules.

And she'll be so happy when I bring Father home, Cordelia thought.

She dashed upstairs and fetched a bouquet of exotic feathers from the Hatmaking Workshop. She fanned them out for the actor and he promptly chose the glossiest one in the bunch.

'The tail feather of an Upstart Crow,' she informed him. Then she thought for a moment. 'You know what would go beautifully with it . . .'

'More feathers?' the actor suggested.

'No . . .'

She darted up the spiral stairs, all the way to the glasshouse. It was lush with the green tendrils of vines and the warm, damp air was perfumed. A new Loquacious Lily had opened, dropping fragrant pollen from its golden stamens. Carefully, Cordelia picked the lily and carried it out as gently as if she was carrying a live butterfly.

On her way back down the spiral staircase, the glint of instruments in the Alchemy Parlour made her pause. She should really be weighing and measuring, checking star charts and calculating . . . How would this lily behave side by side with the Singing Sapphire? Would Braggart Buttons *and* the tail feather of an Upstart Crow be too much for one hat?

Then something infinitely more interesting than Hatmaking equations caught her eye. Lying on the alchemy workbench were a dozen little star-shaped sequins, cut from thin gold. Their points, snip-sharp and sparkling, were pure glory. They would look magnificent on the actor's hat.

She won't miss three of them, Cordelia told herself, peering into the dark parlour to check that her great-aunt was sleeping.

Softly, she slid three sequins into her pocket, sneaked from the room and sped downstairs to the shop.

'Ah!' the actor exclaimed when he saw the beautiful lily. 'Plucked from the lofty heights of heaven itself!'

Cordelia beamed and put her hand in her pocket. The actor's eyes lit up when he saw the golden stars.

It was excellent fun adding things to hats.

She stood at the counter and sewed the sequins, feather and lily on to the turquoise tricorn. As she sewed, the actor entertained her with a zestful series of his favourite speeches. He flung himself to the floor (again) and cried about a girl called Juliet. Then, standing on the chair, in a voice as high as a tight violin string, he whined about a boy named Romeo. He plotted to kill someone by the name of Caesar, sang a song called 'Hey Nonny Nonny', and finally put on an alarming Scottish accent and pretended to see a ghost.

When Cordelia presented him with the finished hat, he

swept it on to his head and struck a gallant pose. The Impression Measurer read, *Splendid Swaggerer!*

'Aah!' he exclaimed. 'You have truly made me a hat fit for an emperor, my lady!'

There was a rather long pause as he admired himself in the mirror. Cordelia was reminded of a pigeon cooing at its own reflection in a window. The stars on the hat flashed and winked.

'I, Sir Hugo Gushforth, am ever in your debt, Mistress Hatmaker,' he eventually said, in a voice choked with emotion.

He kissed Cordelia's hand and the new feather in his hat tickled her nose.

'If you give me a ticket to the play tonight, your debt is repaid,' she said, trying not to sneeze. 'And can I also bring my friend Goose?'

'My bountiful lady, any friend of yours shall be treated as a prince among paupers!' he declared. 'Give your name at the theatre and you shall have the second-best box in the house!'

And, with that, Sir Hugo Gushforth swaggered from the shop. She could hear him bellowing poetry all the way down the street.

Sir Hugo's verses had not quite faded from the air when Cordelia heard the rumble of the carriage pulling up at the front door of Hatmaker House.

Aunt Ariadne and Uncle Tiberius hurried into the shop.

'What ingredients do we need?' Uncle Tiberius was saying.

'Lullwool felt from the Welsh mountains,' Aunt Ariadne answered.

'Paxpearl Shells, from Ease Bay.' Uncle Tiberius was rolling up his sleeves with purpose.

'Cordial Blossoms,' Aunt Ariadne added. 'And a little sifted starlight.'

'What's happening?' Cordelia asked.

Aunt Ariadne kissed Cordelia on the forehead, while Uncle Tiberius turned a serious face to her. Both seemed so distracted that they did not notice what a state of turmoil the shop was in, with Sir Hugo's rejected hats scattered everywhere.

'Princess Georgina has called for peace talks,' Aunt Ariadne told Cordelia. 'With that wild youth the king of France.'

'He has been sending ruder and ruder letters to her,' Uncle Tiberius growled.

'Sage Ribbons. And Politic Cord too,' interrupted her aunt.

Her uncle nodded. 'We shall need them post-haste.'

'We have been ordered by the princess to make a Peace Hat, Cordelia,' her aunt explained. 'It must be ready by noon, three days from now. And the other Makers are to make Peace Clothes too –'

'Hah! Much good the *boots* will do!' Uncle Tiberius exploded. 'More likely they will cause the princess to ride roughshod over diplomacy – stamp out any chance of peace! The hat's the important thing! The head is where the thinking is done and the hat is what goes on the head!'

'Now, now, Tiberius, we should lay aside our differences in times like these,' Aunt Ariadne said. 'We hope that *all* the Peace Clothes will have the desired effect, and there is no war.'

'Where will the peace talks take place?' asked Cordelia.

'On a ship in the English Channel,' Aunt Ariadne told her.

'That's not what the French call it,' Uncle Tiberius muttered darkly.

Aunt Ariadne fished a silver astronomic watch out of her pocket to consult it.

'When Venus rises this evening, we will begin,' she announced. 'And Aquarius is in the ascendant, so that will help Great-aunt Petronella. She must distil some *Esprit de corps.*'

Uncle Tiberius went thundering up the stairs.

'I shall consult the Orrery!' he called down. 'Before beginning the ribbons!'

'We must close the shop for the rest of the day,' Aunt Ariadne told Cordelia, locking the door. 'All our efforts must go towards making the Peace Hat!'

Cordelia felt suddenly uncertain.

'Will there really be a – a war?' she stammered. 'I must rescue Father before it starts!'

Aunt Ariadne gazed down at her.

'If we make the Peace Hat the best we can,' she murmured, 'perhaps war can be avoided.'

'What can I do to help?' Cordelia asked.

Her aunt hesitated, so Cordelia fixed her most determined expression on her face. It was a mixture of very earnest and decidedly stubborn. It seemed to convince her aunt.

'Look in the books and find the runic symbol for peace. Trace it on to paper and your uncle will stitch it inside the brim with silver thread,' her aunt said, and hurried upstairs.

Alone in the shop, Cordelia felt cold and shaky, as though she had just been plunged into the icy sea.

She wondered if the peace talks would stop the princess lending her a boat so she could search for her father.

She shook her head. *No.* She would set sail on the midnight tide and would probably find him before noon tomorrow.

'I'm coming to find you, Father,' she said.

Then she hurtled upstairs to the Library and began pulling books from the shelves, hunting for the peace rune.

Then she hurtled upstairs to the Library and began pulling
books from the shelves, hunting for the peace rune.

CHAPTER 11

She found the rune in the fourth book she looked in and traced the spiky diamond shape on to a strip of fragile paper.

'Here, Uncle, I've got it!' she shouted, tumbling into the Hatmaking Workshop.

'Shhh!' Aunt Ariadne hushed her.

Uncle Tiberius was bent over a small wooden loom, weaving fine strands of silver into a ribbon. His large hands worked deftly with the delicate threads and his tongue poked out of his mouth in concentration.

'Thing is . . .' he muttered, as much to himself as anybody else, 'it requires tact and politeness to bring these threads together . . . and *silence* is vital, Dilly . . .'

'*Sorry*,' Cordelia whispered.

'Lay the paper there, Cordelia, thank you.' Aunt Ariadne's

arms had turned pale blue: she was up to her elbows in a vat of dye. Cordelia could smell camomile and woad steeping in the hot water.

'Can I do anything else?' Cordelia asked, but her aunt shook her head.

'Run along. Go and play. *Quietly.*'

Cordelia laid the rune on the table and backed reluctantly out of the workshop. She closed the door as softly as she could. There was still an hour to go before it was time to set out for the theatre. She felt restless, keen to do something useful to make the time go quicker.

In the Alchemy Parlour, she found Great-aunt Petronella squinting into one of her telescopes while tying a piece of copper wire in complicated knots.

'Great-aunt, can I help you with anything?'

'Για να δώσετε μια ασημένια γλώσσα στην πριγκίπισσα,' Great-aunt Petronella said, screwing her eye into the telescope again and swivelling the dials.

Cordelia sighed. When her great-aunt started speaking Ancient Greek, it was time to leave. She would not get an English word out of her for several hours.

She hurried back to the Library and threw open the window, searching the sky for Agatha. Nothing.

'I wish she'd hurry up,' Cordelia said, stroking Margaret's wing. 'It would be useful to have a note from Father before I set off tonight, with his location, so I can find him by the stars.'

Margaret cooed in an understanding sort of way.

Suddenly Cordelia remembered that she hadn't told Goose about their trip to the theatre. She scrawled a message, with instructions to be ready on the corner of his street at seven o'clock.

'You're looking for a boy,' she whispered to Margaret, rolling the note up. 'About this tall, and quite clever, with a slightly strange haircut. He has a timid expression, except when he's talking about boats. He's only three streets away, at Bootmaker Mansion, probably in his schoolroom. Make sure his mother doesn't see you. Tap on his window with your beak.'

She stood watching Margaret flit into the dusk. The sky was growing dark, ocean-deep. She searched the heavens until her eyes watered for a sign of the speckle-winged Agatha flying back to her. How wide was the world? How long would it take the bird to wing her way through the sky to her father?

A little while later, Cordelia softly pushed open the workshop door to discover that her aunt and uncle were still busily occupied. Venus winked outside the window and they were steaming and pinning felt on to the hatblock in the middle of the workbench. For several awed moments, Cordelia watched as the hat began to take shape in front of her eyes. Then she tiptoed away.

In her Alchemy Parlour Great-aunt Petronella was stirring her fire, and in the kitchen Cook was stirring her saucepans.

Cordelia left a note in the front hall:

Gone to the theatre! To see a play about a nunnery.
Love, Dilly

Then she slipped out of the door. She was wearing her best cape and a handsome hat that she had borrowed from the shop window, decorated with a plumy Moonwing feather.

She walked quickly to the bottom of Bulstrode Street. Because Hatmakers and Bootmakers were sworn enemies, Cordelia was not welcome at Goose's house. Not that it looked very welcoming anyway. It was a tall grey building with dark windows and complicated carving on the stonework. She dawdled on the corner at a safe distance.

Nearby St Auspice's Church struck seven and a small figure emerged from the front door of the mansion and hared down the street towards her.

'Evening, Cordelia!' Goose panted, out of breath already. 'This is exciting!'

Cordelia smiled.

'Hello, Goose! You got away all right, then. What excuse did you give your parents?' she asked, glancing back at gloomy Bootmaker Mansion.

Goose waved his hand. 'Oh, they're both really busy working on – um – on some important things,' he replied. 'They won't even notice I'm gone.'

'Here, put this on.'

Cordelia pulled a Camouflage Cap from under her cape. Even though it looked like a normal black top hat, it had a cleverly concealed wire that wrapped around the chin. A bushy beard and impressive moustache (made of crimped sheep's wool dyed rusty red) was attached to the wire. When Goose put it on, he looked as though he had sprouted a full face of hair. Cordelia snorted with laughter.

'You look very grown-up all of a sudden!'

'This is so clever!' Goose enthused, twirling the tips of his new moustache. 'I've never worn a Hatmaker hat before!'

They set off for the theatre through the streets and squares of London. Halfway along Bond Street, they saw Sam Lightfinger hawking a newspaper called *The Evening Sneer*.

'GETCHA *EVENIN' SNEER*! READ ALL ABOUT THE STINKY FRENCH!'

'Let's cross over,' Goose urged, pulling Cordelia by the elbow. 'That's Cloakmaker Hall – I don't want to walk past the front door.'

So Cordelia contented herself with waving to Sam from across the road. Sam waved back.

'Need any NEWS?' he yelled. 'It's extra-bad tonight!'

'No thanks!' Cordelia called, hurrying after Goose.

Hatmaker and Bootmaker were just passing through leafy Berkeley Square when a shout rang out.

'Hey, sir! I demand that you face me!'

Cordelia and Goose swung round, surprised.

'Ah! You lily-livered scoundrel!' another voice yelped. 'I have been looking everywhere for you!'

It was the young men who had come into the shop earlier, each demanding a hat to win a duel. They were marching towards each other, red in the face. Cordelia was glad to see they were both clutching their hatboxes. One of the boys had a girl following him. She was dressed in a frilly frock and trying to look dramatic.

'Oh, Archibald! Please do not duel on my account!' she cried, waving a lace handkerchief around. 'Have mercy!'

'Stay out of this, Janet,' the boy called Archibald snapped.

Janet looked miffed.

'*You!*' Archibald pointed at the other boy. 'Ferdinand Spouter! You have been a thorn in my side for too long!'

'HAH!' bellowed Ferdinand. 'You are not sharp enough to be a thorn, Baldie Bluntwort. You are a pebble in my shoe! And a dull, grey one at that!'

''Tis time for the pistols!' Archibald announced, shaking Janet off his arm. He never took his eyes from Ferdinand.

Cordelia pulled Goose behind a tree in case things went badly wrong.

Janet was wailing, 'Ay, me!' in a very shrill voice.

'Oh, do shut up your *bleating*, Sniffy Goat Gruff,' Ferdinand barked at her, taking a pistol.

'How dare you!' Janet bawled.

'Ten paces!' Archibald yelled.

Cordelia peered out from behind the tree.

The boys, each gripping a pistol, took ten long strides in opposite directions, and turned to face each other. Then they opened their hatboxes and pulled out the hats. Cordelia saw the gleam of the pale cap and the flash of the red beret as they jammed them on their heads.

Janet was watching with an eager, triumphant look on her face. Goose groaned. Cordelia held her breath.

There was a moment when the gunshots should have come.

The moment passed.

Archibald blinked several times, the Love Beetle wings glinting on his hat. Ferdinand gasped quietly, one hand went to his chest and the other (the hand holding the pistol) fell limply to his side.

Archibald dropped his pistol on the grass. He was gazing at Ferdinand with the kind of eyes that idolize. Ferdinand looked tenderly back at him.

The boys walked bashfully towards each other.

'What on earth are you doing?' Janet hissed at Archibald, who ignored her.

Goose, crouching behind the tree, had his eyes screwed shut and his fingers in his ears. Cordelia tapped his arm.

'Goose!' she whispered. 'The hats worked!'

The boys were face to face now.

'Oh, Baldie,' Ferdinand breathed.

'Ferdie,' Archibald answered softly. 'You are not a thorn; you are a beautiful rose.'

'And you are no dull pebble – you are a diamond!' Ferdinand whispered.

He reached up and tenderly touched Archibald's cheek. Archibald blushed and, in one sweeping rush, Ferdinand kissed him.

'WHAT?' Janet shrieked. 'This is *not* what was meant to happen!'

Ferdinand and Archibald kissed so passionately that their hats came off.

Cordelia gulped as the boys pulled apart, staring at each other in surprise. For a terrible, frozen moment Cordelia thought they would kill each other with their bare hands.

Then Archibald did something nobody expected. He leaned forward and kissed Ferdinand again.

A church bell bonged triumphantly. It was quarter past the hour and Cordelia grabbed Goose's hand and pulled him up.

'Come on, Goose! We can't be late for the theatre!' she cried, running full pelt along the street.

CHAPTER 12

The Theatre Royal, Drury Lane, was a towering building with soaring pillars and golden statues of angels round the grand doors. Inside, jewel-encrusted ladies and grand gentlemen in white wigs milled around the candle-lit foyer.

'Cordelia Hatmaker,' Cordelia said when asked for her name by a stern doorman in a gold-trimmed jacket.

Immediately he bowed very low and said, 'This way, Miss Hatmaker, and sir. We have the second-best box in the house ready for you.'

He led them up the red-carpeted stairs and ushered them into the box, lush with velvet finery. They threw themselves into squishy armchairs and peered over the railing at the dazzling scene below.

The theatre was packed and buzzing. Cordelia searched

the crowd for the princess but could not see her anywhere. She recognized many Hatmaker hats bobbing around on the heads below them. In the pit, lads threw handfuls of peanuts at each other and jostled to impress ladies wearing jewel-coloured silks that Cordelia thought made them look like Birds of Paradise. The whole auditorium was a great breathing beast, panting for the play to begin.

A young man stepped on to the stage and blasted a brass trumpet.

'Pray be upstanding for Her Royal Highness, Princess Georgina!' he cried.

He continued to blow loudly on the trumpet until a long stick with a bent end appeared from off stage, hooked itself around his middle and yanked him back behind the curtain.

A hush descended and all eyes in the audience turned towards Cordelia. For a strange moment Cordelia thought the crowd below was looking up at her and Goose. Then she realized that Princess Georgina was in the box next to theirs – the royal box!

'Perfect!' Cordelia whispered.

The partition between the boxes meant they couldn't see more than the princess's delicate nose as she nodded to the adoring audience. Cordelia decided that she would ask to speak to her during the interval.

Around the theatre, the candles were snuffed out until everything but the stage was in darkness. The purple velvet curtains swept aside and Sir Hugo Gushforth was revealed, posing heroically in the middle of the stage. He was wearing the magnificent hat that Cordelia had made him and a frilly outfit to go with it.

The audience burst into applause. The golden stars on the hat twinkled in response and the Upstart Crow feather dipped and wagged as Sir Hugo took bow after bow.

'Isn't he meant to bow at the end?' Goose whispered to Cordelia as the actor blew a kiss to the princess.

'Maybe if you're a sir, you bow at the beginning,' Cordelia suggested.

They heard a sigh from the royal box.

'Are you quite all right, Princess?' said a man's voice. He sounded important and somewhat familiar.

'I told you I did not wish to come to the theatre tonight,' the princess answered. 'It is far too frivolous an activity when there is serious talk of war.'

'But, Your Highness, your presence reassures the people that all will be well,' the important voice replied.

'You are right, Lord Witloof,' the princess said with a sigh. 'As you keep reminding me, I am sadly lacking in political expertise.'

Cordelia frowned. If Lord Witloof was with the princess, he might again stop her from lending Cordelia a ship. She would have to get the princess on her own.

Before she could formulate a plan, Sir Hugo threw himself flat on the stage and began wailing. For a dreadful moment Cordelia thought her hat had malfunctioned. Then she realized he was acting. The play had begun!

First a powder-white ghost swooped on to the stage, wailing and moaning. Then a damsel wailed and moaned a bit too. A scheming uncle plotted in plain sight and a pair of young chaps were slapped and tripped up by Sir Hugo and danced around the stage trying to avoid him.

Cordelia was pleased to see that her hat was working wonderfully: Sir Hugo showed no trace of stage fright. In fact, he frequently stopped in the middle of scenes to take bows and blow kisses to members of the audience. During these pauses the other actors were left shuffling their feet upstage, until Sir Hugo deigned to rejoin them and carry on with the acting. He even appeared in some scenes that Cordelia suspected he had no business being in.

Halfway through the play there was an interval. The curtain went down and the theatre filled with an excited hubbub and a haze of pipe smoke. Cordelia and Goose were given strawberry ices in silver bowls. As Goose ate his, Cordelia peered round the partition between their box and the royal box. Neither Lord Witloof nor the princess looked as though they were going to move. Cordelia chewed her lip, thinking. How to speak to the princess alone?

She then heard Lord Witloof announce, 'Your Highness, you have just received another letter from the French king.'

There was the clink of a silver spoon in a bowl as the princess said, 'I hope it isn't as rude and unkind as the last two letters he sent.' There was a rather long pause before she continued: 'I gather from your silence, my Lord, that the letter is indeed rude and unkind?'

Lord Witloof coughed delicately.

'The French king is an insufferable popinjay,' he declared. 'He has a dangerous ego and a pathological obsession with exotic fruits.'

The princess sighed. 'Read me the letter, please.'

'I do not think that Your Highness's delicate ears should hear such words.'

'But if I stop communication with King Louis,' Princess Georgina said patiently, 'there will be no hope of making things better between England and France.'

Lord Witloof rustled the pages and said, 'Your Highness should enjoy your strawberry ice unbothered by the insults of the French nincompoop.'

'If I am to be a good leader, I need to listen to the people who disagree with me,' the princess reasoned. 'Besides, when I was five, Lady Elsa Clustertrunce (who was five and a half at the time) called me a "stinky snivel-whinge" for riding too long on her rocking horse. I am sure the French king can do no worse.'

Lord Witloof gave a small sigh and began to read.

Princess Georgina,

*You are little more than a girl playing in the palace with a china
tea set. And your father is as giddy as a spinning jenny. My
spies tell me you are afraid of talking to me, most likely because
I am the king of the greatest country on earth – France.
Perhaps you should allow a man to take charge of England,
which was a brave and powerful nation when a man ruled. If
no man can be found, I suggest that one of my mother's poodles,
Frou-Frou, take the job. Frou-Frou the Poodle is a very good
dog. He sits on command and can count up to ten, which is
more than I have heard about you.*

Yours respectfully,
King Louis of France

Silence followed. Then the dry sound of paper being
folded.

'Well. This is a new vista of impudence,' the princess said.
Though she sounded calm, there was a catch in her voice like
a thread that might unravel.

'Indeed,' Lord Witloof answered gravely. 'It is one thing to
send spies to spy upon one's neighbours; it is quite another
thing to admit to it.'

'I thought spies were meant to be secret, yet he has told me about them . . . How very strange,' the princess said.

'And he has insulted you! *And* insulted your father, and spinning jennies, and, frankly, everybody in England!' Lord Witloof cried.

'He *is* very cruel and unkind,' the princess admitted, her voice quavering.

'There now, Princess,' Lord Witloof said, his tone suddenly soothing. 'Perhaps he will be less rude if you write back to him and tell him that you can count up to ten thousand. And that you have counted each of your new cannons personally.'

'New cannons?' the princess murmured. 'What new cannons?'

'If you sign this paper, Your Highness, I can order ten thousand new cannons from the Ironfire factory tonight,' Lord Witloof announced. 'Your father was meant to sign this paper yesterday.'

'But I have commissioned Peace Clothes from the Makers,' the princess said. 'I would like the peace talks to succeed.'

'As would I, Princess. But the Makers failed us before. Should we really put our faith in them yet again? Their ways are rather old-fashioned, you know . . .'

'The Makers' clothes are an important tradition in my family,' the princess said. 'I do not intend to give them up at the drop of a hat, so to speak.'

'Indeed. But some might say there are more sensible inventions to be concentrating on that will help achieve peace,' Lord Witloof ventured. 'Like guns.'

Cordelia leaned forward so she could see the princess's profile. There was a wrinkle of concern creasing her forehead. Lord Witloof waved a piece of paper under her nose and held out a quill, its nib already slick with ink. 'The peace talks should go ahead as planned. But the French king will talk far more politely when you have a great number of cannons pointing in his direction.'

The princess hesitated. The quill dripped a black ink-spot on to her pale gown.

'The Ironfire Cannon Factory is ready, Your Highness,' Lord Witloof pressed. 'It has the very latest in modern technology. All that is needed is your royal commission to take the money from the coffers, and the cannons will be ready within three days.'

The princess paused, watching as the candles were snuffed out around the auditorium again.

'War is a terrible thing,' she eventually said. 'And my father believes in peace. I am meant to be honouring his wishes while he recovers at the seaside. So I will *not* order any cannons from the Ironfire factory. I would like to try for peace first. And at the peace talks I'll show King Louis that I am not afraid of speaking to him.'

Lord Witloof began, 'But it is foolish, Princess, to –'

'Hush, my lord, the play is starting again!'

Cordelia heard a lordly sigh and a frustrated shuffling of papers. She turned to look at Goose. Behind his impressive moustache, Goose looked worried.

'Your Highness! Ladies and gentlemen! The Very Dramatic Tragedy of *Hamlet* is about to continue!' the boy with the trumpet shouted as the curtains rose.

The second half of the play featured more yelling and groaning from Sir Hugo, even louder wailing from the damsel and, most exciting of all, a sword fight.

Sir Hugo swished his silver sword with violent flourishes. His opponent seemed anxious to avoid the wide arcs of the weapon, so the fight was more of a chase around the stage as Sir Hugo brandished his glinting blade and his enemy dodged and ducked out of the way.

Perhaps, thought Cordelia, *the enemy is frightened because he has a sword made of wood painted grey, while Sir Hugo's seems to be made of real steel.*

Cordelia jumped up as soon as the curtains closed, ready to waylay the princess. But Sir Hugo reappeared between the curtains and took nineteen bows before he finally went away.

Goose got out of his seat, hands red from clapping, as

The second half of the play featured more yelling and groaning from Sir Hugo,
even louder wailing from the damsel and, most exciting of all, a sword fight.

Cordelia threw open the door. She found herself face to face with a guard who was standing outside the royal box.

'Good evening,' she said politely. 'I don't suppose I can see the princess for a minute?'

Her request was met with a scowl.

CHAPTER 13

Cordelia and Goose squeezed between the rustling dresses of women in hooped skirts and ducked under the elbows of fops.

'Let's stand here by the door, so when the princess comes past we can stop her and talk,' Cordelia said. 'Can you distract Lord Witloof?'

Goose looked uncertain. 'How?'

'I don't know. Maybe compliment him on his wig?'

Sir Hugo sashayed into the foyer, still wearing his spectacular hat. The starry sequins winked and the Loquacious Lily filled the air around the actor's head with a halo of golden pollen. He was immediately encircled by an admiring gaggle of aristocrats, all giving him compliments and flowers and blowing him kisses.

'Ah! Some have already said 'tis my finest performance yet!' Sir Hugo announced loudly. He caught sight of Cordelia and winked. The lady next to her keeled over, taken by a fit of the vapours.

'Make way for Her Highness!' a guard barked.

The princess appeared and a swathe of ladies curtsied and whole legions of gentlemen in white wigs and gold-buttoned jackets bowed. Everyone crowded forward, eager to compliment her. Cordelia was jostled in the mob and Sir Hugo managed to end up at the front of the crowd.

'O Royal Highness!' he began. 'Upon thy pale cheek, a lily of Eden would seem shabby —'

'Yes, yes,' Lord Witloof said, taking the princess by the elbow and ushering her along.

Cordelia struggled to see through the horde. The princess was almost at the door, and Cordelia was going to miss her chance — there were a dozen people pushing in front of her. Then the crowd surged, and Lord Witloof was swept away from the princess.

'It's now or never, Goose!' Cordelia hissed.

She crouched down as low as she could and pushed her way through a thicket of stockinged legs and swishing skirts. She heard Goose struggling along behind her. They popped up right in the princess's path.

'Your Highness!' Cordelia cried.

'Oh, Miss Hatmaker!' the princess gasped. 'What a relief to see a familiar face . . . All these people are a little *too* friendly.'

Cordelia wasted no time. 'Please can you lend me a boat?' she asked. 'I'm *certain* my father is alive but I need a boat to go and find him!'

The foyer was loud. The princess leaned in close.

'I wish I could help you,' she whispered.

'I'll only need to borrow the boat for a little while,' Cordelia urged. 'Just long enough to find my father. He's been out there for nearly three days.'

Princess Georgina put her hand on Cordelia's arm and said quietly, 'This afternoon the palace received word that the *Jolly Bonnet*'s cabin boy survived the wreck.'

Cordelia felt her eyes widen. 'Jack?' she gasped. 'Is he all right? Where is he?'

'He is at the sailor's sickbay at Wapping Docks,' the princess said. 'Lord Witloof went to visit him as soon as we heard there was a survivor. The poor lad was delirious, speaking nonsense – but from what Lord Witloof managed to piece together . . . Miss Hatmaker, I am so sorry, but –'

'O most esteemed Highness!' Sir Hugo swept towards them with a flourish, somehow getting himself between Cordelia and the princess.

And that was when it happened.

There was a shout. '*Sacré bleu!*'

And a gunshot rang out. The air ripped down the middle as though it was made of cloth.

Around Cordelia, everybody slowed. The hubbub thickened into blunt sounds till all she could hear was her own heartbeat.

People were silently pulling grotesque faces, faces like theatre masks, hands splayed in the air.

Was that somebody screaming?

'*Goose!*' Cordelia tried to say, but her tongue was too big for her mouth.

Her eyes stung as plaster dust fell from the ceiling.

And suddenly she was in the middle of a seething sea of people. The crowd swelled, panic rising in a riptide. The air was choked with screams.

'ASSASSIN!'

Cordelia saw a guard scythe through the crowd. Lord Witloof, white with shock, was right behind him.

'Georgina! *Are you hurt?*' he cried.

The princess shook her head.

'An assassination attempt! Look! The bullet!' Lord Witloof pointed.

In the ceiling right above the princess's head, the black O of a musketball was wedged in the bare bottom of a plaster cherub.

The princess turned a terrified face to Lord Witloof. 'But – *why?*' she whispered.

'The French, I'm certain of it,' he barked. 'Guards! The carriage!'

A dozen guards crashed into the foyer, flinging fops and ladies aside to get to the princess. They seized her and carried her out, Lord Witloof hastening behind. Cordelia staggered to the door and saw the carriage thunder off towards the palace, horses at a gallop.

Then Goose was at her shoulder.

'Come on – let's get out of here!' he puffed, pulling her by the hand out into the London night.

They ran the length of several streets. Only when a sharp pain speared Cordelia in the side did they stop. She bent double, clutching the stitch.

Goose collapsed against the wall and slid slowly to the ground.

'*Assass-in-ation*,' he panted.

'Did you see him?' Cordelia asked. 'The assassin?'

Goose shook his head.

'Me neither.'

'Did they catch him?'

'I don't think so.'

'Is she . . . all right? The princess?' Goose managed.

Cordelia nodded. 'Just scared. Not hurt.'

She did not trust her legs not to wobble, so she sat down next to Goose. Goose managed a wonky smile. She smiled shakily back.

She waited until her voice was certain not to tremble.

'Well, my plan didn't work,' she said eventually. 'No boat.'

Goose groaned. 'I'm sorry, Cordelia.'

'But – Jack!' She suddenly remembered. 'The cabin boy from the *Jolly Bonnet*!'

She jumped up. 'Which way is Wapping?'

'You can't go *now*! It's really late,' Goose said, scrambling to his feet.

'I need to see him as soon as possible, Goose,' Cordelia cried. 'He might know where my father is!'

Goose took her by the shoulders. 'Let's go first thing in the morning,' he said. 'I'll explain to Miss Starebottom when she arrives at my house for lessons. We'll go together. All right?'

Cordelia sighed.

'All right,' she agreed. 'First thing in the morning.'

At the corner of Wimpole Street, Goose took the Camouflage Cap off and his bristly face was smooth again. Cordelia was still so wrapped in her own thoughts that she did not protest when Goose gave her a peck on the cheek and gabbled, 'Thank you for a – a very . . . um . . . a wonderful evening!' before rushing off home.

Hatmaker House was dark and quiet. Still lost in a tangle of thoughts, Cordelia climbed into bed and fell headlong into dreams.

They were dreams so deep and distracting that she did not hear the tread of the thief on the stairs, nor the creak of the door to the Hatmaking Workshop as it was eased open.

CHAPTER 14

'THIEVES AND VILLAINS!' somebody was shouting.

Which was strange, because she was alone, shipwrecked on a desert island. A scarlet parrot flapped in the palm tree above her.

'BURGLARS AND HOUSEBREAKERS!' the parrot squawked.

The sea on the shore sounded like doors slamming. The sun beating on the waves sounded – could light make noise? – like a clanging bell.

'WAKE UP, CORDELIA!'

Cordelia sat up in bed.

Uncle Tiberius's head was sticking into her bedroom through the trapdoor hole.

'WE'VE BEEN ROBBED!' the head shouted, before disappearing.

On the bench in the middle of the Hatmaking Workshop, there was nothing.

The wooden hat block was bald and shiny. The Peace Hat was gone.

'I locked the workshop before bed,' Aunt Ariadne was saying as she tore through all the drawers and cabinets. 'And the key was on my belt all night!'

Buttons, feathers and ribbons flew everywhere. In the Alchemy Parlour, Great-aunt Petronella, in her armchair, poked anything she could reach with her walking stick.

'Call the Thieftaker!' Cook screeched from the kitchen doorway, waving her wooden spoon and spraying flecks of hot porridge around.

'I'll go and fetch him now!' Jones shouted, striding down the hall.

Cordelia frowned at the brass lock on the door to the Hatmaking Workshop. Aunt Ariadne had the only key, but around the keyhole itself there were several scratches.

Uncle Tiberius was frantically upending hatboxes, and Aunt Ariadne was pacing around the room, saying firmly,

'I *locked* . . . The clock struck eleven and I *locked* the door.'

'By the Great Horned Helmet of Odin!' Uncle Tiberius cried. 'They've broken into the Menacing Cabinet!'

The strong iron doors of the Menacing Cabinet were swinging on their hinges.

'Empty!' Uncle Tiberius wailed. 'The bottle of Lightning Strife, gone! And the Orcus Fox claws! Even the *master key*!'

He crumpled in a cold faint and Cordelia backed out of the room. Everybody had lost their heads, it seemed, as well as the Peace Hat. She scrambled back upstairs to her bedroom.

'I can't get distracted,' she said aloud, dressing at speed. 'I've got to get to Wapping as soon as possible. I won't bother Aunt and Uncle with it, in the middle of everything. I'll just go now and tell them later.'

She hurried downstairs. As she passed the Library, she felt a breeze coming from the room. She poked her head round the door. Still no Agatha. The other Quest Pigeons were huddled together in a corner of their aviary, looking ruffled and cold. The window was wide open, which explained the breeze.

'How long has the window been open?' Cordelia asked them.

Tabitha cooed in a dispirited sort of way.

'A long time?' Cordelia asked. 'All night?'

Coo.

Cordelia reached up to close the window and noticed two sooty black handprints on the windowsill. The fingers of the handprints were pointing *into* the room. It looked as though a shadow had clambered in through the window and left a trace of itself behind.

'How strange.'

Cordelia stuck her head out into the morning air.

The street was a long way down. There was a thin drainpipe and a narrow ledge of brickwork on the sheer side of the building. It would surely be impossible to climb up the outside of the house and through the Library window . . .

Uncle Tiberius was brought round from his fainting fit and given a thimbleful of Reviving Dew.

Just as Cordelia was about to slip out of the house, Jones clattered into the hall followed by a tall man, chest puffed out to show off his shiny badge.

Aunt Ariadne and Uncle Tiberius appeared at the top of the stairs.

'Thieftaker Sternlaw at your service,' the man announced, rocking on his polished boots.

Cordelia edged towards the front door.

'Oh, Thieftaker! Thank you for coming,' Uncle Tiberius said, clutching an Ice Cap to his head.

'This way, Mr Sternlaw.' Aunt Ariadne ushered him upstairs.

'I need everyone present who was in the house at the time of the burglary,' the Thieftaker boomed.

'Come along, Cordelia,' Aunt Ariadne commanded.

'But . . .' Cordelia lingered reluctantly by the front door.

'Don't keep the Law waiting!' the Thieftaker barked from the landing.

Cordelia sighed as she traipsed back up the stairs.

'Ah! The scene of the crime, as we call it!' the Thieftaker announced in the doorway to the topsy-turvy workshop.

The Hatmakers all watched the Thieftaker prowl around. He inspected the floor, the ceiling and everything in between.

'Am I right in thinking the hat was here last night?' he asked, pointing at the bald hat block.

Aunt Ariadne nodded.

'But it is not here this morning?' he continued.

She nodded again.

He was silent for several minutes, staring at the hat block.

'The evidence would suggest,' he said, 'that you have been robbed.'

There was a stunned pause.

'Yes,' said Aunt Ariadne. 'We had worked that much out already.'

'My sources inform me that the French assassin has been very active in the last few days,' the Thieftaker pronounced.

'Assassin?' Uncle Tiberius repeated.

'Yes. I'm sure you heard about the assassination attempt at the theatre last night?'

Aunt Ariadne shook her head, turning surprised eyes to Cordelia.

'Is it true?' she asked.

'Yes, but only a plaster cherub got hurt,' Cordelia assured her aunt.

'And the scoundrel got away,' the Thieftaker told them. 'Like smoke in the night. Crafty devil.'

'Um . . . sir?' Cordelia said, pointing at the keyhole. 'Have you seen these scratches?'

Thieftaker Sternlaw blinked down at Cordelia.

'Ah, an enquiring mind – that's good,' he said. 'But, sadly, the mind of a child.' He wagged a finger at her, continuing, 'You see, little girl, those scratches are on the *outside* of the door. The crime happened on the *inside* of this room.'

Cordelia – and the other Hatmakers, from the looks on their faces – failed to follow his logic.

'But there are handprints on the windowsill in the Library,' Cordelia said. 'That could be where the thief broke in!'

Her aunt gasped, but the Thieftaker held up his hand for silence.

'Again,' he said, 'the Library, presumably, is a *different* room from this one. I am concerned with what has happened on the *inside* of *this* room.'

'But –' Cordelia began as the Thieftaker turned to the grown-ups.

'Is there anything else you have noticed is missing?' he asked them.

Great-aunt Petronella, who had been carried downstairs in her armchair by Jones, was poking through the ribbons.

'Three gold star sequins have gone from my Alchemy Parlour,' she croaked. 'They're made of Pyrite and forged in Vesuvian lava, so they're rather unstable without the Angelite enamel I was going to put on them.'

Cordelia felt herself blush. She turned to search busily among the buttons for signs of the thief, while her cheeks cooled down. The three missing star sequins now adorned the hat of London's most celebrated actor . . .

'One Peace Hat. Contents of Menacing Cabinet. Three gold sequins,' Thieftaker Sternlaw muttered, writing in his notebook.

'It's those Bootmakers!' Uncle Tiberius burst out. 'They've always been jealous of the Hatmakers! Ever since Great-great-grandfather Makepeace Hatmaker be-hatted King James the First and put a silver buckle on his hat! Old Plumbago Bootmaker couldn't stand the fact, said buckles were strictly for boots! The Bootmakers have been out for revenge since 1611!'

Uncle Tiberius looked as though he had swallowed a river of Great-aunt Petronella's Vesuvian lava and was filling up from the inside with burning fury. Then he suddenly went white and fainted again.

Over Uncle Tiberius's horizontal form, the Thieftaker told Aunt Ariadne that he would have to go back to his headquarters and fill out a report.

'It will take a rather long time for the ink to dry,' he explained. 'So I shall deliver the report in two to three weeks.'

'B-but the Peace Hat?' Aunt Ariadne faltered. 'What about finding the stolen Peace Hat?'

The Thieftaker assumed an expression of great wisdom and said, 'The trouble with finding stolen goods, Madam Hatmaker, is that very often they are gone.'

This logic was so undeniable that Aunt Ariadne was rendered speechless.

'And whoever stole your hat is the sneakiest thief London has ever seen,' the Thieftaker said, into the baffled silence. 'Or, rather, *not* seen. Good day.'

With that, Thieftaker Sternlaw departed. Cordelia revived Uncle Tiberius with a little more dew.

'There's nothing else for it,' Aunt Ariadne announced, when she had recovered the power of speech. 'The Peace Hat is needed in two days. We shall have to begin again. Luckily I have a little more Lullwool felt.'

'I shall spin more Politic Cord,' Uncle Tiberius said woozily from the floor. 'All this, on the heels of Prospero's loss. It really is too much.'

'More starlight can be gathered tonight,' Aunt Ariadne added determinedly. 'Fresh starlight is best, anyway.'

'Mars is rising, Ariadne,' Great-aunt Petronella warned. 'Be careful not to gather any Mars-light with the starlight.'

Aunt Ariadne nodded, frowning.

Cordelia saw an opportunity and jumped at it. 'I could find some Mellow Daisies,' she suggested brightly.

'Excellent idea, Cordelia!' Aunt Ariadne said. 'Run along and gather some!'

Cordelia grabbed a basket and a large piece of fruitcake from the kitchen table and hurried into the street.

She was *finally* on the way to Wapping.

CHAPTER 15

Cordelia had arranged to meet Goose on the street at nine o'clock sharp, but she was rather late because of all the turmoil at Hatmaker House. Goose would be having his lessons with Miss Starebottom by now, in his schoolroom at the back of Bootmaker Mansion.

She was slinking down the street behind the gloomy grey mansion when she heard a familiar squawking.

'SAAAS-AAA-NAAA-SHAA!'

It was Sam Lightfinger. He was standing on the pavement opposite Goose's schoolroom, wagging newspapers at passers-by. Perhaps if she lingered outside talking to Sam, Goose would look out of the window and see she was ready to go.

'Hello again!' Cordelia said loudly.

Sam spun round, clutching his oversized cap to his head.

'Oh! 'Ello!' he said, grinning. 'SAAAS-AAA-NAAA-SHAA!'

'What is *Saaas-aaa-naaa-shaa*?' Cordelia enquired.

'Assassination,' Sam said, holding up a newspaper with a grubby paw.

~ THE DAILY SLAPP ~
ASSASSINATION DRAMA
AT THE THEATRE*!*

Princess escapes death but Shakespeare is butchered!

'Why do they say Shakespeare was butchered?' Cordelia wondered aloud. 'He died a long time ago!'

Then she remembered Hamlet swaggering about the stage, yowling every speech. 'Oh, perhaps they're being rude about Sir Hugo's acting.'

'What's it say?' Sam asked, squinting at the headline.

'Can't you read?' Cordelia blurted.

Sam squinted at her. 'It ain't like I turned down lessons,' he said. 'Never got the chance to 'ave any.'

'Oh.' Cordelia blushed. 'Sorry – I didn't mean to be rude.'

'Ah, well.' Sam grinned ruefully. 'An orphan who can read's nuffin' but trouble, I bin told.'

He scuffed the pavement with a holey boot that was, in truth, more hole than boot.

Cordelia glanced casually up at Goose's window. There was still no sign of him. She turned back to Sam.

'How do you decide what to shout for the headline?' she asked, trying for a polite, conversational tone to make up for her accidental rudeness.

'I get told what to yell every morning, then I yell it, see? SAAAS-AAA-NAAA-SHAA!' Sam yelled, to demonstrate.

A footman stalked up and gave Sam a penny, holding out his hand for a paper.

'Aw, sir, price 'as gone up,' Sam said happily. 'Paper's two pennies now.'

The footman scowled but dropped a second penny into Sam's hand and stalked away with a newspaper.

Still nothing from Goose's window.

'Why's the price gone up?' Cordelia asked.

Sam scratched his nose, leaving a sooty smudge, and said, 'The news today is twice as bad, so it costs twice as much.' Then he leaned in close to Cordelia and whispered, 'Me boss says that when there's a war I'll sell *three times* as many newspapers at *four times* the price. Cos grown-ups always want to hear bad news, see?'

Cordelia could not help but wonder at the strange habits of grown-ups.

Suddenly the back door of Bootmaker Mansion slammed open, making Cordelia and Sam jump.

'Goo—' Cordelia stopped herself mid-word.

It was not Goose. It was his mother, Mrs Bootmaker, wearing an irate expression that reminded Cordelia of the saying 'a face like an old boot'. Mrs Bootmaker stood there glowering, a leather mallet clutched in one hand.

'Skulking!' she bellowed. 'Lurking! Loitering with intent!'

Sam pasted a winning grin on to his face.

'He's only selling newspapers!' Cordelia objected, as the angry woman advanced.

But it was not Sam Lightfinger who was causing Mrs Bootmaker such outrage. She strode up to Cordelia and towered over her, blocking out the sun.

'I suppose your Aunt Hatmaker sent you, didn't she?' growled Mrs Bootmaker. 'To *spy* on us! To see what excellent Peace Boots the Bootmakers are making for the princess!'

Out of the corner of Cordelia's eye – finally! – she saw Goose's face peeking through his schoolroom window. He looked horrified at the sight of his mother threatening his secret friend. Miss Starebottom hovered anxiously behind him.

'No, ma'am,' Cordelia said, trying to sound polite but firm. 'I simply came to buy a newspaper.'

'Hah!' Mrs Bootmaker snorted. 'That story's about as honest as the claptrap they print in *The Daily Slapp*!'

With that, Mrs Bootmaker dropped two pennies into Sam's hand and snatched a newspaper.

'Get out of here, nosey little Hatmaker!' she spat. 'Tell

your aunt she's not to send snoops around here trying to steal our ideas!'

THWACK!

The Daily Slapp, true to its name, slapped Cordelia squarely round the head before Mrs Bootmaker retreated. Luckily it was not the leather mallet.

Cordelia glimpsed Goose grimacing and mouthing '*Sorry!*' at her through the window before Miss Starebottom yanked him out of sight.

'Phew! She's a battleaxe, in't she?' Sam grinned. 'Think I'll find somewhere a bit more friendly ta sell me papers.'

They walked along two streets together, Sam doing a lively impression of Mrs Bootmaker bearing down on Cordelia. She couldn't help grinning as Sam windmilled his arms and bawled.

'Wapping's south-east, isn't it?' she asked him at the corner of Bond Street.

Sam nodded. 'Yup.'

'This way, then,' Cordelia decided.

'Hold on a mo.' Sam caught Cordelia's arm, peering down the street.

A little way down the road, a big commotion was kicking off. There was a clanging, then a figure in a flowing white nightgown ran into the street.

'CALAMITY!' the figure shouted.

Someone else was leaning out of an upstairs window, banging copper pots together.

'Call the Thieftaker! *We've been robbed!*'

'Is that . . .' She could not be sure. 'Is that the *Cloakmakers*?'

'Come on,' Sam muttered, pulling Cordelia away down a side street. 'Let's not get tangled up in all that.'

'That's *two* robberies,' Cordelia panted, jogging beside Sam as he marched along. 'Us last night and now them this morning! Do you think it was the same person?'

Sam frowned. 'Prob'ly.'

They passed the Glovemakers on Henrietta Place. Cordelia glanced at Glovemaker House (which was actually two identical pink houses, side by side) and wondered how such a sweet-looking home could contain such odious children as the two sets of Glovemaker twins.

Sam shuffled his newspapers back into a neat stack. 'This looks like a good place ta hawk a bit more bad news,' he announced.

'I've got to go,' Cordelia said. 'With or without Goose, I've got to get to Wapping!'

'Bye, Cor!' Sam called after her.

As Cordelia hurried away down the street, she heard Sam shout, 'GETCHA *SLAPP* 'ERE!'

CHAPTER 16

Cordelia smelled the docks at Wapping before she saw them: the tang of tarry ship's rigging combined with the muddy reek of the Thames.

A girl selling cockles from a handcart swerved round her, sailors heaving heavy sacks stumped past. Mules brayed, complaining, as they hauled wagons loaded with barrels. Cordelia goggled at the sheer volume of goods being carried in and out of Wapping. It seemed everything that came into London came through the docks.

She wove through the crowds and out on to the quayside. Moored at the wharves were several huge ships. They were ocean-going vessels, their enormous bodies stirring like sleeping giants on the tidal swell of the river.

Sailors whistled instructions to each other as they winched

crates from the decks to the dockside. Girls sang ditties to advertise their wares.

'Fresh briny winkles!'

'Sugarcane of Caribbee!'

'Baccy from the New World!'

'Excuse me!' Cordelia called up to a sailor, lounging on top of a bale of cotton the size of a carriage. 'Which way to the sickbay?'

The sailor pointed, and Cordelia pushed through the crowd. The sickbay was nothing more than a ramshackle shed. Inside, she found coils of thick rope stacked by the door and masses of slimy rigging abandoned in tangled heaps.

'Hello?' she called.

The air was stale and stifling. A dirty old piece of canvas sail was draped over a railing to make a curtain. She reached out towards it –

'ARRR!'

Cordelia jumped. Something stirred in the shadows. She squinted into the darkness.

Splayed on a pile of rope was an old seadog. He was a man, not a dog, but he was so grizzled and unkempt that Cordelia immediately felt he should be thought of as a seadog. She peered at him. He clutched a bottle to his chest and twitched in his sleep.

'*RAR . . . arrr*,' he growled, huddling down into his rope-nest.

She considered waking him, but thought it was probably

best to let sleeping seadogs lie. She pulled aside the sail-curtain and there, in a bed made from shipping crates and old sacking, lay Jack Fortescue: the cabin boy from the *Jolly Bonnet*.

Cordelia had last seen him scrambling up the rigging to the crow's nest. Now he lay small and still, his sleeping face puckered in a distressed expression.

'Jack?' she whispered.

She crept to his bedside, glad she had brought something for him. From her basket she took out the slab of fruitcake she had stolen from the kitchen and unwrapped it.

'Jack?' she whispered again. 'You awake?'

She held the fruitcake near his face, hoping the sweet smell would wake him up.

'*Jack?*'

She wafted it under his nose but he did not stir. She shook him gently. His body was heavy like a sack of flour. Her heart started to pound. The cabin boy was in a deep sleep – *too* deep.

'JACK!' she shouted, shaking him harder. 'WAKE UP!'

She looked around desperately. Perched on a nearby barrel was a jug of water and a small, dark bottle that looked like medicine. She snatched up the jug and threw the contents on Jack's face.

'WATER!' he wailed, lurching upright. 'WATER!' His face was dripping wet and terrified, his mouth a black O gasping for breath.

'It's all right, Jack! You're all right!' Cordelia cried.

'TOO MUCH WATER!'

'I'm sorry! I'm sorry!' she said, sobbing. 'I didn't mean to –'

'Everywhere! *It's everywhere!*' Jack scrabbled frantically, as though he was trying to fight a great wave bearing down on him.

'You're safe!' Cordelia whispered. '*You're safe!*'

She caught his arms and held them steady. His breath came in shuddering gasps. She looked into his frightened eyes and tried to smile in a reassuring way.

'You're all right, Jack,' she murmured. 'You're safe, you're on dry land. See? Here, I've brought you some fruitcake.'

He clung to her as if she was saving him from drowning. His ragged gasping calmed a little, but he was still delirious.

'Jack?'

He blinked woozily at her and collapsed back on to the sacking. 'In the drink,' he muttered.

Cordelia nodded. *The drink* was what sailors sometimes called the sea.

'I know you were, but you survived,' she said soothingly.

He shuddered and closed his eyes.

'I know this isn't an ideal time to talk about this,' she said, stroking his hand gently. 'But it's really important. It's about my father, Captain Hatmaker.'

Jack's eyes snapped open. 'Hat – Hatmaker! Captain Hatmaker!'

'Yes!' Cordelia cried, hope and fear shooting through her belly. She was on her feet. 'He's alive, isn't he?'

Jack was agitated, struggling to sit up. 'Cor – Cor–' he stammered. *'Dil-ly!'*

'Yes! It's me! Can you tell me where Father is?'

Jack reached a shaking hand into his shirt. He pulled something out, burbling words Cordelia could not fathom. He was clutching a leather tube. She reached for it, but he swung it wildly to the side. The medicine bottle fell to the floor and smashed. A dark, bitter smell burned Cordelia's nostrils.

'Oh, no!'

Exhausted, Jack dropped the leather tube on to his lap.

'For you,' he murmured. 'From him.'

And he was asleep.

From him. For her! Cordelia snatched up the leather tube. It was heavier than it looked, capped at one end, and still damp from the sea. Fingers trembling, she pulled off the cap and tipped the tube upside down.

A shiny brass instrument slid out on to the bed. It was her father's treasured telescope! He carried it at his side whenever he was on board ship.

She picked it up. The hands that had last held this instrument were her father's. But why had he sent it to her?

'It must be a message,' she whispered. 'Or some kind of sign?' She paused, almost expecting it to speak its message to her.

Carefully, she put her eye to the spying end of it. The pile of ropes near the bed was so close she could see the individual strands in the coarse twist of hemp. She took her eye away and blinked.

It was, as far as Cordelia could tell, just a normal telescope. All her hope and fear and excitement were ebbing away, leaving her empty and confused.

She put it back to her eye and swung it round.

'YAARRR!'

Bared yellow teeth and one popping eye!

'AAH!' Cordelia jerked the telescope away from her face. It was the old seadog. He stood swaying beside the dirty sail, his single, bloodshot eye fixed on Cordelia.

'What's this, missy?' he rasped.

Cordelia caught a whiff of stale rum. 'I – I'm his sister,' she invented. 'I've come to visit him.'

The seadog tilted his head woozily. 'Arr.' He caught sight of the broken medicine bottle on the ground and kicked it. 'Blast. He'll be in a bate 'bout it.'

'Is he going to be all right?' Cordelia asked, tucking the telescope safely out of sight inside her jacket.

The seadog swivelled his eye towards her.

'The sea does strange things to folk,' he muttered, before turning and lurching back past the sail-curtain. She heard glugging, then rattling snores a moment later.

She gazed down at Jack's sleeping face.

'You know the truth, I'm certain of it,' she said softly to him. 'But it's all swirled up inside your head at the moment.'

'*Cordelia!*'

She swung round.

'Miss Starebottom!'

It was her governess, looking very out of place in her prim grey dress among all the rotting ship's equipment.

'What on earth are you doing here, child?' she cried. 'When Master Bootmaker told me that you were likely on the way to Wapping, I barely believed him. Nevertheless, I hurried here as soon as I could!'

Miss Starebottom picked her way delicately through the slimy ropes, looking around in disgust.

'This is no place for a young lady, Miss Hatmaker!' she said, pinching her nose closed. She took a pretty bottle out of her purse and splashed Cordelia liberally with lavender water.

'Am I – in – trouble?' Cordelia coughed as the sweet scent tickled her throat.

'Oh, yes, you are in a great deal of trouble,' Miss Starebottom confirmed. 'But I am at least happy to have found you before something dreadful happened. Come along – I'm taking you home. I have a phaeton waiting.'

Cordelia hesitated. She had been so close to finding out the truth about her father. She looked from her governess to Jack.

'Can we bring him with us?' she asked. 'He needs looking after.'

Miss Starebottom peered at the sleeping cabin boy.

'He looks rather grubby,' she said disapprovingly. 'You can ask your aunt when we get home.'

'But he needs looking after *now*! He's sick!' Cordelia insisted.

Miss Starebottom raised one eyebrow. Cordelia knew this warning sign – one eyebrow meant *Danger ahead*, while two eyebrows meant *Too late*.

'*Please?*' Cordelia begged, in spite of the eyebrow.

In answer, Miss Starebottom took Cordelia's hand and pulled her towards the door. The seadog snorted awake as they passed, but the governess emptied her entire bottle of lavender water on him and he collapsed in a cacophony of coughs.

Miss Starebottom whisked Cordelia out of the shed and along the docks, towards the phaeton. They were going at a very unladylike pace indeed, but Miss Starebottom did not appear to care.

CHAPTER 17

As the phaeton turned up Wimpole Street, Miss Starebottom cleared her throat delicately.

'Of course, today is Tuesday,' she said. 'And technically I am governess to Master Bootmaker today. Therefore, I could not possibly have been in Wapping with Miss Hatmaker.'

Her eyes twinkled conspiratorially. Cordelia grinned and tapped her nose.

'Not a word, Miss Starebottom. I promise.'

The carriage rolled to a halt and Cordelia jumped out.

'Good luck,' the governess whispered, rapping the side of the carriage. It whisked her away down the street.

Cordelia bounded up the front steps of Hatmaker House and threw open the door.

'Aunt!' she called, galloping through the hall and up the stairs. 'Aunt! Where are you?'

Aunt Ariadne appeared in the workshop doorway, holding a steaming kettle in her hand.

'There you are!' she exclaimed. 'You've been a terribly long time! Do you have the Mellow Daisies?'

'What?' Cordelia had forgotten all about collecting Mellow Daisies. 'Oh! No – I didn't get any. But, Aunt, there's something much more important! I found Jack Fortescue. He's alive – he's in Wapping!'

Uncle Tiberius appeared, frowning.

'You've been to Wapping?' Aunt Ariadne said.

'Yes!' Cordelia said breathlessly. 'Cos the princess told me –'

'Jack Fortescue?' Uncle Tiberius rumbled.

'*Yes!*' Cordelia was impatient to tell them about him. 'But he's sick. He needs looking after, and not by a seadog who smells of rum.' Her aunt and uncle stared down at her. Their slowness was infuriating. 'And he knows something about my father. He can tell me how to find him, I am absolutely sure of it!'

Cordelia's whole body and soul were tensed.

'Jack survived the wreck?' said Aunt Ariadne.

Cordelia nodded. She felt her eyes widen, pleading.

'And now he's in a sickbay in Wapping?'

'It's more of a shed than a sickbay,' Cordelia said.

'We must fetch him here and nurse him back to health,' Aunt Ariadne said decisively. 'Go and tell Jones to ready the carriage.'

Cordelia's soul soared. She flew back down the stairs, tore through the kitchen and out into the mews behind Hatmaker House. 'Jones!' she shouted. 'Ready the carriage!'

She rushed back inside and began to collect things that she thought Jack might need for the journey – a blanket, the rest of the fruitcake, a bottle of milk.

'*You* won't be going, Cordelia,' Aunt Ariadne told her. 'I need you to tidy the workshop. It's in a terrible state after the robbery. An unruly workshop makes for unruly hats. We can't have an unruly Peace Hat on the princess's head. That would make for an unruly peace.'

'But –'

'Jones is perfectly capable of collecting Jack without your help.'

Very reluctantly, Cordelia bundled her collection of supplies into the carriage, gave Jones detailed directions to the sickbay in Wapping and waved him off.

Aunt Ariadne ushered her upstairs. 'You've got your work cut out for you, Dilly,' she said. 'And I've got to start steaming the felt for the new Peace Hat while your uncle goes to collect those Mellow Daisies.'

Cordelia sighed and rolled up her sleeves. She began by tidying away all the buttons and beetle wings that had been thrown to the floor in the mad search for the missing hat. She had not had time to go up to her room to put her father's telescope away, so it poked her in the ribs as she worked.

What does it mean? she wondered, untangling a muddle of wriggly ribbons. *Why did he give the telescope to Jack to give to me? What for?*

Tidying the workshop took a very long time, although Hatmaker House did give Cordelia a little help with her chores. Her aunt did not approve of the ingredients or cupboards in the workshop getting 'too involved' in Hatmaking, but when she was out of the room, the bobbins helpfully rolled around on the floor, neatly re-spooling their Dwam Threads. A flock of feathers drifted back up to their places on the wall and some Risible Mushrooms hopped back into their box of their own accord.

'Thank you,' Cordelia whispered to them, just as her aunt marched back into the workshop with Uncle Tiberius behind her, arms full of Mellow Daisies.

'Don't forget my filing system, Dilly!' he said.

Uncle Tiberius's filing system was extremely complicated and involved about a thousand small sandalwood boxes all labelled with tiny writing. You could not simply put an azure-blue Moonwing feather into a box that said:

Feathers

Or even:

Feathers ~ Blue

You had to find exactly the right box, which in the case of an azure-blue Moonwing feather was the box inscribed:

Feathers ~ Blue ~ (strong, light)
Avi-ornithological ~ Northern Europe
Tranquil ~ Lunal ~ Phoenix Rising
Dream-Benevolent ~ Aspect-Providential
Silver-mark Felicitous
✷ ✷ ✷ ☾

The little diagram of moons and stars on the label meant something important.

Squinting at the spidery writing, Cordelia felt it would be a lot more fun to make a hat using pure instinct, rather than consulting all the tiny labels and poring over books for hours before starting. But she did not think it wise to suggest this to her uncle, whose frustrated sighs ruffled the silence as he tried to weave an uncooperative strand of Concord Moss into a hatband.

Cordelia put the seashells back in their saltwater tank, polished the Sooth Crystals and laid them carefully in their velvet-lined box, swept the floor (the ticklish floorboard shivered as the broom touched it), and rearranged the wooden hat blocks on the shelves. But she was still nowhere near coming up with a sensible answer to the question of the telescope.

When he's feeling better, Jack will be able to tell me why he sent it, she thought. *And where Father is.*

But Jones was still not back from Wapping with Jack.

Cordelia pressed her face to the window. It was getting dark. 'They should have been back *ages* ago!' she said.

Her uncle shrugged, weaving the last flower into a delicate Mellow Daisy chain. Aunt Ariadne looked up, pink-faced from the steam. She wiped her damp forehead.

'Well done, Cordelia,' she said. 'Beautifully tidy.'

Cordelia nodded. 'Much more ruly.'

'Ruly?'

'You said it was *un*ruly before,' Cordelia reasoned. 'So now I've tidied it, it must be ruly.'

Cook rang the supper bell.

Cordelia fidgeted at the kitchen table. She tried to concentrate on eating, but every carriage that rolled down the street made her jump up and run to the window.

'Cordelia,' Aunt Ariadne barked the ninth time it happened. '*Please* sit down.'

'It's really them this time!' Cordelia cried, rushing to open the door.

Cook was already dishing up a bowl of stew for Jack, but Jones came inside alone.

'Where is he?' Cordelia exclaimed.

Jones shook his head, took his hat off and slumped down heavily on the bench.

'I searched all over Wapping for him,' he said. 'High and low, asked everyone I saw. Couldn't find him anywhere.'

'Did you go to the sickbay?' Cordelia frowned.

Jones nodded. 'Yes. There was an old drunk sailor asleep and a broken medicine bottle on the floor, like you described.'

'But Jack wasn't there?'

'Nowhere to be seen. And all the ships have now been forbidden from leaving port, on account of the assassination attempt. The last one allowed out was just setting sail for Jamaica when I arrived at the docks,' Jones told them.

Cordelia shook her head.

'It doesn't make sense,' she whispered. 'He was all muzzy and confused – he couldn't have gone anywhere.'

She felt her aunt's comforting hand on her shoulder, but she shook it off. Jones looked from Cordelia to her aunt.

'On my way back, as I passed the Glovemakers, they were calling for the Thieftaker. They were robbed too, this afternoon. And the Cloakmakers this morning, I heard.'

Cook gasped and Uncle Tiberius snorted.

'The Cloakmakers, the Glovemakers and us,' Aunt Ariadne said grimly.

'All Makers are in danger,' Great-aunt Petronella croaked.

'It's got to be those Bootmakers –' Uncle Tiberius began.

'But *Jack*!' Cordelia interrupted. 'He knows something about my father. I need – I need –' She felt the chance of finding her father slipping like water through her fists. 'We need to find Jack!'

'Sometimes when something terrible and frightening has happened to someone, they aren't themselves,' Uncle Tiberius said softly. 'And the easiest thing is to run away.'

'But Jack couldn't have! He wasn't even strong enough to sit up!' Cordelia protested.

Uncle Tiberius pulled her to him and crushed her into a bear hug, murmuring words of comfort, but all she could hear was the sound of waves on rocks. Or it might have been blood pounding in her ears.

She unscrunched from her uncle's arms.

'But . . . there's still hope?' she whispered.

'My dearest,' Aunt Ariadne began, her voice full of unbearable sympathy.

Cordelia did not want to hear it.

'No!' she wailed, whirling round and running from the room. 'There *is* hope! There's . . .'

Agatha!

Agatha would be back by now.

Cordelia's feet pounded up the stairs. Her heart tore in her chest. In the Library, she threw open the window and leaned out into the night, listening for the hush of wings bringing Agatha back with a message from her father.

Nothing. Nothing but a terrible emptiness in the sky.

'*What can I do now?*' Cordelia sobbed.

There was a soft footstep in the doorway and Aunt Ariadne was there.

'Cordelia? Can you help me set the Starbowl on the roof?' she asked gently. 'And then I think we should all have an early night. We need to be at our very best to work on the hat. The day after tomorrow it must be finished and delivered to the palace. We must not forget our duties even in this difficulty.' She took Cordelia by the hand.

Uncle Tiberius carefully tied a Boltfast rope in complicated knots around the doors of the Hatmaking Workshop as Cordelia helped her aunt carry the Starbowl out on to the roof.

It was a deep silver bowl with a domed glass lid. They set it carefully on the brick ledge by the chimney. Mars winked red in the western sky, so Aunt Ariadne tilted the bowl eastwards.

'By morning, it will be full of fresh starlight,' she whispered.

Its glass dome was speckled with reflected stars.

'They help us find our way, littlest one,' Prospero had once said to her, sitting on the very same chimney. 'The stars guide us through this world. They're always above us, but we can only see them when it's dark. So, if you're ever lost, you have to wait for it to be dark – so dark that you can't even see your nose in front of your face. Then you can look up at the stars and begin to find yourself.'

'They help us find our way, littlest one,' Prospero had
once said to her, sitting on the very same chimney.

Cordelia had snuggled in her father's arms, wondering at his heaven-deep wisdom.

Tonight she looked up, but her eyes prickled and a hot tear slipped down her cheek. She was grateful that the dark was hiding her face from her aunt.

When she climbed into bed, she did not shut her eyes. She held her father's telescope tightly to her chest and lay hoping – *hoping* – for a miracle, like the moon shining in the dark of the night.

Perhaps, said a small voice inside her head, *perhaps it was the last thing he did before he went under the waves. Perhaps he threw it to Jack, like my mother threw me in the hatbox, right before she died. Just so I could have something special of his –*

'No,' Cordelia said sternly. 'There's *got* to be another reason.'

She slipped out of bed and went to the window with the telescope. She extended it as far as it would go. It was almost too long for her to hold, and very heavy. When she put it to her eye, it brought the chimneys across the street close enough to touch.

She swung the telescope up towards the star-speckled sky.

It looked as though someone with starlight on their fingers had smudged the glass. The stars were daubed and splotched across a black canvas. Cordelia twisted the telescope, as her father had taught her to do, and the blurry stars snapped into sparkling focus.

With a soft whisper, a piece of paper unfurled from a thin slit in the brass casing and drifted to the floor, landing at Cordelia's feet. She snatched up the paper and bounded across the room to the fireplace, where the embers still gave enough light to read by.

She stared at it, turned it over, then turned it over again. It was blank.

'It *can't* be!'

She stirred the embers and held the paper closer. Nothing but a smooth, empty page.

'*Father!*' Cordelia cried.

Heart sinking like a stone in the ocean, she remembered: the leather telescope case had been damp from the seawater. Jack had tucked it inside his shirt as he swam to safety, so surely anything written on the paper would have been washed away by the remorseless waves.

Cordelia knelt on the hearth in front of the dying fire, clutching the blank paper in her hand. She wondered, with a great aching heart, what words her father had written for her that had been lost to the sea.

She did not know how long she sat there. Eventually the soft murmur of the wind swirling around Hatmaker House and the ever-so-faint tinkle of starlight falling into the bowl on the roof made Cordelia's head feel heavy. She laid her cheek on the warm tiles of the fireplace.

'There's still *hope*,' she muttered, already half dreaming

that she would find those lost words from her father drifting in the ocean of sleep.

The embers burned low and slowly faded to ash.

In a mansion not far away, a shadow was scrambling through a schoolroom window. A shadow that left a print of itself behind on the windowsill.

CHAPTER 18

Cordelia woke on her bedroom floor, her cheek cold on the fireplace tiles. Musical chimes tinkled through Hatmaker House. It sounded as though Great-aunt Petronella had spilled a jar of moonbeams down the stairs.

Cordelia followed the sound all the way to the front hall, but there were no spilled moonbeams anywhere.

Aunt Ariadne appeared from the workshop, clutching an armful of Pax Palm leaves.

Uncle Tiberius leaned over the staircase and called down, 'By Methuselah's bicorn! It can't be the Summoning Clock?'

'I haven't heard that sound in thirty years,' Aunt Ariadne whispered.

Cordelia was about to ask what on earth a Summoning Clock was, when her mouth fell open in surprise.

The ancient clock in the corner of the hall was moving.

Never, in all of Cordelia's life, had the clock moved. It had stood there, upright and inscrutable, like a sentry guard with a secret, since before she was born. It was built into the very walls of Hatmaker House and Cordelia was sure she had seen Uncle Tiberius glance darkly at it from time to time. But if she tried to touch it or turn the key to wind it up, her aunt or uncle, or Cook, and even once her father, would say, 'Leave it be, Cordelia.'

Now the hands on its face were moving smoothly round, and melodic chimes were sounding a tune from somewhere inside its ancient body, and –

'Oh!' Cordelia cried.

A tiny wooden door opened and a little carved figure glided out. It was exquisitely dressed, with miniature polished boots, a flowing cloak, a pair of gloves, a fob watch the size of an apple seed, and an old-fashioned black hat, trimmed with a tiny feather. The figure carried an elegant walking stick in one hand, as thin as a twig, with a fine silver handle.

Aunt Ariadne and Uncle Tiberius joined Cordelia in the hall. They all watched as the clock's secret resident raised his hat in salute, turned on the spot and disappeared back inside.

The tiny door snapped shut and the hands on the clock face froze. The chimes fell silent.

'You know what this means, Ariadne,' Uncle Tiberius muttered.

'Indeed I do,' Aunt Ariadne replied grimly.

'What –' Cordelia began.

'Cordelia, go and put on your finest clothes,' her aunt ordered.

She had such a stern look on her face that Cordelia ran straight up the stairs without asking any of the questions running through her head.

Twenty minutes later, the Hatmakers marched along Bond Street, all dressed in their smartest clothes, with their most spectacular hats jammed on their heads.

'Where are we going?' Cordelia asked, half jogging to keep up with her aunt.

'The Guildhall,' Aunt Ariadne answered, cutting along the pavement with the surging purpose of a battleship in full sail.

'What's the Guildhall?' Cordelia panted, feeling like a rowing boat struggling along in her wake.

'You'll see when we get there,' Uncle Tiberius puffed, coming up behind them. He was pushing Great-aunt Petronella in a wheeled chair. Great-aunt Petronella squawked with glee as the wind flapped her black shawls around her face.

'But why did the clock chime?' Cordelia demanded. 'Did you wind it, Uncle?'

Her uncle kept ploughing down the pavement, using Great-aunt Petronella and her chair to make headway through the crowds. 'No, I did not wind that clock,' he huffed. 'That clock is made from a Kingsland Oak, which was struck by lightning in the great storm of 1492. Six identical clocks were carved from it, so when one clock is wound up, all six clocks chime at the same time. That is why you were instructed never to touch it. You'd have set off chimes throughout the city.'

Cordelia stopped in the street, in wonder.

'But where are the other five clocks?' she called, bounding after her uncle.

He appeared not to hear her.

Across the gully of the muddy road, through a shuffle of carts and carriages, Cordelia spotted the Cloakmakers on the opposite pavement. They were a large family, eight of them in total, walking together in an elegant procession. They were heading in the same direction as the Hatmakers, wearing what looked like their finest clothes and their stoniest expressions.

Strange.

'Uncle – look –' Cordelia pointed at them.

He grunted and narrowed his eyes, but he did not seem surprised.

'This way!' Aunt Ariadne called, taking a corner at speed. Cordelia scampered after her.

They were striding down an alley now, the backs of buildings rising on either side of them like the cliffs of a canyon. Round one corner, then another, the alley zig-zagged, getting darker and narrower.

After a hairpin bend Aunt Ariadne stopped suddenly. Cordelia collided with her. The wheels on Great-aunt Petronella's chair squealed as Uncle Tiberius pulled her to a halt.

The Hatmakers were standing in a shabby square, staring up at a very old building. It was vast and grand, with ruby-red brick walls, wide diamond-paned windows and twisting chimneys.

On a plinth above the studded oak door was a statue of a man. It was identical to the little carved figure that had appeared out of the clock in the Hatmakers' hall, except this one was life-size. He wore a triumphant smile on his stone face and did not seem to mind that his hat had crumbled a little, or that his elegant cane had been broken off.

In spite of its grandeur, the building had a sad, abandoned air, as if its walls and empty windows were wishing for something.

'Aunt Ariadne, what is this place?' Cordelia asked, rather breathless.

Her aunt looked down at her with a curious mixture of sadness and pride.

'Only Makers and monarchs can open these doors,' she answered, reaching out and taking hold of the brass handle. She twisted it.

The door groaned open, revealing a dark hallway.

Cordelia stepped inside.

CHAPTER 19

The air was thick with dust and magic.

Before her eyes adjusted to the gloom, Cordelia could smell the history in the building around her: there was the chalky scent of marble floors and the resin sweetness of wood-panelled walls. She felt her way forward and brushed through velvet curtains, prickly with age.

She was in a colossal circular chamber. Jewel-coloured light spilled through a vast stained-glass window, scattering a dazzling pattern on the wide wooden floor. Soaring pillars circled the room and a domed ceiling rose high above her, garlanded with plaster flowers. Tapestries and paintings adorned the walls, carved wooden crests hung above the doors, and a sweeping mahogany staircase curled in an elegant arc to a gallery above.

Cordelia walked into the middle of the enormous room,

leaving a track of footprints in the dust. Around her, the air hummed with unspoken magic. She felt like she was standing inside a secret.

'I am sorry we've never told you about the Guildhall,' Aunt Ariadne murmured as she drew up behind Cordelia, 'but we did not really know how to begin . . . Besides, a meeting of Makers has not been called for thirty years.'

'It was built more than two hundred and fifty years ago, by King Henry the Eighth.' Uncle Tiberius beckoned her over to look at a large oil painting on the wall. 'There he is. Notoriously vain, was King Henry. He appointed families to be Makers of the Royal Garb and every few weeks he'd come riding up and want to try on new outfits. This is where our ancestors worked, making hats for the king.'

Cordelia peered up at the painting. It depicted the familiar broad-faced king surrounded by industrious Makers, all busily decorating him with magnificent accessories.

'Oh, King Henry was rather naughty.' Great-aunt Petronella sighed, gazing up at the painting. 'I remember, after he beheaded his second wife, my mother made me hide in the garderobe when he came for his fittings. She was worried he'd take a shine to me.'

Cordelia turned to her great-aunt. 'But – that was over two hundred years ago!'

'Yes.' Great-aunt Petronella nodded. 'I was a pretty young thing, wasn't I?'

*Cordelia walked into the middle of the enormous
room, leaving a track of footprints in the dust.*

Cordelia stared at the graceful young lady in the painting who was placing an ornately embroidered cap on the king's head. She turned to study her great-aunt's parchment-pale face, her wrinkles so deep they could have been carved from marble.

'Great-aunt, exactly *how* old are you, if I might be permitted to ask?' Cordelia said, careful to sound as polite as she possibly could.

Her great-aunt turned twinkling eyes to Cordelia. 'Oh, once I got to a hundred I stopped counting.'

'But when *was* that?' Cordelia asked.

'Ah, dearest, time is relative, you know!'

Cordelia could not tell whether or not her great-aunt was joking. She turned back to the painting, still puzzling. Then she noticed something else strange about it.

'But – there are *six* Makers in this picture!' she exclaimed. 'Hat – Cloak – Glove – Watch – Boot – and . . . is that a walking stick?'

'Cane,' her uncle said through a tight jaw. 'The Canemakers.'

'Who are the *Canemakers*? Why are they in this picture? I thought there were only five Maker families!'

'There were six,' Aunt Ariadne admitted, her footsteps echoing as she marched across the great empty chamber. 'King Henry appointed six Maker families in total. As well as being vain, he was also paranoid – he constantly worried about his enemies trying to overthrow him and take his throne – so he gave the six greatest Maker families a royal charter and banned all other makers from working.'

'There were other makers?'

'Oh, yes,' Great-aunt Petronella said. 'There was once a time when everyone in England was free to make whatever they chose, and not just clothes. Then the king decided he wanted to keep that power all for himself and anyone caught making anything without a royal charter was thrown in prison.'

'Why?' Cordelia cried.

'The king was afraid that somebody else might invent a hat that would give them great cleverness, or make gloves to gain the upper hand, or a cloak of compelling elegance, and then they would be able to throw him off the throne. He made the six chosen families sign a pledge to do no harm. That's where the Maker motto comes from: *Noli nocere*, do no harm.'

'I thought that was the *Hatmaker* family motto?' Cordelia asked.

Her aunt shook her head. 'It belongs to *all* the Maker families,' she said, ignoring Uncle Tiberius grinding his teeth behind her.

Cordelia frowned. 'And ... the Canemakers – what happened to them?'

'After King Henry died, we kept on making,' Great-aunt Petronella said. 'All six royal-appointed Maker families would come every day to the Guildhall to make things for the king or queen. In 1632, King Charles the First gave permission for us to make things for members of the aristocracy. We made things for the lords and ladies, but always had to keep the most magnificent things for the king himself. That way, he made sure he was always the grandest and most powerful person. Each family of Makers had an individual workshop leading off this grand chamber. That's the Hatmaking Workshop there –'

She pointed to a tall door with a crest carved over it: a shield with a plume-feathered hat, surrounded by seven stars.

'Oh!' Cordelia was surprised to see the familiar Hatmaker emblem looking perfectly at home in this strange, ancient place.

'Do you know why there are seven stars on the Hatmaker crest?' Aunt Ariadne asked her.

Cordelia shook her head.

'There's one for each Maker family,' her aunt told her. 'And the seventh star represents the idea that the Makers shine brightest when they all work together. You can have a hat, or a pair of gloves, or a cloak, but alone they have less power. The most potent magic is said to ignite when all six Makers unite.'

Uncle Tiberius growled low in his throat and narrowed his eyes at a portrait of a plump Glovemaker smiling benignly from the wall.

'We all shared our secrets and ingredients and new techniques and discoveries very happily,' Great-aunt Petronella told Cordelia. 'There was a slight disagreement between the Hatmakers and the Bootmakers in the early 1600s, and a spot of bother in the middle of the century, with a chap called Oliver Cromwell. But, generally speaking, generations of Makers got along very well for about two hundred years . . .' Her great-aunt stopped.

'Then – what happened?' Cordelia asked.

'Thirty years ago . . . Solomon Canemaker broke the Makers' pledge.'

'You mean the pledge to do no harm?'

Great-aunt Petronella nodded gravely. 'He began secretly making swordsticks. He would encrust the handles of his canes with jewels and carvings to encourage hot-headedness or excessive pride or vanity, and hide a thin blade inside the cane.'

Cordelia looked around the great room for the Canemaker crest. She saw it, mounted over the door opposite the Hatmakers' crest: two crossed walking sticks that sharpened into lightning bolts at the bottom.

'He was using Menacing ingredients in his creations,' Great-aunt Petronella said, and Cordelia felt her eyes widen. 'Back then, every evil ingredient a Maker found on their travels was locked in the Menacing Cabinet here, at the Guildhall.'

Her great-aunt extended a pale finger and pointed to the

far wall. Set into the wood panelling was a tall iron door. Cordelia shuddered: carved into the door was a grinning skull.

'Is it like the Menacing Cabinet at Hatmaker House?' she asked.

'Yes.' Her great-aunt nodded. 'But this one is much bigger. And it was locked with six locks – do you see the keyholes?'

Cordelia crept closer to the cabinet. There was a row of six bones beneath the skull, each with a keyhole.

'Each family of Makers was entrusted with a master key, so the Menacing Cabinet could never be opened without everyone's consent. The purpose of the six keys was to keep the evil ingredients from ever being used.'

Cordelia nodded. The skull stared at her out of empty eye sockets.

'But Solomon Canemaker wanted something different. He went out searching for Menacing ingredients. He collected them secretly. He didn't tell the other Makers about the wicked things he had plundered from around the world.'

Cordelia turned to her great-aunt. 'Why?'

'He was greedy. He wanted everyone in London to own a Canemaker cane. He secretly turned the ingredients into weapons, so that everybody would be frightened of walking around *without* the protection of their own cane. Perhaps the most dangerous ingredient he used was his own bad intentions: he twisted evil into each swordstick. He made hundreds before he was caught.'

'How was he caught?'

Great-aunt Petronella's face clouded.

'A young man was killed,' she said quietly. 'He wasn't much more than a boy, really. His name was Abel Dudlook, youngest son of the Duke of Dudlook. One night young Abel exchanged angry words with the son of a squire, on Piccadilly. Witnesses said the quarrel quickly became a fight. Both boys were carrying Canemaker swordsticks. There was the clunk of wood hitting wood, then a stripe of silver flashed out of one cane, then the other, and within a minute one boy lay dying on the pavement and the other had fled. Both boys, it turned out, had bought their new canes that very day.'

Cordelia was cold with horror. *Making* had made that happen.

'The duke would not rest until his son's murderer was found,' Great-aunt Petronella went on heavily. 'The poor foolish boy was discovered and hanged at Newgate. When the Lord Privy Councillor found the swordstick used in the fatal fight, he realized the Canemakers' treachery. The Canemaker family was stripped of the royal charter and Solomon was branded a traitor and executed on Tower Hill. Mrs Canemaker and the two children were thrown into a workhouse, penniless and in disgrace. They all died less than a year later. The young Miss Canemaker was a little younger than you are now. It was a terrible tragedy.'

Cordelia gazed at the carved Canemaker crest. There was

something chilling about it: something furious about the way the lightning bolts struck down, like vengeance. She thought of the young Canemaker girl – ripped away from the enchanted life she knew and thrown into a dingy, stinking workhouse. And she had died there.

Cordelia shivered with sorrow.

'But why is the Guildhall empty now?' she asked, looking across the abandoned room to the glowing stained-glass window. The window depicted six Makers in Elizabethan clothing holding their creations aloft, but someone had smashed the Canemaker's face, so the body was creepily headless. 'Why did everyone leave, if just the Canemakers were disgraced?'

'Well, dearest, old tensions tend to surface in times of crisis,' her great-aunt said wisely. 'Everybody was shocked by what had happened, and emotions were a little raw. Then the Bootmakers accused the Hatmakers of stealing ideas –'

'BAH!' Uncle Tiberius exploded, his voice echoing around the vast chamber. 'Those Bootmakers were keeping secrets. And the Cloakmakers weren't sharing either! The Watchmakers were the first to go. Said they couldn't hear their precious watches tick, what with other Makers having shouting matches in the grand hall. After them, the Cloakmakers packed up and left. The Glovemakers weren't far behind. Then it was just Hatmakers and Bootmakers, and *we* couldn't stand the sight of those useless –'

'*Tiberius!*' Aunt Ariadne hissed.

Uncle Tiberius broke off mid-sentence, and Cordelia turned round.

Every Maker in London was standing in the great chamber.

CHAPTER 20

The ten Glovemakers glared in a group. The old Watchmaker stood silently beside a pillar, holding the hands of his two little grandchildren. The Cloakmakers all loomed by the staircase. And the four Bootmakers glowered in the doorway.

Cordelia, on the point of waving hello to Goose, caught herself just in time. They would have to pretend to be enemies. He looked very stone-faced and she tried to follow his example, jutting out her bottom jaw and knitting her eyebrows together in a frown. He was doing a very good impression of being furious to see her.

'Tiberius Hatmaker!' Mrs Bootmaker boomed across the room. 'As usual, your voice is even louder than your hat. Quite impressive.'

Cordelia thought she heard Uncle Tiberius growl. The red

Flabbercrest feather that topped off his extremely tall hat quivered.

'Nigella Bootmaker,' he retorted, sweeping his hat off and bowing flamboyantly in her direction, 'your expression, as ever, resembles one of your finest pieces of footwear.'

Mrs Bootmaker's nose twitched. Cordelia stole a glance at Goose, who scowled at Uncle Tiberius.

One of the Glovemaker twins swivelled his head to waggle his tongue at Cordelia. She retaliated with the wickedest grimace she could manage.

'Now, now, let's try and be civil,' the tallest Cloakmaker drawled, flicking his shimmering cloak so it shivered through the air. 'Fighting really is beneath us.'

Mrs Glovemaker said 'HAH!' very loudly, which caused the Cloakmaker to snap his head round to glare at her. 'We know you think *everything*'s beneath you, Cloakmakers,' she sneered. 'Including all of us.'

The old Watchmaker tutted fretfully. The two junior Watchmakers blinked, like owls. The younger one was sucking his thumb.

'Somebody here *is* beneath the rest of us,' the tall Cloakmaker hissed, narrowing his eyes at each family of Makers in turn. 'Somebody here is a thieving scoundrel of the murkiest variety.'

'Don't look at *us*!' Mr Bootmaker exploded. '*We're* the ones who got robbed last night!'

'*We* were robbed yesterday afternoon!' a pair of Glove-makers cried.

'And us, yesterday morning!' snapped the tall Cloakmaker.

'We were burgled the night before last!' Uncle Tiberius bellowed. 'Don't you dare point your gloved fingers at the Hatmakers!'

'The Watchmaker's the only one who *hasn't* been robbed,' a young Cloakmaker spat. 'He must be the thief!'

Everybody turned to the elderly Watchmaker, who shrank against the pillar in fright. There was a moment of silence, then:

'Don't be ridiculous!' Goose's older brother, Ignatius, scoffed. 'He's ancient! He couldn't rob a biscuit out of his own biscuit tin!'

'I beg your pardon –' the Watchmaker began, tremulously, but he was drowned out by the clamour.

'How do we know you didn't rob *yourself*, Old Boot?' Uncle Tiberius shouted. 'To make yourself look innocent!'

'That's *absurd*!'

'Nonsensical!'

'Our Peace Gloves are *gone*!'

'The Cloak was almost finished!'

'Our Menacing Cabinet was broken into!'

'Who's the sneak-thief?'

'Rapscallion!'

'VAGABOND!'

Cordelia surveyed the raging Makers around the hall. Every face was contorted with wrath as Maker bellowed bitter blame at Maker.

Perhaps this was what the Guildhall had been like thirty years ago, she thought, when the Canemaker's villainy was revealed and everybody's friendships were smashed by grief and distrust.

Cordelia chewed her lip, watching Goose hurl hurtful words in her direction. He really was giving a most convincing performance.

'Who wound the Summoning Clock?' Aunt Ariadne's question cut through the din. 'WHO wound the SUMMONING CLOCK?'

All the Makers fell silent.

BANG! BANG! BANG!

Somebody was hammering on the Guildhall door.

'Who could that be?' Mrs Bootmaker barked. 'Lucas, go and see.'

Goose scuttled out of the hall.

'Is nobody going to admit to calling us all here?' Aunt Ariadne asked crisply. 'Or explain the reason why?'

Cordelia studied the Makers' faces. Everybody glared at each other, waiting for the culprit to reveal themselves. She thought she heard a faint, snickering laugh echo around the domed chamber. She glowered at the Glovemaker girls, who sneered silently in reply.

Goose trotted back into the chamber, followed swiftly by Lord Witloof. The Thieftaker stalked in behind them.

'Lord Witloof!' Mrs Bootmaker sank into a low curtsey.

Not to be outdone, every other Maker bowed and curtseyed too. One Glovemaker's nose almost touched the floor, he bowed so low.

'You grace us with your presence this morning, my lord,' Mrs Bootmaker began. 'I am most humbled –'

But Lord Witloof waved a flustered hand for silence. He cut a path through the Makers and climbed two steps up the sweeping staircase so that he could see everybody clearly. Sternlaw Thieftaker lingered by the door.

Lord Witloof cleared his throat. 'I am surprised that all of you are standing around having a party when the Peace Clothes are so distressingly delayed,' he said.

Mrs Bootmaker puffed herself up like a pigeon, opened her mouth to reply, and slowly deflated as Lord Witloof went on: 'The peace talks are the day after tomorrow and you Makers are slacking. Never, in my years as Lord Privy Councillor, have I witnessed such vexatious and troubling behaviour.'

'But, my lord,' began the tallest Cloakmaker, looking peeved. 'We have all been *burgled* –'

Lord Witloof crinkled his forehead and blinked several times at the Cloakmaker.

'*Burgled!*' the Thieftaker repeated. 'I suspect you could all have *faked* these burglaries to make yourselves look like victims.'

The Cloakmaker's mouth fell open.

'Indeed! Have you actually been making the Peace Clothes at all?' Lord Witloof said querulously, twisting his hands in agitation. 'Do you *care* about your duties to the Crown?'

'My Lord, we have been working on the Peace Clothes day and night —' Aunt Ariadne began, but Lord Witloof's indignant voice continued over her.

'Do you *wish* these peace talks to fail? Will you *cheer* if England succumbs to the French? Would you *welcome* an invasion, so you can sell more gloves, more cloaks, more hats?'

'And boots!' Ignatius Bootmaker added. His mother elbowed him in the ribs.

Lord Witloof bristled with anger. 'First you failed to help the king, and now you are failing to make the Peace Clothes. Her Highness has told me she is seriously considering scrapping the royal charter of Makers.'

Cordelia heard her aunt's sharp gasp, her uncle's moan of despair. A swell of noise began, but Lord Witloof held up his hand for silence.

'You know what that means, don't you?' he said. 'Without a royal charter, you will no longer be allowed to make at all. It will be an end of the ancient tradition of Makers in England.'

Cordelia's stomach plummeted. *No more Making!* She felt sick just thinking about it.

'Lord Witloof, you must believe us!' Mrs Bootmaker burst out. 'We left our workshop at midnight last night and when I opened the doors again at dawn this morning the Peace Boots were gone. And our Menacing Cabinet was broken open, everything *stolen*!'

Her voice was taut and quivering, like a fiddle string about to snap . . . and suddenly it snapped.

'It was HER!' Mrs Bootmaker bawled, pointing one furious finger at Cordelia. 'SHE'S THE THIEF!'

The room gasped like one big animal and all eyes turned to Cordelia. She felt as though the collective gasp had sucked all the air out of her body.

'That is an outrageous allegation!' Aunt Ariadne snapped.

'Preposterous!' Uncle Tiberius barked.

'*Derisible!*' wheezed Great-aunt Petronella.

'She was beneath our workshop window yesterday morning! Before we were robbed! She was *skulking*! Lurking! LOITERING WITH MALICIOUS INTENT!' Mrs Bootmaker screeched. Her eyes were knives and her mouth was all teeth.

The Thieftaker stalked towards Cordelia. She felt light and shaky, and her heart was beating horribly hard.

'Skulking? Lurking? *Loitering with malicious intent?*' the Thieftaker intoned, leaning down to inspect Cordelia. His nose was an inch from hers and he had the unblinking eyes of a fish.

Cordelia's voice had slipped down to somewhere under her stomach. She dredged it up. It did not come willingly.

'I – I – I would never do anything with *malicious intent* – whatever that means!' she choked. 'And I've *never* robbed or burgled or stolen anything!'

She felt the prickle of everybody's eyes: some narrowed in suspicion, some wide with surprise. Lord Witloof peered from the stairs.

'I do not know who is responsible for the thefts, but Cordelia is not guilty of this *absurd* accusation,' Aunt Ariadne declared, in a voice nobody could hope to win an argument against. 'It is pure hysteria.'

'If I find you skulking, or lurking, or, indeed, *loitering*, anywhere you have no business being, Miss Hatmaker,' the Thieftaker growled, his voice heavy with menace, 'you'll be inside my prison-wagon before you can say *nicked*.'

He straightened up, but continued to stare down at her from his great height. Cordelia searched for Goose in the blur of people. She saw him, frowning stoutly at his boots. She wished he would look at her. She could do with seeing a friendly face.

'I think the strain of Making has got the better of you, Mrs Bootmaker,' Aunt Ariadne said, her voice like a drawn sword. 'Perhaps you are in need of a holiday.'

'Nice try, Hatmaker!' Mrs Bootmaker spat back daggers. 'I can make a better boot than you can make a hat, any day of the week.'

'Then I beg you to do so!' Lord Witloof pleaded, looking completely exhausted. 'By order of the Crown Princess, I command all of you Makers to go home and get to work! You have until noon tomorrow to produce the Peace Clothes. If you fail, the peace talks will fail, and our country will be at war. And you will all be forbidden from Making anything ever again!'

There was a surge of Makers heading for the exit as Lord Witloof shooed them out. In the scramble, Cordelia felt the eyes of the Thieftaker still watching her. She stared defiantly back at him, jutting her chin out to make herself feel braver, even though her legs were a bit wobbly.

'Come along, Cordelia!' Aunt Ariadne grabbed her hand and towed her away, scattering a gaggle of Glovemakers.

'I've always been curious,' Uncle Tiberius said loudly, pushing Great-aunt Petronella. 'Which came first: an old boot that looks like a face, or having a face like an old boot?'

Mrs Bootmaker glared at him as she marched past, Goose trailing in her wake. Cordelia tried to catch his eye, but he stared stonily at the floor.

In the pitch-black entrance hall, everybody got bunched together. The main doors were stuck closed and Makers started shouting instructions and making irritated comments about wasting time. The dark was full of elbows and impatience.

Cordelia took her chance. She yanked her hand out of her aunt's and threw herself forward, as though she was stumbling over somebody's foot. A squash of bodies staggered and gave way. Amid the shouts of protest, she heard Goose yelp, 'Ouch! My toe!'

Cordelia grabbed him and pushed him behind the prickly velvet curtains as a scrum of Makers jostled in the dark. 'Goose!' she whispered. 'It's me.'

There was a silence that was pricklier than the curtains.

'Goose?' Cordelia repeated. 'It's *me*, Cordelia!'

'What do you want?' he said, in a small, surly voice.

Cordelia paused. 'Um . . .'

'*I thought you were my friend!*'

Cordelia could barely hear Goose over the squabbling of the Makers.

'I *am* your friend, Goose!' she whispered.

'Then why did you rob us?'

'*Rob* you? I didn't — you don't believe —' Cordelia began, but Goose interrupted —

'You stole our Peace Boots! I know you did!'

'I didn't steal your Peace Boots, Goose!' Cordelia spluttered. 'I would *never*!'

'You're lying!' Goose spat. 'My mother is *right*! She *always* says Hatmakers are no good.'

Cordelia shook her head. 'Goose, I promise I didn't –'

'Hah!' Goose snapped. 'You can't lie to *me* about it. Here – I found this on the floor in my schoolroom this morning. I suppose you want it back.'

He pushed a tiny bundle into Cordelia's hands, but it was too dark to see.

'What's this?'

'*Evidence*,' Goose hissed. 'You're lucky I didn't give it to the Thieftaker – cos it proves you're a lying, thieving Hatmaker!'

Cordelia was so stunned by the bitterness in Goose's voice that she could not answer. She felt her own voice bunching up painfully in her throat.

With a loud creak, the front doors were wrenched open and light spilled into the entrance hall. Cordelia caught a terrible glimpse of Goose's furious face before he blundered out from behind the curtains and into the crowd of Makers rushing away from the Guildhall.

Cordelia looked at what Goose had thrust into her hand. It was just a scrap of dirty grey cloth. But when she unfolded it, she was so surprised that she almost dropped it.

'My handkerchief!'

Embroidered in the corner were her initials: *C.H.*

'Cordelia! Cor-*delia*!'

The alleyway was almost empty by the time Cordelia stumbled out of the Guildhall.

'There you are!' Aunt Ariadne exclaimed. 'Come here at once! We've got to get straight back to work on the new Peace Hat! Oh my, this is a disaster! How shall we ever make a Peace Hat in this state of mind?'

She towed Cordelia back through the maze of narrow alleys. They caught up with Uncle Tiberius pushing Great-aunt Petronella along Bond Street. Cordelia was grateful to be rushed home at a pace that meant all she could feel was the painful stitch in her side. She had lost her best friend. He believed she was a thief! His eyes had been so full of dislike.

'FRENCH SPIES IN LAAAANDAAAAN!'

Cordelia stopped dead.

On a side street, Sam Lightfinger stood waving a newspaper in each hand. He was right beneath the Watchmakers' window.

'Pardon me.' Someone elbowed past her.

It was the old Watchmaker himself. He and his two grandchildren tottered past Cordelia towards their front door. The smaller child stared wide-eyed at Cordelia and she smiled back.

'Come along, Grasshopper,' the old man muttered, jerking the boy away.

Cordelia watched from the corner as Sam grinned and flapped a newspaper at the Watchmaker, who unlocked his door and went inside. As Sam's eyes flicked from the shop door to the window above it, the truth leaped to life like a fire inside Cordelia's head:

Sam Lightfinger was the thief!

'Cor*delia!* Come along!' her aunt cried from down the road.

It all made sense. Sam had been beneath every Maker's window in the past two days: in the street below the Library of Hatmaker House, of course. Then she had seen him outside Cloakmaker Hall that evening, on her way to the theatre with Goose. Then yesterday morning – the injustice rankled – he had been outside the Bootmakers'. And Cordelia had walked along with him, leaving him loitering near the Glovemakers'!

And now here he was at the Watchmakers'.

'CorDELIA!' Aunt Ariadne barked again.

'Coming, Aunt!' Cordelia cried, haring along the street. Her legs were a whirl and her mind whirled faster. The handprints on the windowsill must have been black with ink from the newspapers – not soot. And one thing seemed certain: Sam was going to rob the Watchmakers tonight.

BAM! Cordelia collided with her aunt, who was standing stock-still on the pavement. Uncle Tiberius had stopped next to her, with Great-aunt Petronella in her chair.

Cordelia picked herself up, her mind still spinning with shock: *Sam was the thief!* She was about to turn in the street, and run and confront him right there –

But then she saw what the Hatmakers were all staring at.

Oh, no.

It was Sir Hugo Gushforth, wielding a lute, in the middle of the road. He was still wearing the hat she had added things to without permission . . .

The plinking of his instrument drifted down the street.

Cordelia looked closer. Sir Hugo was somewhat crumpled. His face was scrubby with stubble, the hat looked a little dented, and the Loquacious Lily had gone brown around the edges. None of this seemed to bother him, though. He roamed around the road, carriages veering past him on both sides.

'Shall I compare thee to a SUMMER'S DAY?' the actor roared at a passing lady, who jumped in alarm and tried to shoo him away. 'Thou art more LOVELY! And more TEMPERATE!'

The lady hurried off, so Sir Hugo turned his attention to an advancing cart.

'Rough winds do shake the DARLING BUDS OF MAY!' he bawled at the horse, which spooked and cantered sideways, nearly flattening the actor. The driver swore and yanked the reins. The cart lurched and hundreds of apples tumbled out of it, bouncing over the road.

But Sir Hugo had spotted a group of wimpled nuns, milling on the steps of St Auspice's Church. He loped over to them, ignoring the apples rolling around his feet.

'FAIR DAMSELS!' he declared, kneeling in the street

and strumming his lute. 'Let me serenade you with a SONG OF LONGING.'

The nuns looked around. Some of them blushed. One giggled.

As the Mother Superior descended on Sir Hugo, brandishing a crucifix, Aunt Ariadne turned blazing eyes on Cordelia.

'Cordelia Hatmaker, please explain.'

Cordelia quailed, but thought she ought to attempt an answer. Unfortunately, no words that seemed likely to soothe her aunt came to mind. She was distracted by the vicious swish of rosary beads and the resulting yelps coming from the steps of St Auspice's Church.

'Well . . .' Cordelia began valiantly. 'He – he came in wanting a hat, you see – for stage fright . . .'

'And I see you gave him one. The turquoise tricorn with a Singing Sapphire and brass Braggart Buttons. I made that hat myself, a month ago.'

'Yes.' Uncle Tiberius nodded, narrowing his eyes. 'I distinctly remember weighing it. It contained exactly three mettles of Confidence and half an ounce of Bravado. Just enough for a little boost.'

Cordelia's aunt and uncle could remember the details of every hat they had ever made. She was usually very proud of this impressive skill, but at that particular moment it was highly inconvenient.

'Well, I . . .' Cordelia tried again. 'He wanted – It didn't have a feather on it . . . and . . .'

'You thought a feather from an Upstart Crow would be suitable,' Aunt Ariadne growled. 'Along with a bloom from the Loquacious Lily *and* –'

Cordelia gritted her teeth.

'My star sequins!' Great-aunt Petronella crowed.

The Mother Superior was now mercilessly battering Sir Hugo with the *Book of Common Prayer*. The actor abandoned his instrument and scrambled for cover. Two men carrying a sedan chair kicked him in the shins and the angry cart driver lobbed an apple at his head.

'We have here,' Aunt Ariadne pronounced dispassionately, 'a perfect example of what happens when Hatmaking is attempted by somebody unqualified for the task.'

Cordelia flushed. She felt shame flip and wriggle in her belly like a tadpole.

'I beg you, noble crone, *forbear*!' Sir Hugo was on his hands and knees, pleading with the Mother Superior, but the prayer book came swinging through the air to hit him again.

'Poor soul,' Uncle Tiberius murmured. 'I'll go and help.'

'And *you*, Cordelia, will come straight home *now*.'

Cordelia suspected that she was in quite a lot of trouble.

CHAPTER 22

The air inside the Hatmakers' hallway was cool on Cordelia's burning face as Aunt Ariadne slammed the door behind her.

'I can explain,' Cordelia began.

'*For shame!*' Aunt Ariadne gasped. 'Cordelia, I am deeply disappointed in you.'

Cordelia shook her head. 'No!' she protested. 'I was only trying to –'

'There are principles of Hatmaking that you have no idea about. Principles of balance, of equanimity. Did you know this? No!' Aunt Ariadne snapped.

'I wanted to *help*! I wanted to *do* something!' The tadpole of shame in Cordelia's belly squirmed and she felt sick. 'It was the only way I could think of to get to the princess – I *had* to do it –'

'You heard Lord Witloof,' her aunt went on. 'These are treacherous times. The Makers' fates hang in the balance. We cannot afford to have the Hatmaker name smeared by scandal! How many hats did you add things to that afternoon?'

'Only that one, I promise!'

'Cordelia, this is very serious.'

'YES!' Cordelia found herself shouting. 'It *is* serious! My father's life is at stake! And nobody *cares*! Nobody except me has done ANYTHING to try to find him!'

A terrible silence filled the hall. It ate up all the air. The kitchen door opened a crack and Cook peeped through. Miss Starebottom craned over the bannister upstairs.

Cordelia felt the squirm of shame again. It bloated into a gloating toad, crouching heavy in her belly.

'*I'm* the one who tried to get a boat from the princess!' she cried. '*I'm* the one who went to find Jack! I'M THE ONLY ONE WHO'S TRYING TO GET MY FATHER BACK!'

Aunt Ariadne's lips flattened into a line as straight as a cane.

'Jones told us last night that he woke up the old seadog in the sickbay,' she snapped. 'He said there had never been a cabin boy there at all.'

'What?'

'You wasted our time with a made-up story, Cordelia, and you made us hope for a moment –'

'But it's *true*!' Cordelia wailed. 'He gave me my father's tel–'

'ENOUGH!' Aunt Ariadne shouted.

More silence followed, frayed by Cordelia's ragged breathing.

'I care very much about your father, Cordelia,' her aunt finally managed to say, though it seemed to take a great effort. 'And it may be some time before you accept that he is —'

'He isn't *dead*!' Cordelia howled. '*He isn't!*'

Hot tears welled up in her eyes. She pushed them angrily off her cheeks. She wanted her aunt to shout back at her, but she just stood there, so still and so grey-faced that she seemed to be made of stone.

It was a long time before Aunt Ariadne spoke. When she did, it was in a whisper so thin and sharp that it cut the air like a blade. 'The Peace Hat demands complete calm and utter tranquillity until it is done. You are creating discord and atmospheric strife in this house, so you will go to your room. You will stay there quietly until noon tomorrow, when we have finished our work and delivered the Peace Hat.'

'*No!* I don't —'

The front door swung open. Uncle Tiberius pushed a dozing Great-aunt Petronella into the hallway. He paused when he saw Cordelia, her cheeks wet and fists balled, facing the implacable statue of Aunt Ariadne.

'Ah,' Uncle Tiberius whispered. 'Everything all right?'

He sidled past them and laid a sad handful of things on the

hall table: the tattered remains of the Loquacious Lily, the bent feather from the Upstart Crow and the three star sequins.

'All cleared up!' he announced. 'I managed to convince Sir Hugo to let me look at his hat. As soon as he took it off, he fell asleep on the steps of the church. The nuns are looking after him now. Mother Superior has been persuaded to take pity on the poor fool, though she did try to lock him in the confession box.'

Ariadne and Cordelia ignored him, still glaring at each other with identical expressions of fierce stubbornness on their faces.

Uncle Tiberius milled around the hallway, attempting to dispel the tension.

'You know, I made a hat without permission when I was eight,' he said conversationally. 'I gave it to a stable boy. He started clucking like a chicken, ran around backwards reciting rude poems and then tried to pick a fight with a donkey. I got into such trouble.'

Nobody said a word. Great-aunt Petronella snored gently in her chair.

'So!' Uncle Tiberius cried, overly jovial. 'Naughty Cordelia! But no harm done! Tell you what, let's see if Cook has made some *tea* –'

'Upstairs, Cordelia. Now,' Aunt Ariadne ordered. 'And when you come down tomorrow, I will expect a very sincere and well-thought-out apology.'

Cordelia considered putting up a fight. But her aunt glowered so ferociously that she knew she had no choice. She turned and marched straight up the stairs, head held high and fingernails digging into her palms.

Behind her, Uncle Tiberius sighed. She thought she heard Aunt Ariadne let out one small, stifled sob.

In her room, Cordelia pushed away thoughts of remorse for making the hat without permission. She knew she should not have done it: it was forbidden.

How unfair that the forbidden things were always the most interesting.

'It was the only way I could think of to get to the princess,' she said to herself. 'I *had* to do it.'

She threw herself belly-down on the floor, reached under her bed and pulled out a tattered hatbox. It was the hatbox that had been her cradle when she was born. Her father had saved her from the sea in this hatbox and brought her home to London nestled in it. Its paper was puckered from the salt-water, curling at the edges. She stroked the crinkled lid.

Inside lay all her treasures: her baby blanket made from a piece of sailcloth, a shiny knot of nutmeg her father had brought back from Ceylon, the fragile orb of a Venetian glass song-bottle, a clear quartz crystal that scattered shards of rainbow light across the floor, a bowl made from a polished coconut shell, an ancient book that her father loved to read aloud called *The Mythmaker*, an iridescent feather from an Elysian Eagle, and her jar of Sicilian Leaping Beans.

She felt tears sting her eyes and wanted, more than anything, to outrun the wave of misery threatening to engulf her.

'I *know* you're alive, Father!' Cordelia burst out. 'You've *got* to be!'

A door slammed downstairs.

'And it's no good being stuck in here till tomorrow!' she groaned. 'There's no time to waste!'

She snatched up the jar of Leaping Beans. They hopped and bounced against the glass and she felt the patter of them in her fingertips . . .

'I'm finished with waiting for help,' Cordelia announced to the empty room. 'I can't get a boat from the princess, and Jack's disappeared, so I'll have to find another way.'

Goose believed she was the thief, her aunt was furious with her, and she had no allies left. So she would go out on to the ocean by herself and rescue her father.

'If I get to the coast at Rivermouth, that's a start,' she said. 'There'll be a boat there I can borrow.'

She chewed her lip, thinking.

'I'll have to wait till nightfall. And before I leave London I will make sure at least Goose knows the truth – that I am *not* a thief!'

She put the Leaping Beans carefully back into the hatbox with her other precious treasures. Then she lay down and tried to sleep. She would need to be wide awake tonight, so sleeping in the daytime seemed sensible.

But she could not stop her mind snicking and circling like a wound-up clock as she went over and over her (rather flimsy) plan.

Eventually, she fell into a doze as the sun was sinking among the chimneys. When she woke again, velvety night had gathered outside.

'Dilly?'

Her uncle was at the trapdoor. Cordelia kept her eyes shut even when he whispered her name again.

'Dilly? Are you asleep?'

She did not answer. The smell of roast chicken wafted through the room and made her mouth water.

'I've brought you some dinner,' Uncle Tiberius said gently. 'And there's a chocolate pudding too – your favourite. I asked Cook to make it for you, secretly.'

Sickly shame about Sir Hugo's hat bubbled in Cordelia's stomach again and she squeezed herself tighter into a ball to try to smother it.

'It's probably a good thing you're up here, little Hatmaker,' he whispered. 'Not much fun downstairs. Lots of stress and a fair bit of strain . . . and Ariadne used a *very* rude word when the grosgrain wouldn't lie flat.'

Cordelia kept clenched in a ball.

Her uncle sighed. 'For both our sakes, Dilly, please eat the chocolate pudding. Best get rid of the evidence before your aunt finds out about it.'

She heard the trapdoor shunt shut and opened her eyes.

The chocolate pudding *was* delicious.

And it was the perfect meal to eat before an adventure.

The hat hoist was large for a hat but small for a person.

Cordelia knew her aunt and uncle would be up until dawn, bent over the Peace Hat in the workshop. Her uncle would be stitching ribbons with his delicate silver needle, pins clamped between his lips. Her aunt, gilded with lamplight, was probably coaxing the felt into an elegant shape.

Cordelia banished the thought.

They don't believe my father is alive! She made her voice as fierce as she could inside her own head. *I'm going to go and find him and prove them wrong.*

Being fierce seemed to help burn away the feeling of clammy guilt that chilled her. She refused to imagine how her family would feel when they found her bed empty. She slipped down her ladder on to the landing. Great-aunt Petronella was asleep in her chair, her face lit palest mauve by the embers from her fire.

Cordelia knew that there were several squeaky stairs right outside the Hatmaking Workshop, and she also knew that sliding down the bannister to get past them would be very risky. Aunt Ariadne's hearing was as keen as an owl's. There was only one way down to the ground floor . . .

She sneaked past the door to the Alchemy Parlour, slunk into the Hat-weighing Room and folded herself into the hat hoist. She perched on the purple velvet cushion, knees under her chin. A tiny brass crank handle glinted on the wall next to her.

This was the tricky part.

Cordelia reached for the handle and turned it. The hoist jolted, she pulled the door shut and, for a breathless second, nothing happened. Cordelia opened her eyes wide but it was black as ink inside the hoist.

The dark lurched – then she felt herself sinking smoothly downwards. She breathed a small sigh of relief.

Outside, anybody who might have been watching (although nobody was) would have seen an elegant wooden box, large enough to hold the most flamboyantly feathered hats, slowly descending to the ground floor of Hatmaker House.

Ding!

The tiny glass bell pinged as the hat hoist came to a stop on the shop level. Had Aunt Ariadne's owl-ears heard it?

Cordelia waited a hundred heartbeats to make sure nobody was coming to investigate, then she opened the little door.

The shop was shadowy and strange in the dark. Hats threw weird shapes on the walls. Dove feathers became the crests of monsters and frilled ribbons were suddenly dragons' tails.

Cordelia took a deep breath. She squeezed herself out of the hoist.

With steps as soft as velvet, she moved across the shop.

She unlocked the door and eased it open slowly so the brass bell didn't ring.

Foggy London was framed in the doorway. A church bell donged quarter to midnight.

She went out into the night.

CHAPTER 23

The Watchmakers' was dark. An upstairs window yawned open like a hungry mouth.

Sam Lightfinger was already inside.

Cordelia opened her eyes wide as moons but the sprinkled starlight was not bright enough to see much by. A faint scratching sound and a silvery tinkle came in a wisp through the open window.

She stretched up, but the wall below the window was too high to climb. It would take a jump to a brick ledge, a shimmy up a drainpipe, then a dangerous inching along to reach the windowsill.

I'll just have to wait here for him to come out, she decided.

After a minute, an uncomfortable realization dawned on Cordelia: she was *loitering*. The very thing she had been accused of doing by Mrs Bootmaker. She tried to look purposeful and not at all suspicious, which was hard while skulking in a dark side street.

Oh no! Now I'm skulking too! she thought.

A lantern-lit carriage rolled past on the main street. The soles of Cordelia's feet itched as she made herself stand still and not bolt.

Her whole plan had been:

1. Break out of Hatmaker House.
2. Catch Sam Lightfinger in the act of climbing through the Watchmakers' window.
3. Extract a promise from Sam to tell Goose the truth.
4. Hitch a ride on a cart to the coast.
5. Borrow a fishing boat to go and find her father.

But this unexpected lull between stages 1 and 2 was making her nervous.

A lamp flared further up the road. Round the corner a horse whinnied softly. Cordelia's palms were sweaty. She was just about to decide that she would wait for twelve more seconds when a foot appeared in the open window.

Then the rest of Sam Lightfinger reversed into view.

Cordelia could not help but admire Sam as he inched, shimmied and leaped with surprising grace down from the window. But when the orphan landed lightly on the street, Cordelia was waiting, arms folded.

'Well, well, well,' said a voice.

A voice that did not belong to Cordelia or Sam.

Both children looked up. Thieftaker Sternlaw's face flared above them, flickering flame-red and black in the lantern light.

Sam bolted.

The Thieftaker lunged for Cordelia and she dived out of the way. She heard him curse as he lumbered into the iron railings. She whipped round and spied Sam sprinting across the main street and into an alley. She darted after him, fast as a bird.

Sam's silhouette stood stark for a second at the end of the alley.

'Hey!' Cordelia cried. 'I want to talk!'

He fled. Cordelia followed.

The Thieftaker was pounding the pavement behind her, long arms reaching for her like a mad marionette.

'COME BACK HERE!' he bellowed.

Sam pelted down Oxford Street and into the shadows of Soho Square. He scuttled round a corner, Cordelia galloping behind him. But the Thieftaker could not turn the corner as quick. He slipped in a pile of horse dung and went sprawling into the gutter.

Cordelia heard him thud to the ground with a squelch and yell, 'BLAST!'

But she did not stop. Sam Lightfinger was almost lost in

the gloomy streets. Then she caught a flash of silver – the Peace Watch! It was like a taunt. She put on a spurt of speed.

She was gaining on him.

They burst on to Piccadilly Circus. There were very-late-night or very-early-morning carts rolling along the street. A pair of dandies, ruddy with brandy, reeled around, singing. They paused when they saw two kids run hell for leather in front of them, the boy a blur of rags, the girl a whirl of skirts.

'Wait!' Cordelia panted. She could almost touch him. She reached out –

But Sam sprang across the street in front of a carriage. The horses reared, eyes rolling, and Cordelia skidded to a stop.

'Oi! Wotcha plying at?' the driver snarled, flicking his whip.

'Sorry!' Cordelia gasped, doing a sort of dance around the lurching carriage. Through the spokes of the wheels she could see Sam getting away.

She dodged round the pawing hooves as Sam bolted down a wide side street.

'Please come back!' Cordelia called. 'I want to talk to you!'

He swung round and stared at her for a moment, eyes wide. 'Don't follow me!' he yelled. 'Go home!'

He slipped down a dingy alley and, for a second, Cordelia paused. There was something feral about him, a shadow stealing beneath the black shoulder of the building.

She felt a little shiver of fear. She could just let him go, into the dark of the London night. Now was her chance: she could turn tail and run for the light that was her father.

She stood there in the dark street, gritting her teeth. As Sam slipped away, he was stealing more than the Peace Watch. He was stealing her friendship with Goose. He might even be stealing the last chance for peace itself.

Cordelia took a deep breath and took a step. Then she was following him – along the twisting alleyway, pressing herself against the brick wall when he glanced back.

He started to climb, scaling the sheer face of a building like a sailor climbing to the top of a mast. But, unlike a rope-swagged ship, there was no rigging on the building. He was holding on to notches in the crumbling brick wall with just the tips of his fingers. He climbed lightly, as though the earth would not pull him back down if he slipped.

Cordelia held her breath as Sam climbed past a vast stained-glass window and continued up a thin tower, stupefyingly high. When he clambered inside through a narrow window, Cordelia sighed with relief.

It was only then that she recognized the building: the Elizabethan Makers in the stained-glass window were unmistakable.

Sam was inside the Guildhall.

Cordelia held her breath as Sam climbed past a vast stained-glass
window and continued up a thin tower, stupefyingly high.

CHAPTER 24

Cordelia did not have a hope of pursuing Sam up the side of the building, like a spider. It took her several minutes to follow the zig-zag alley round to the front of the Guildhall.

Only Makers and monarchs can open these doors, her aunt had told her.

Cordelia reached out and turned the handle. It was warm to her touch.

The door opened.

She was ready for the dark and it did not frighten her.

She felt her way across the hallway, through the dusty magic and the prickly curtains, into the big space of the great chamber.

An ashy taste hung in the air and a wisp of smoke burned her nostrils. Sam must have lit a fire in one of the ancient grates.

As her eyes adjusted to the dark, she saw the enormous mahogany staircase rising, like the spine of a great dragon, to the upper floors. She began to climb.

At the top was a long gallery. Cordelia froze, her heart clapping in her chest.

Dozens of people stood waiting for her in the moonlight. They stared, silent and perfectly still.

She gasped. One of the silent people was headless.

Then she realized.

They were not people waiting for her: they were life-sized mannequins, dressed in slivers of old capes. Creepily, even the ones *with* heads did not have faces. Pale plaster models of hands were strewn across the floor and carved wooden lasts for shoes had tumbled off the shelves. Snapped canes littered the floor like spilled matchsticks.

A lilting song lifted through the air. Someone was humming. It was a tune faintly familiar to Cordelia, soft and sad and slightly disquieting. Like a lullaby about dying.

At the end of the gallery was a staircase – up to the tower! A shaft of moonlight lay on the narrow stairs like a silver carpet. Sam must be up there, singing to himself.

Cordelia crept upwards. Strangely, the soft song faded as she climbed. She reached a door at the top of the stairs and pushed it open.

It creaked and Sam turned, saying, 'I gotcha the Peace Watch, Boss –'

He saw Cordelia and his face fell.

'You!'

Cordelia stepped into the room. Six Cordelias were reflected back at her, and six Sams looked dismayed from every angle: there were mirrors hung on all the walls of the hexagonal tower. An old wooden trunk stood open in the middle of the room and a narrow wardrobe fitted neatly between two of the mirrors. Cordelia supposed this must have been a fitting-room in the heyday of the Guildhall. Now the only clothes in here were heaped in a corner, where someone had made a kind of child-sized nest.

'Is this where you sleep?' Cordelia asked, aghast.

Two of the windows were broken and the wind whistled around the ceiling.

'I told ya to go home!' Sam whispered. 'You shouldn't be here.'

Cordelia looked steadily at Sam.

'I've come for the Peace Watch,' she said. 'You have to give it back to the Watchmaker. And you have to tell Goose I'm not the thief, and admit you stole my handkerchief and put it on his schoolroom floor.'

'I never!' Sam protested. 'What handkerchief?'

'You know the one I mean,' Cordelia said sternly. 'The one with my initials on it. You have to promise not to steal things any more. It's bad. You should do something more honest with your life.'

Sam blinked at her. Slowly, he sank on to the edge of the trunk and sat there, studying his knees.

'Easy for a Maker to say,' he murmured. 'Do somefing more honest . . . It's hard to be honest when you're hungry and cold and ya got no safe place to sleep.' He hugged himself miserably and sniffed.

This was not the scene Cordelia had imagined. She had imagined Sam, sheepish and full of cheerful remorse, promising to do the right thing. But here he was, hunched wretchedly on the trunk, looking sick and ashamed.

'D-don't you have any family?' Cordelia asked, patting his back. His ragged clothes were rough against her hand.

Sam shook his head.

'Me brother's gone. We used ta live in the bell tower of St Rigobert's in Seven Dials. It was cold and we got all the worst of the rain and wind, but it was better than sleepin' on the street. He'd go out 'n' get food and try ta earn a penny or two. I'd try 'n' sell flowers, if I could get 'em. But one day I got sick. I was feverish 'n' shaking and there was no food and Len, me brother, got desperate and nicked a chicken off a market stall.'

Cordelia's eyes were round. 'What happened?'

Sam's mouth twisted as he tried not to cry. 'You dunno what happens to thieves? They get thrown in the bellies of ships and sent to the underneath of the world. They never come back.'

Cordelia felt an ocean of sadness contained in Sam's thin ribcage. She tried to think of something kind and hopeful to say, but what words could bring a ship back around the world?

Sam wiped his eyes on his sleeve.

'Ya shouldn't have followed me here!' He was suddenly on his feet. 'I told ya to go home! It ain't safe. If he catches ya –'

Sam's head went up, like a fox sensing a hunter. He turned terrified eyes to Cordelia.

'Ya gotta hide!'

Sam looked frantically around. There was the thud of boots on the stairs.

'Here!' He hustled Cordelia into the tall wardrobe. 'Keep dead quiet.'

Cordelia managed to nod. She felt sick. Bile rose in her throat, but she swallowed the bitterness back down. The last thing she saw was a sliver of Sam's frightened face as he closed the wardrobe door.

CHAPTER 25

It was stuffy and dusty inside the wardrobe. Cordelia shuddered as the ribbon of an old cloak brushed her cheek.

'Lightfinger!' A cold voice rang through the room.

'G-good evenin', sir,' she heard Sam reply.

Very slowly, so she did not make a sound, Cordelia crouched down and carefully put her eye to the keyhole.

A figure stood in the doorway. A sinister black hood shrouded his face and the cloak swept down so low that only the shiny tips of his boots could be seen. He prowled into the room. Sam cringed as he advanced.

'I got the watch, sir,' Sam mumbled.

He fished in his pocket and, with a whisper of silver chain, drew out the Peace Watch.

The stranger swathed in the cloak chuckled softly. 'Well done, well done.'

His voice was a growl.

A meaty red hand with thick gold rings emerged from the black folds and wrapped itself round the beautiful watch.

Cordelia clenched her fists, helplessly furious.

The stranger dangled the watch from its silver chain, walking softly away from Sam, who watched him like a mouse watches a cat. He got nearer and nearer to Cordelia's hiding place. She shivered as the silver watch arced to and fro.

'Excellent work, little criminal,' the stranger whispered. 'That's all the Peace Clothes stolen. The full set.'

He was so close to the wardrobe now that Cordelia could hear the click of clockwork as the watch ticked.

Tick.

She did not dare breathe.

Tock.

In one violent motion, the stranger flung the Peace Watch to the floor and stamped on it.

It crunched like the bones of a bird under his black boot. Cordelia clamped a hand to her mouth. The beautiful Peace Watch was crushed into a sad mess of spilled cogs and mashed metal. The stranger kicked its remains with his toe.

'And the Watchmaker's Menacing Cabinet?' he demanded, rounding on Sam.

As the stranger turned, both of his boots were visible, and their gold buckles flashed from beneath his cloak:

MM

Cordelia frowned at the bright letters on the boots.

Sam reached inside his jacket. 'There wasn't anything in the Menacing Cabinet,' he muttered. 'Only this.'

He pulled out a heavy iron key, bearded with brown rust. The stranger took it.

'The final master key,' he breathed. 'Most excellent thievery.'

He loomed over Sam, tucking the key into the folds of his cloak.

'Sir, p-please,' Sam stuttered. 'I done everyfing you asked. I stole all the stuff you wanted me to steal.'

'Indeed you have, my little cutpurse,' the stranger purred.

'So — so — can I go free now?' Sam asked. 'Like you promised?'

The stranger's laugh shivered through the room.

'Ah, Master Lightfinger,' he said, closing his heavy red hands around Sam's shoulders. 'If only life were kind to lawbreaking orphans.'

'What d'ya mean?' Sam went pale.

'I can't very well put you back where I found you, can I, little delinquent? Back to stealing ladies' handkerchiefs in

Covent Garden,' the stranger whispered. 'You might tell somebody what you've been up to. You could ruin all my plans.'

'I – I promise I won't! Thieves' honour!'

The stranger gave a mirthless shout of laughter and flung Sam into the open trunk. Before Sam could stumble up, the man crashed the lid down over his head and shot the heavy iron bolt across, locking him inside.

'NOOOOO!' Sam howled. 'LEMME OUT!'

'Quiet!' the stranger snarled, thumping the heavy oak lid.

Sam stopped howling but Cordelia heard muffled sobs.

'In the morning, I shall announce I've found the culprit,' the stranger hissed with horrible relish. 'And you'll be thrown in prison. By then, all those traitorous Makers will be locked in the dungeon of the Tower of London. Another excellent headline to feed to the newspapers: MAKERS MAKE NOTHING BUT TROUBLE.'

Cordelia scrabbled at the wardrobe wall for support as her head swam. *The Makers – traitors? Locked in the Tower of London?*

The stranger paused. For a terrible second, Cordelia thought he had heard her. But then the cloak twitched, as if he was thinking, and he said, 'Perhaps I shall wait a few days before telling anyone you're here, Lightfinger. I don't want you blabbing before the Makers are sentenced . . . and if you're no more than a skeleton when the Thieftaker eventually comes to get you, well, that's one less ragamuffin burdening the city.'

The stranger stalked from the room. Cordelia heard him stumping down the stairs, chuckling softly to himself. She forced herself to wait, heart pounding in the dark, for several minutes after his footsteps had faded. It was torturous. She could hear Sam whimpering in the locked trunk.

When she was sure the stranger had gone, Cordelia lurched out of the wardrobe in a shower of dust. She fell on her knees beside the trunk and tugged at the iron bolt, grazing her knuckles as she dragged it back.

She heaved the heavy lid open and Sam staggered to his feet, gulping great lungfuls of air.

'Thank you, Cor – you saved my life – *thank you*,' he gasped between grateful breaths.

Cordelia's hands were shaking. 'He said the Makers were going to be locked in the Tower!' she whispered. 'Why? *Who is he?*'

Sam shook his head wretchedly.

'I dunno, I never seen 'is face. He's never took 'is cloak off.'

'We've got to get home,' Cordelia muttered desperately. 'I've got to warn my family!'

CHAPTER 26

Cordelia made for the tower door but Sam grabbed her hand.

'Not that way! She'll see us!' he hissed.

'Who?' Cordelia whispered back.

'The one who sings while she works. Downstairs.'

Cordelia remembered the lullaby lilting through the great chamber. 'Is there someone else hiding out here?'

Sam nodded.

'I get in and out through the window, cos I can't open the front door. But *she* uses it. I never seen 'er, but she always sings that song when she's workin'.'

'But how does she get in?' Cordelia frowned. 'My aunt told me only Makers and monarchs can open the front doors.'

Sam vaulted to the top of the wardrobe and leaned out of the window. He turned to look doubtfully at Cordelia.

'I dunno if you'll make the climb,' he said. 'How are you with heights?'

'I'm all right with heights if there's something to hold on to,' Cordelia said.

Sam shook his head. 'It's sheer.'

'We've got to *go*,' Cordelia urged in a low moan. 'There's no time! My family's going to be thrown in the *Tower*!'

Sam leaped lightly down and padded across to the door. His mouth was set in a grim line.

'Nuffin' for it, we gotta go this way. Foller me.'

They crept down the silvered stairs back on to the gallery populated with the silent mannequins.

Cordelia peered over the wooden balcony. A rectangle of flickering light stretched across the floor of the chamber below. One of the old workshop doors was open and there was a fire crackling in the fireplace. She heard two voices mingling. One belonged to the stranger in the cloak. The other was a woman's.

In the darkness of the vast chamber, their shapes moved like sharks in a deep sea. They reached the far wall and stopped. Then the woman lit a lantern and her shadow splayed, massive, across the floor. Distant, but distinct, came the clinking of keys and a scraping screech of metal on metal.

Cordelia frowned. She turned to Sam, fretting silently beside her.

'The keys — did you steal them from *every* Maker family?'
Cordelia whispered.

Clink — scrape.

Sam nodded tersely.

'We gotta get *outta* here, Cor,' he muttered.

Clink — scrape.

A wailing shriek split the room in two.

A moment later, the air had claws and teeth. It surged and
snapped around her, and a scorched, sulphuric stink — like
rotten eggs laid by Firechickens — blackened the atmosphere
in a foul tidal wave. Cordelia choked, clapping her hand over
her mouth to stop herself coughing.

Down in the depths of the Great Chamber, the woman
gave a howl of vicious delight. The man's triumphant laughter
rang round the domed ceiling.

Sam sprang to the window, gesturing silently for Cordelia
to join him. She scrambled after Sam, who eased the window
open. They took grateful gulps of the fresh night air.

'It's gonna have ta be this way out,' Sam muttered, hoisting
himself up.

He stretched a hand out to Cordelia. She clambered up
beside him on to the windowsill and felt her stomach churn.
The ground was a long way down.

But a little way below the window was the stone statue of
the Maker. They were above the front doors.

'Jus' foller my lead,' Sam whispered. 'You'll be all right.'

Cordelia tried to nod, but it was more of a nervous jerk of her head. She felt dizzy from the sickening mixture of curdled air and sudden space beneath her feet.

Sam swung his legs out over the space and tentacled a leg into the air as he reached for a foothold. His toe brushed the stone feather of the statue's hat.

'Right,' he murmured. 'Bit of a stretch. Gonna have ta jump it.'

'What?' Cordelia gulped, but Sam had already leaped –

– and was wrapped around the statue's shoulders like a living cloak.

He slid down on to the narrow stone ledge and turned his face up to Cordelia.

'*Come on!*' His voice floated up to her.

Cordelia silently cursed her skirts, which flapped heavily around her legs as she pulled herself round to face out over the abyss. As she stared at the statue, it seemed to get further and further away.

'Don't think – jus' jump!'

Her hands slipped with sweat and her mouth was dry and her stomach was knotty as Eelweeds.

'*You can do it, Cor!*' Sam's voice was a red thread made of courage.

She screwed up all her guts and heart and muscles into a tight bundle – and everything else she was made of, too: bravery and imagination, wildness and wits and her spark of magic –

– and she jumped!

'Oof!' The statue knocked all the air out of her, but she clung on.

'You done it!' Sam whispered joyfully.

The doors to the Guildhall, just inches beneath their feet, opened. The children froze.

Cordelia felt the night shift around her as the cloaked stranger emerged on to the steps. The rotten stink came with him in a revolting surge. Cordelia took a tiny sip of air and the vile taste – like vomit and old milk – made her gag.

If the man looked up now, he would see her wrapped in a strange embrace with the stone Maker, and Sam splayed against the wall behind her, desperately clinging on with his fingertips.

She slid an inch down the statue and Sam gave the tiniest of whimpers. They were trapped halfway up the bare face of the building. She clung to the cold stone figure, feet dangling helplessly.

Cordelia felt hope ebb from her heart just as surely as she felt the strength ebbing from her muscles. The stranger slowly turned his head. He would spot them in a second – he would wait for them to fall, like shot birds, to the ground, and drag them away to the Tower.

'I say, Archie, darling, you are *such* a flash at the card table. I'm terribly proud of you!' A voice, brighter than the moonlight, rang through the gloomy alley.

'Well, my love, Lord Buncle was just *begging* to gamble away all his cash,' another voice replied. 'And I was very happy to help him do it!'

Two young men burst, laughing, from the dark mouth of the alleyway.

Cordelia recognized them, even though there was cold sweat trickling into her eyes. It was Archibald and Ferdinand, the boys who had almost duelled in Berkeley Square.

They stopped dead when they saw the situation they had stumbled into: the ominous stranger in a black cloak and two terrified children clinging to the building right above his head.

Help! Cordelia mouthed without a sound. *Help!*

Both boys leaped into action at once.

'Good sir!' Ferdinand cried, stepping sideways so that the stranger, watching him, turned his back on the children. 'We are lost in this maze of alleyways! Can you tell us the way to – ah – the Sargasso Chocolate House?'

'Ah, yes!' Archibald said, leaping in front of the stranger too. 'We are *hopelessly* lost. And I'm *craving* a cup of Mrs Tempest's hot chocolate.'

For a moment, the stranger did nothing. The boys froze, smiling uncertainly at him. Then one hand emerged from the deep black cloak and pointed back down the way they had come.

The boys laughed and clapped each other on the back, rolling their eyes.

'I told you we were lost, Archibald!' Ferdinand laughed, bowing to the cloaked stranger. 'Sir, may I humbly beg you to show us the way? I do not trust that my companion here will lead us aright.'

The cloaked stranger growled a word which sounded like 'no'.

'Once we are set on our way, we shall leave you to your business,' Ferdinand insisted. 'This way, you say?'

The boys each took the cloaked stranger by the arm and led him down the alleyway. Just before they were swallowed by the darkness, Archibald glanced back, his face full of concern.

Thank you! Cordelia mouthed.

And the three of them were gone. The Guildhall square was empty and the boys' voices faded as they strode away with the villain into the night.

Sam slid off the ledge, down the wall and sank to the ground, clutching his heart.

Cordelia gingerly let go of the statue and slithered on to the plinth, her whole body shaking with effort and fright. Then, too numb to feel any more fear, she jumped.

The shock of the earth shot up her shins and she tumbled into a slushy puddle. But she did not care. She laid her cheek on the muddy street, profoundly grateful to be on the ground.

Without stopping to congratulate her on her safe arrival, Sam grabbed her hand and tugged her to her feet. They slipped away down the alley, into the safety of the dark.

CHAPTER 27

They were too late.

A heavy black wagon was standing in front of Hatmaker House. Silver-and-black guards glinted around it in the pale dawn light.

That was all Cordelia saw before Sam pulled her back round the corner.

'Let me go!' Cordelia fought Sam, but the orphan pinned her to the wall.

'You wanna get arrested?' Sam hissed.

Cordelia forced herself to calm down, but her stomach felt as though she had a swarm of Frenzy Bees buzzing inside it, and her mouth was desert-dry.

'I'll see what's goin' on,' Sam said. '*Stay 'ere.*'

Cordelia could only watch, trying not to panic, as Sam

casually sauntered round the corner, glancing along the street. Moments later he returned looking sombre.

'They've got 'em,' he said.

'Who? Aunt Ariadne? Uncle Tiberius?'

'Both of 'em,' Sam said.

Before he could stop her, Cordelia dodged round him and into plain view. The soldiers were shoving her uncle into the wagon. She could see Aunt Ariadne already inside, wearing her nightclothes, looking aghast. Cordelia's insides turned to water.

Four guards struggled out of the front door, carrying Great-aunt Petronella, still throned in her big red armchair, between them. With a surge of pride, Cordelia saw her great-aunt poking all the guards as hard as she could with her Knobble Oak walking stick.

'Blunderbusses! Wretches!' she squawked. *'Oafs! Blaggards!'*

'Where's the smallest one?' a guard demanded. 'We got orders to take you all.'

Great-aunt Petronella glanced up and looked straight at Cordelia. The ancient lady's eyes flashed bright.

The guard turned his head and Great-aunt Petronella swung her stick and thwacked him as hard as she could.

'She's run away, you clodpole!' she crowed. 'You won't find Dilly here!'

In a rage, the guard seized Great-aunt Petronella's walking

stick and snapped it in half. The broken pieces clattered to the ground and Cordelia felt furious tears sting her eyes. She started forward, only to be pulled back by Sam.

'She's protecting ya, don't ya see?' he hissed.

Once Great-aunt Petronella had been wrestled into the wagon, it trundled away down the street, soldiers mounted on the outside like flies. Cordelia saw the pale faces of her family staring out of the tiny barred windows.

In a flurry of flour, Cook burst from the house and staggered into the road. But the wagon was gone and she collapsed in the middle of the street, sobbing and clutching her side.

Cordelia and Sam ran over and pulled Cook to her feet. They steered her, still sobbing, through the wide-open doors of Hatmaker House and into the kitchen.

'What happened, Cook?' Cordelia asked, poking the big kitchen fire so it threw sparks up. She was trembling as violently as Cook.

'Dilly? Is that you under all that muck?'

Cordelia tried to wipe her face clean with a dirty hand. 'Yes, Cook, it's me! Please tell me, what happened?'

'There was a terrible banging on the door and your uncle went to open it, and a dozen soldiers were waiting on the front step,' Cook said. 'They came barging in, seized hold of your uncle and dragged your aunt out of her bed! I couldn't stop them! There were so many of them swarming all over the house! They've t-t-took them to the T-T-Tower!'

Cook succumbed to a storm of sobs. Cordelia patted her on the back. Sam hovered in the doorway, looking morose.

'Who was that man in the Guildhall?' Cordelia demanded, suddenly angry. 'How did he know my family was going to be thrown in the Tower?'

Sam shook his head and hugged himself miserably.

'I don't know,' he whispered. 'I never seen 'is face. He caught me one day, nicking ladies' handkerchiefs in Covent Garden. Said he'd watched me thieving fer an hour. I was guilty all right – 'ad a dozen stolen fings in me pockets. He said I 'ad a choice: work fer him or get chucked in Newgate Prison. Newgate's a hellhole. I'd take anyfing over that.'

Sam's eyes brimmed with bright tears and they fell, leaving two pale tracks down his dirty face. Cordelia's anger melted.

The back door crashed open. Cordelia and Sam dived under the table and Cook leaped to her feet, seizing her rolling pin. 'You won't take ANOTHER SOUL from this house!' Cook howled, charging to the door.

There was a clatter and –

'AAAAAAAARGH!'

'NOOOOO!'

'GOOSE!' Cordelia yelled, scrambling out from under the table.

Goose was cowering beneath Cook's raised rolling pin.

'Cook! He's my friend!'

'But he's a *Bootmaker*!' Cook bellowed.

'I know he's a Bootmaker,' Cordelia said soothingly. 'He's also my friend.'

Goose was in his nightclothes. He looked very small standing in the doorway.

'Cor-Cordelia,' he whimpered. 'They've taken my family away to the Tower! They said they were going to throw the Peace Boots in the river! I hid in the Bootlace cupboard and when I came out my family was gone!'

Cordelia rushed to him and hugged him.

'Mine too, Goose,' she said softly, squeezing him so hard she heard him squeak.

'I'm so sorry for everything I said,' Goose whispered into her shoulder. 'I don't know who stole the Peace Boots or how your handkerchief ended up in my schoolroom, but I *do* know I was stupid to ever think it could have been you.'

Cordelia glanced under the table. Sam's sparrow-bright eyes blinked back at her.

Now was not the time to tell everyone the truth about Sam. Instead, she took her friend gently by the shoulders. 'It's all right, Goose.'

Cook was staring at them. Cordelia could not tell if it was in disapproval or disbelief.

'We'll get them back, Goose,' she said. 'We'll get our families back.'

CHAPTER 28

Cook cooked. It calmed her down, and Sam emerged from under the kitchen table fifteen minutes later when she laid out a big sizzling breakfast for all of them.

'Can't do anything properly on an empty stomach,' she said, handing plates to everyone.

Goose looked curiously at Sam. Sam gave him an awkward smile, then copied how Goose used the cutlery.

As they ate, Cordelia filled Goose in on almost everything she had overheard in the Guildhall. She took care to avoid any mention of Sam, who blushed furiously right the way through the story but still managed to eat three times as much as everyone else.

'He said "traitorous Makers",' Cordelia repeated, buttering toast.

'Traitorous! I ask you,' grumbled Cook, digging out the

marmalade. 'How your poor aunt and uncle are meant to finish the hat when they're stuck in the Tower, I don't know. And how they're meant to get out of the Tower when they can't finish the Peace Hat —'

'So the king threw them in the Tower?' Goose asked, helping himself to more sausages. 'People are traitors if they betray the king.'

'The princess,' Cordelia corrected, reaching for the jam. 'She's in charge while the king is away for his health at the seaside. But . . . I think that man in the Guildhall has something to do with it.'

'Was he the thief?' Goose asked.

Sam tensed.

'Yes,' Cordelia said.

Out of the corner of her eye, she saw Sam sigh with relief.

'And you didn't see *anything* to give a clue who he was?' Goose asked.

Sam gave a tiny shake of his head.

'No – oh, wait! He had gold buckles on his shoes!' Cordelia remembered. 'They were strangely shaped. Like two Ms.'

'Could be his initials!' Goose suggested, waving a bit of egg on the end of his fork. 'When we make boots for really rich people, we sometimes make their initials specially!'

'MM,' Cordelia said. 'MM?'

Everybody shook their heads.

'I can't remember any MM pairs we Bootmakers have made,' Goose admitted.

Cordelia frowned. 'There's something else strange about all this,' she said slowly. 'Cook's right. Why tell our families that they had to deliver the Peace Clothes by noon today, only to arrest them at dawn, before they even had a chance to deliver them? They can't very well finish them in the Tower, can they? And why throw what they've got into the river, if the princess is so desperate for them? It makes no sense!'

'Well, they may have thrown *most* of the Peace Clothes into the river,' Cook said, looking as smug as a hen sitting on a golden egg. 'But not *all*.'

She got to her feet, bustled over to the cold oven and, with a flourish like a baker producing a magnificent cake, she pulled out –

'The *Peace Hat*!' Cordelia cried, jumping up. 'You hid it from them!' She looked around at everyone. 'D'you see what this means? We can finish making it and take it to the princess! She'll have to let my family go – and I can explain that none of the Makers are traitors at all!'

'You'll finish your breakfast first,' Cook decreed, placing the hat gently on the table.

After breakfast, Cook made Cordelia wash.

'You're filthy from head to foot, Dilly. I won't ask why, nor will I ask where that ragamuffin comes from.' Cook narrowed her eyes at Sam, who was inspecting a silver spoon. 'But you are to wash. *Before* touching the Peace Hat. Your aunt would say so, sure as I.'

So Cordelia hopped from foot to foot in the copper tub as Cook poured buckets of chilly water from the pump over her and scrubbed her with soap and a sea sponge.

'It's FREEZING!' Cordelia shrieked.

'If you'd given me two shakes, I'd have warmed the water over the fire for you, Dilly!' Cook tutted.

'That would take too long! We have very important work to do!' Cordelia gritted her teeth as the next bucketful came.

Goose was staring determinedly out of the window. Sam climbed on top of the cupboard and looked edgily at the washing going on below him.

'Come on – it's your turn!' Cook barked.

But Sam shook his head and clung to the cupboard, while Cook threatened to climb up and fetch him down.

Fearing an eruption of hostilities, Cordelia negotiated a truce. Cook agreed not to pursue Sam up the furniture if Sam agreed to scrub his hands and face. A damp cloth was passed to him on the end of a broom handle and he even cleaned behind his ears. Still, only when Cook had poured all the water away and put the soap back in the dish did Sam decide it was safe to descend.

Cordelia, Goose, Sam and Cook all studied the Peace Hat.

This second attempt was a delicate creation made of pale-blue felt from the Snowdonian Lullwool Sheep. A Sage Ribbon (woven from some beard-hairs of the famous philosopher Professor Pondergood and seven silver strands from the head of an Irish wise woman) was already fastened around the band. Uncle Tiberius had sewn three sheeny Paxpearl Shells on to the ribbon. But the Cordial Blossoms had withered to black papery saucers, with only thin crescents of yellow left (like old bitten fingernails). An olive branch, twisting around the crown, had been snapped in the rush to hide the hat.

Cordelia dusted a bit of soot from the oven off its brim.

As she touched it, she felt a flash of sadness – and drew her hand back. It was as though her fingers had been burned by a cold fire.

Her aunt had been so sad after they had argued.

Cordelia carefully pulled the broken olive branch off the hat. She felt stress in the buttons around the brim, and a thread of anger in the stitches. The Cordial Blossoms crumbled into black ash at her touch.

All the discord she had caused was infused in the hat.
She shook her head.

'What's wrong?' Goose asked.

Cordelia sighed. 'It's *all* wrong – it's full of stress and sadness. Not what we want at all. It needs to be overflowing with peace.'

Her fingers still tingled with her aunt's sorrow. 'We can't take any chances,' she said. 'We have to start again.'

Goose, Cook and Sam stared at her with round eyes, but Cordelia gritted her teeth and picked up the hat.

'Come on, everyone,' she said, trying to sound confident. 'We've got a lot of work to do!'

Goose stood and stared. He had never been inside Hatmaker House before, let alone in the workshop itself. He gazed at the bright cascade of ribbons hanging from the ceiling and the glittering glass beads and buttons by the windows. He was wonderstruck by the rainbow feathers pinned to the wall, along with shiny beetle wings, precious stones, frothy lace, glinting gold leaf, delicate leaves, flowers, sequins, skeins of cloth and shimmery gauze.

'It's amazing in here, Cordelia!' Goose whispered. 'So much more colourful than the Bootmaking Workshop. We only have stacks of leather and sheets of metal and some wooden models of feet.'

Cook sniffed.

'Yes.' Sam nodded with an air of authority. 'I like the Hatmakers' best too.'

Goose looked sharply at Sam.

Before he could begin to wonder how Sam could know anything about the Makers' workshops, Cordelia plucked a Merrybird feather from the wall and put it in Goose's hands. She watched his smile come back as the Merrybird feather worked its sweet magic.

She carefully unpicked the Paxpearl Shells from the brim of the hat and unwound the ribbon. As the ingredients came off, she felt the stress and sadness fall away. A few minutes later, she placed the un-decorated hat on the hat block. She felt the eyes of the others on her, waiting for instructions.

'I've never really made a hat on my own before,' she admitted. 'I'm too young. I don't know all the stuff. I haven't had enough lessons, I haven't read all the books . . . Things could go badly wrong . . .'

She wanted to add 'again', but she did not think it would be good for morale to admit that she had already had one disastrous adventure in illicit Hatmaking.

She suddenly wished, with a great ache, that her father

would come striding through the door, tanned from his adventures and still smelling of the sea. He would take charge and fix everything with smiling ease. But there was no musical sound of a carriage pulling up at the front door, no tread on the stairs.

Cordelia looked down at her feet so that nobody would see the despair in her eyes. Now was not the time to give in to hopelessness.

Then the ticklish floorboard quivered and something rolled out from under the table, glinting gold like a thin shard of hope. She bent down to look at it.

It was Aunt Ariadne's hatpin.

She picked it up. It was cool and sharp, and it gleamed with power. The emerald on its tip winked at her. Fingers shaking, Cordelia slid the hatpin into her hair, just as she had seen her aunt do a hundred times. She could feel the hatpin humming with possibilities; they sang through her hair, into her head, through her chest and right to the tips of her fingers.

Magic!

Cordelia took a deep breath and raised her head, a new hope shining in her eyes.

'I'm the last free Hatmaker,' she announced. 'So I'm going to give it my best shot. And you're all going to help me. We're going to make this hat together.'

'But . . .' Goose faltered, 'what about all the secrets? Aren't Makers meant to keep their secrets safe?'

Cordelia looked at Goose, who looked sideways at Sam and Cook.

'Isn't keeping secrets sort of what got everyone into this big mess in the first place?' Cordelia asked.

Goose shifted in his boots.

'My aunt told me that the seventh star on the Makers' crests means we're stronger when we all work together: we're best when we're united,' Cordelia said decisively, twiddling the hatpin in her hair. 'Let's get to work!'

The Politic Cord was spooled and ready to be put on the hat, and the garland of Mellow Daisies her uncle had made lay next to it. There was the silver bowl of sifted starlight too – Cordelia saw the serene glimmer of the evening star when she tipped the bowl.

'We'll use all these ingredients,' Cordelia said. 'But it needs something more.'

She looked thoughtfully at the wall of sandalwood boxes with their minuscule labels, then shook her head. All the rules and all the usual ingredients were not enough. It would have to be a hat like none that had ever been. They needed to break the rules and throw them out of the window.

She turned to Cook and Sam.

'What makes you most peaceful?' she asked. 'In the whole world?'

Sam stared blankly, but a dreamy expression came over Cook.

'The smell of Sunsugar when it's caramelizing,' she crooned. 'Just as it turns golden and starts to taste like sunlight.'

'Can you make some?' Cordelia asked. 'To go on the Peace Hat?'

'But – food doesn't go on hats!' Cook protested.

'You told me once that food is a kind of magic,' Cordelia replied. 'It might be one of the kinds of magic we need.'

'I . . . I . . .' Cook began, apparently struggling to wrap her head round this astonishing logic. 'All right! Yes, I will!' And, with that, she bustled out of the workshop, muttering, 'I will get my best copper pot out and start right away.'

Cordelia turned to Sam.

'I – I can't help you with this,' he stammered. 'All I'm good for's thieving. I ain't got any kinda learning –'

'Nonsense,' said Cordelia, taking his hand. 'Everyone has the magic in them to make things. Most people have just forgotten or got distracted or don't believe they can.'

'I can't even read!' Sam protested, his eyes roving over all the spidery labels on the sandalwood boxes.

'You don't need to learn stuff to know how you feel, in your belly,' Cordelia replied. 'In fact, sometimes learning too much stuff gets in the way. Remember what you said to me last night? *Don't think – just jump!*'

Sam squirmed, as though his belly was causing him some discomfort.

'What makes you feel at peace? That's all you need to tell me,' Cordelia said gently.

Sam was silent, his face a little scrunched. Then, on a shelf just above his head, a round-bottomed bottle rocked and toppled over. Its cork popped and smoke billowed out, surrounding Sam's head in a cloud of violet mist. Cordelia smelled a faint spiciness and recognized it at once.

Vapour of Valour! Just what he needs. Well done, House!

'It might sound silly,' Sam began. 'But . . . I feel most peaceful lookin' at the sky just before a lightning storm – that moment when everyfing goes quiet.'

Cordelia was glad to see that his eyes were shining. The Vapour of Valour had melted into the air.

'So,' she said, 'you need to find something that has that feeling in it: the sky before lightning.'

Sam hopped up on to the windowsill, all his swagger back.

'Righto!' he crowed. 'I know just where to go. Back in a jiffy!'

And he was off out of the window with a duck and a spring.

Goose, still holding the plumy Merrybird feather, said, 'Your new friend is . . . unusual.'

'He is, isn't he?' Cordelia grinned. 'All right, Goose –'

But, before she could decide what Goose should do to help, he was swallowed by a colourful avalanche.

'Aaah!' he yelped, his voice muffled.

Every one of the exotic feathers pinned to the wall had dropped on top of Goose.

'I think it's your job to decide which feathers we should put on the Peace Hat,' Cordelia laughed as he re-emerged from the storm of whirling colours. 'Hold each of those feathers in your hand and whichever ones make you feel most peaceful, we'll use those.'

Goose nodded, eyes wide. He picked the first feather gently from the floor and balanced it seriously in the palm of his hand. He closed his eyes in concentration.

Cordelia looked down at the Peace Hat.

'Benevolence Buttons?' she wondered aloud.

A cupboard door popped open and some sky-blue buttons rolled out.

'Thank you,' Cordelia said, picking them up. 'And perhaps also an Angelus Shell chime?'

A soft tinkle rang through the room. Cordelia followed the sound to find the Angelus Shell jingling among a collection of sea-green glass bubbles hanging in the window. She took the shell down gently and laid it on the workbench. She surveyed the ingredients laid out ready.

To get my family back, she thought, *this has to be the most peace-filled hat we can possibly make.*

'What brings me peace?' she whispered. 'In my heart and head and belly?'

She closed her eyes and dived into a sea of images: the

smooth seashell painted with her mother's portrait, the spicy-smoke smell that hung like a garland around her father, the seven freckles on her own nose, the feeling of magic right at the tips of her fingers . . .

Her eyes were still closed and she was still trying to decide, when an earthy, tangy smell sneaked like a finger up her nose and tickled her brain.

Horse dung.

CHAPTER 29

Cordelia's eyes snapped open. The Thieftaker loomed in the doorway, looking exhausted and furious. His left elbow was crusted with a brown substance that smelled very suspicious. Cordelia had the impression that, like her, he had been up all night.

'Ah! Miss *Hat*maker!' he drawled in a horribly triumphant voice. 'How *nice* to see you again!'

He made the word 'nice' sound terribly nasty. Goose dropped the feather he was holding.

'Hello, Thieftaker Sternlaw,' Cordelia said politely, backing away from him. 'You're looking well.'

'You can't run,' the Thieftaker snapped. 'Don't try to hide. I'm putting you under arrest.'

Cordelia moved so the workbench was between the two of

them. Out of the corner of her eye, she saw the hat ribbons wriggling restlessly.

'Goose,' she muttered out of the side of her mouth. 'Dark blue ribbon.'

A thick indigo ribbon hung, heavy as a python, among the others. The Thieftaker advanced on Cordelia and she backed away. He dived for her and she sprang across the workshop.

Goose was ready. He held out the end of the wiggling ribbon and Cordelia snatched it. She swerved, holding the ribbon tight, and the Thieftaker ran straight into it. Cordelia ducked and darted and wove, nimble as a needle in her uncle's hand. In the time it took the Thieftaker to say, 'OOF – ARGH! – NO! – GRRR!' Cordelia had wrapped the ribbon five times around him, binding his arms to his sides.

Thieftaker Sternlaw struggled. But he was not fighting to free himself; he was struggling to keep his eyes open. The ribbon that bound him was made of Drowslip Silk, which the Hatmakers used in nightcaps to help the wearer fall asleep.

He blinked with heavy eyelids and yawned. 'N-n-now, s-seeee h-h-here, Miss – ooh – Miss – H-h-h-haaaat – maaaa–'

Cordelia pointed at an inky velvet ribbon shimmying beside Goose's shoulder. 'Wrap that round him too, Goose!'

Scampering around the Thieftaker, whose head was dropping on to his chest, Goose trussed the man in the black ribbon. By the time he was finished, the Thieftaker was soundly asleep. With the ribbons still attached to the wall and holding him up, he snored and swayed gently like the bough of a tree. Several other ribbons snaked round the slumbering Thieftaker and tied themselves in a smart double bow. He looked like a present nobody would want to be given.

Goose turned shining eyes to Cordelia and whispered, 'That was *so much fun*!'

Cordelia grinned at him. 'Keep wildness in your wits, Goose, and magic in your fingertips!'

And she knew in that instant what she wanted to put on the Peace Hat.

The Sicilian Leaping Bean wriggled in her hand. She held it tight between thumb and finger as she wrapped a strand of spider silk round it. When she was sure it was tied tight enough, she let the bean go and it jiggled gleefully on the end of the thread.

'What is it?' Goose asked.

'It's something my father taught me,' Cordelia said.

She tied the spider silk carefully round the three feathers Goose had chosen and fixed them into the ribbon on the hat. The Leaping Bean bounded and skipped proudly along the brim and back again.

'Now all we need is –' Cordelia began, but she stopped as

the most delicious smell wafted in through the workshop door. It was the smell of hot sunshine.

Cook appeared, carrying a honey-coloured halo, just like the circles of gold round the heads of saints in stained-glass windows.

'Oh, *Cook*!' Cordelia breathed. 'It's *beautiful*!'

'I hummed a Serene Shanty while I made it.' Cook beamed. 'To help the peace along. Seen your aunt do that before, y'know.'

She carefully placed the halo on the hat. It shone like a woven ray of sunshine round the crown. Cook was so enthralled with her own amazing creation that she completely ignored the snoring Thieftaker.

As Cordelia was draping the Mellow Daisy chain over the top of the Sunsugar and securing it with the Politic Cord, Sam swung in through the window.

'Cor!' he exclaimed. 'Hat's lookin' dapper!'

He landed lightly on the floor, while Goose frowned at him suspiciously.

'Got me fing here!' he announced, holding out a large golden star. 'It's from the very top of St Auspice's spire.'

'Brilliant!' Cordelia cried. 'That star catches lightning! We might have to put it back afterwards, but it will be perfect to borrow for the Peace Hat.'

She stitched the gleaming star to the very top of the hat.

'The last thing that goes on is the starlight,' Cordelia said.

She picked up the Starbowl and swirled it around. A faint tinkling shivered through the room.

'What does it do?' Sam whispered.

Cordelia gazed into the bowl. 'It gives hope if you have lost your way,' she said. 'And the feeling of not being so alone.'

Sam looked hungry, but not for food.

Cordelia scooped up a handful of the purling starlight and blew it over him. He was suddenly wrapped in a swirl of eddying lights, tiny as pinpricks yet bright as Polaris. The light settled around him, on his shoulders and ears and the tip of his nose.

'See?' she said, smiling at the look of starry-eyed enchantment on Sam's face.

Goose sneezed and looked sideways at Sam. But then Cordelia scooped out another handful and blew it over Goose.

'Oh!' he exclaimed as a thousand bright crumbs of starlight whirled around him.

Cook coughed softly and Cordelia blew some over Cook too.

'My giddy aunt!' she cried, trying to catch the shining specks as they danced over her.

Cordelia threw a handful up into the air and let the dazzling starlight spiral down around herself.

There was a generous sprinkle left in the bowl. She tipped it all over the Peace Hat and it was suddenly star-garbed and glimmering.

The four makers of the hat stood back to admire their work. A feeling of deep peacefulness came over them, sweeping through the air like wings bringing good news.

'We've done it,' Cordelia whispered. 'We've done it together. We've made the Peace Hat.'

CHAPTER 30

The wide gates swung open and the Hatmaker carriage sailed into the palace courtyard. Alone inside it, Cordelia hugged the hatbox, feeling rattly right down to her bones.

She stroked the crinkled lid of the hatbox. It had saved her from the sea when she was a baby. She hoped it would help her save her family now.

A frilly red footman opened the door to the carriage. Cordelia poked her head out and saw twenty silver-and-black soldiers lined up outside the palace doors. Her heart gave a thud, like a warning drum.

She climbed out, still holding the hatbox against her chest. The soldiers all stood to attention. She was relieved that none of them seemed to be about to arrest her.

Cordelia looked up at Jones in the driver's seat. He winked down at her.

'I have come to deliver the Peace Hat to the princess,' Cordelia said to the footman.

The footman reached to take the hatbox from her, but she held on to it.

'A Hatmaker always carries the hat,' she told him, trying to sound as commanding as her aunt. 'And this hat must be hand-delivered to Her Royal Highness.'

At the word 'Hatmaker', one of the silver-and-black soldiers twitched, but the footman nodded to two guards and they pushed open the golden palace doors. Tummy as fluttery as if she had swallowed a dozen Waltz Moths, Cordelia walked inside.

'I'll be waiting right here, Miss Dilly!' Jones called after her.

The palace was quiet and empty. The footman led her quickly along the dim corridors. There were no jewelled ladies or adorned courtiers waiting to gaze at the hatbox. All the way to the throne room Cordelia only glimpsed one maid, who scurried out of sight. Royal portraits frowned down from every wall.

She whispered to herself: *Remember what you are made of, Cordelia Hatmaker!*

Before the doors to the throne room, ten guards glinted. They peeled apart as the footman approached. He opened the doors and bowed Cordelia inside.

The throne room was chilly and cavernous. At the far end

of the vast space, Cordelia could see a small figure sitting in a golden chair, swamped by a heavy red robe.

Cordelia walked forward. It seemed to take a very long time to get closer to the throne.

Princess Georgina's feet did not reach the floor and her face was as pale as the ice-white collar round her neck. Behind her, a wall of silver-and-black guards stood stone-faced and staring.

Cordelia bowed. She wished the satin bow on top of the hatbox would stop jiggling every time she shivered.

'Your Highness,' she said, glad her voice came out strong. 'I have come to deliver the Peace Hat to you, faithfully fulfilling the command you gave to the Hatmaker family.'

'Oh, excellent!' the princess cried, her pale face perking up. 'I have been so anxious for the Peace Clothes to arrive. Yours is the first!'

She shed her heavy robe like an old snakeskin and jumped to her feet.

Cordelia tried to hide her surprise as the princess hurried forward, eager-eyed, and took the hatbox out of her hands. She tugged the ribbon loose and took the lid off the box.

'Oh!' she exclaimed, lifting the magnificent hat. 'It is a marvellous creation! You Hatmakers are all so clever.'

The princess admired the hat from different angles and Cordelia watched tensely. Her Highness seemed pleased. She raised the hat over her head and Cordelia, unable to wait a second longer, burst out, 'Please can I have my family back?'

The princess paused, the hat hovering. She frowned at Cordelia. 'Back from where?'

'From the Tower! All the Makers were taken there!' she said, forgetting to call the princess 'Your Highness'. 'When you had them arrested.'

'Arrested?' the princess repeated, seeming confused.

'Yes! This morning, the soldiers came and . . .' Cordelia felt her nose prickle hot. She gritted her teeth and willed herself not to cry.

With a *BANG*, the doors at the end of the vast room slammed open and a voice rang out: 'Princess! DO NOT PUT ON THAT HAT!'

Cordelia swung round. Lord Witloof was striding towards her, the frilly footman bustling along behind him.

'That child is the French assassin!' Lord Witloof pointed a red finger at her, his rings winking gold.

'I am *not* a French assassin!' Cordelia spluttered. 'I'm a Hatmaker!'

Lord Witloof clapped at the guards. One of them leaped out of line and had his armoured hands around Cordelia's shoulders in a second.

'Honestly, Your Highness, I'm not trying to hurt you!' Cordelia cried.

'That hat is dangerous, Princess,' Lord Witloof said loudly. 'My sources tell me it is concealing a Croakstone. You would drop dead the moment the brim touched your head.'

There was a *thud* as the Peace Hat fell to the floor.

'A *Croakstone*?' Cordelia repeated. 'No! It's the Peace Hat you asked for!' She struggled in the steel grip of the guard.

But the princess was backing away from the hat in horror.

'All the Peace Clothes have been delivered by the Makers already, Your Highness,' Lord Witloof said smoothly. 'The *real* Peace Hat is, even now, being loaded into the second-best royal coach to be taken to the coast and safely placed on the royal galleon in time for your peace talks tomorrow. Along with the *real* Peace Boots, Watch, Cloak and Gloves.'

He smiled at the princess in a reassuring way as Cordelia scrunched up her face in confusion.

'How lucky I arrived in time to stop you from putting on this deadly impostor hat,' Lord Witloof went on, poking the Peace Hat with his foot.

That was when Cordelia saw the buckles flashing on Lord Witloof's boots.

That was the moment she realized.

The buckles were not MM at all.

They were WW.

She had seen them upside down!

'*You!*' Cordelia gasped, staring up into Lord Witloof's glinting eyes. 'It was *you!*'

Her head was hot and her hands were cold and her heart hammered furiously in her chest. She struggled as the guard wrenched her arms behind her back.

'Whatever is the matter, child?' the princess asked.

Lord Witloof's gaze roved over Cordelia's outraged face.

'She is the French assassin, Princess. Remember, as I keep telling you: you are in terrible danger at all times.'

'She can't be the assassin,' the princess said. 'She was right beside me when the shot rang out at the theatre. She couldn't have fired it.'

'Of *course* I didn't –' Cordelia began.

'I have many years of experience in these matters,' Lord Witloof interrupted. 'And *you* know very little.'

The princess blinked.

'Take this assassin to the Tower,' Lord Witloof ordered.

'NO!' Cordelia shrieked. 'I'm *not* an assassin! I'm a *Hatmaker*!'

But she was being hauled away down the long room, the princess's concerned face shrinking to a pale blob in the vast gloom. Cordelia tripped as she was dragged backwards and her feet slid along the polished floor. She could not fight the impossible strength of the guard. She was almost at the door when –

'STOP!' Princess Georgina called.

The guard obeyed, and Cordelia staggered to her feet. Princess Georgina was hurrying towards them, Lord Witloof's mouth a black O of annoyance as he stomped after her.

'Is there a Croakstone hidden in that hat?' the princess asked Cordelia.

'Of course not!' Cordelia replied. 'I'll put it on myself, if you like, to prove it.'

The princess clicked her fingers and a guard gingerly picked up the Peace Hat by the edge of its brim, dropped it quickly into the hatbox and brought it over to them.

'Georgina, we are wasting time!' Lord Witloof bristled at her shoulder, pulling his glass watch out of his pocket. It ticked irritably.

Cordelia recognized the watch at once; she remembered the delicate blue butterfly that decorated the case.

Lord Witloof is horrible to have killed such a beautiful creature, she thought.

Then the butterfly twitched its wings – it was alive, trapped inside the watch! Cordelia was appalled.

'We must set off for the coast!' ordered Lord Witloof. 'Probert, go and order the royal carriage to be prepared. We must leave within the hour, Your Highness, if we are to arrive at the coast by dawn.'

'Release the child,' the princess commanded.

The guard let Cordelia go and she felt hope sing through her.

'WHAT?' Witloof bawled. 'NO! Seize that child!'

Cordelia skipped out of the guard's reach, dodging behind the princess's wide skirts.

'Your Highness, I think there's something strange going on!' she gasped.

'I think you're right, Miss Hatmaker,' the princess replied.

'This is ridiculous!' Lord Witloof thundered, trying to take the princess by the arm.

But she shook him off and snapped her fingers. The guard stopped chasing Cordelia around the royal skirts and jumped to attention. Lord Witloof's heavy breathing frayed the silence as the princess turned solemnly to Cordelia.

'Miss Hatmaker, what has happened to your family?'

'The soldiers came this morning . . .' Cordelia whispered. She glanced at the two sharp Ws on Lord Witloof's boots, flashing as he tapped his feet with impatience. 'I think Lord Witloof is –'

'What is this impostor saying?' Lord Witloof interrupted.

The princess turned to look the lord in the face.

'She is saying that her family have been arrested by soldiers of the Crown, Witloof,' she said. 'Which is strange, since only you and I have the power to give those orders.'

Lord Witloof clapped his hand to his chest, in shock or indignation, Cordelia could not tell.

'As I have told you before,' he blustered, 'spies will say anything to confuse and discombobulate you. Do not make the mistake of believing the vile lies this child is telling you!'

'Guard,' the princess said calmly. 'Please escort Lord Wit–'

In a flash as quick as a snake striking, Lord Witloof pulled his hand out of his jacket – and, with a flick of his wrist, a small crown was glinting on the princess's head.

'*Oh!*' she gasped, as though a bucket of icy water had been tipped over her.

Cordelia stared in horror. The crown was made of twisting tentacles of glass that knotted together across the princess's pale forehead. It was an ugly, deformed thing – somehow warped when it should have been beautiful.

Cordelia knew she should do something – anything – but she was paralysed, staring at the sinuous glass that encircled the princess's head.

And Her Highness's frightened eyes – *run* – seemed to be sinking under water – *run* – and all Cordelia could think – *run* – were thoughts of despair.

'Cordelia – *run!*' the princess whispered with the last of her strength.

Her words snapped Cordelia out of her daze – just as Lord Witloof lunged for her. Cordelia spun away, snatched the hatbox out of the guard's hands and then she was hurtling towards the doors.

'CATCH THAT CHILD!' Lord Witloof roared.

CHAPTER 32

Behind Cordelia, a dozen guards clattered into action. She skidded into the doors, wrenched them open and found herself surrounded by the soldiers guarding the other side.

Fortunately for Cordelia, their heavy uniforms made it difficult for them to move quickly. She was through the black forest of their legs before any of them could grab her.

A shout went up – the hunt had begun! She felt the tip of her hair sing through the steel-clad hand of one guard as she hared down the corridor, clutching the Peace Hat – safe in its hatbox – to her chest. She put on a burst of speed, legs already burning. Darting round the corner, desperately trying to remember the way back to the front doors – left, right, right and left again – Cordelia dodged between a looming duke and a loitering scullery maid.

Ignoring their shrieks, she bolted past a frowning portrait of a king with a forked beard, a painting of a cross-eyed queen, and a golden statue of frolicking fauns. With blood thundering in her ears – or was that the sound of the guards closing in like storm clouds behind her? – she charged down a gloomy corridor and swerved round three maids carrying armfuls of laundry. They threw up their hands in surprise and snow-white linen flurried around them.

'Blimey! A Hatmaker!' the youngest maid exclaimed.

Cordelia skidded through a thick drift of sheets towards the front doors and – three heartbeats from freedom – felt her stomach plummet. A wave of guards surged towards her from the corridor on her left. She whipped round to see a dozen soldiers swarming behind her.

Trapped, she backed away.

The youngest laundry maid tumbled forward – Cordelia glimpsed her face. It was the maid she always waved to when the Hatmakers visited the palace.

'I've got a way out for you, miss!' the maid whispered, throwing a bedsheet over her head.

The last thing Cordelia saw was a grinning guard reaching his metal hand out towards her, before the world turned white.

'This way,' came a hiss, quick, in her ear.

Cordelia was bundled against the wall. Then the wall was not there.

With a creak and a thud, she was flat on her back – the

249

maid had pushed her through a secret hatch! Framed in the square of light above her, an astonished guard was left holding the sheet.

'Go!' the maid cried.

Still clutching the hatbox, Cordelia scrambled backwards as fast as she could, into the dark.

She slithered down a slope and her head cracked against stone. Stars exploded behind her eyes like a great map of the night sky. She scrabbled to her knees, feeling the smooth walls of the passage with her fingers. To her left and right was cold stone – a dead end!

'No!' she moaned, pummelling the wall in despair.

She felt a flash of cold under her palm. She fumbled in the darkness and her hand closed over a metal lever jutting out from the wall. She pulled. The lever did not budge.

Cordelia hauled the lever with both hands.

'Come on!' she cried.

With a sudden judder, the lever inched down. A crack of light appeared as a massive stone panel moved in the wall. It grazed her knuckles but Cordelia kept pushing, and the lever moved another inch. Fresh air breezed through the widening crack, and Cordelia glimpsed the palace courtyard.

Somewhere in the dark behind her, the guards were closing in with deafening cymbal-crashes of armour.

Her ears scraped between the slabs of stone. Her head was out! She twisted her shoulders and slipped like a fish through the crack in the palace wall, tugging the hatbox out after her.

And she was running across the courtyard, whistling loud as a sailor for Jones and the carriage.

But outside the palace doors stood twenty soldiers. Their heads snapped round at Cordelia's whistle and they clanked into action, but Jones was faster. Shaking the reins, he spurred his horses into a canter.

'THE GATE!' Cordelia cried, veering towards it as the carriage arced behind her across the courtyard.

The girl ran – and the carriage rumbled – and the soldiers charged after it.

'STOP HER!' a guard bellowed.

Two sentries tumbled out from their little hut and began to push the gates shut.

Cordelia felt the carriage thundering closer across the cobbles. The gap between the golden gates was growing smaller and smaller.

'MISS CORDELIA!' Jones shouted.

Cordelia felt her feet leave the ground, legs kicking the air, as Jones grabbed her by the collar and hoisted her on to the seat beside him. She held on, knuckles white. He grabbed the hatbox before it tumbled over the side. The gates were almost closed –

'Hang on to your hat, miss!'

They heard metal screeching on wood but Jones yah'ed the

horses onwards and the carriage scraped through the gates, rocking on its wheels.

The next moment they were lurching along London's streets, the furious shouts fading behind them, fainter and fainter.

CHAPTER 33

Cordelia's heart was still hammering when Jones slowed the carriage at the front door of Hatmaker House.

Goose, Sam and Cook were there, bustling her inside, peppering her with questions.

'Did something go wrong?'

'Ya still got the Peace Hat!'

'Why's your dress torn to tatters, Dilly?'

Cordelia held up her hand and they all stopped talking.

'They're coming – the soldiers – to arrest me. They'll be here in a minute.'

A collective gasp and then uproar:

'We won't *let* them!'

'Ya gotta run!'

'Why did you come back?'

Cordelia shook her head, still catching her breath. 'You all have to hide so they don't take you too,' she said.

There was a shout in the street and Jones yelled, 'Miss! They're here!'

Cordelia turned back to Goose, Sam and Cook. 'The princess is in danger – she's being controlled – they're coming to arrest me – someone needs to stop Lord Witloof –'

But Goose and Cook were shaking their heads in confusion – there was no time to explain everything to them, no time to tell them everything that needed to be done! In despair, Cordelia turned to Sam.

'Sam! What shall we do?' she cried.

In response, Sam took off his cap.

For a breathless moment nobody spoke. Sam's hair tumbled around his shoulders and down his back, bright chestnut brown and curly.

Goose's mouth fell open.

Sam Lightfinger was a girl.

'Take off yer coat, Cor, and yer hat,' Sam whispered. 'Quick.'

Head spinning, Cordelia tore off her hat, coat, gloves and dress. Like a strange mirror, Sam peeled off her rags and left them in a grimy heap on the floor.

In a windmill of arms and legs, Sam was dressed in Cordelia's clothes.

They heard soldiers' feet clattering on the street outside.

Sam reached towards Cordelia and plucked her aunt's gold hatpin out of her hair. 'Hide!' Sam hissed.

Cordelia and Cook dived behind the wooden counter.

Sam fed the hatpin up her sleeve.

Cordelia yanked Goose down beside her.

The door crashed open.

Sam took a deep breath –

– and the soldiers were upon her.

Cordelia dug her nails into her palms as Sam screamed and struggled against the mob of soldiers. Goose and Cook hunched against her, making themselves as small as they could. The door banged closed and their brave friend was carried away to the Tower.

A minute passed. When she was very sure every soldier was gone, Cordelia raised her head. She stood up and went to the window. Jones, splayed on the pavement, groaned and rubbed his head. The Hatmaker carriage lay on its side, wheels broken and horses cut loose. The donkey brayed mournfully from the mews.

Goose unfurled slowly, wiping tears off his face. 'He – she – is very brave,' he uttered solemnly.

'Yes,' Cordelia said fiercely, 'she is.'

Goose sniffed loudly and said, 'What do we do now?'

Cordelia gingerly lifted the lid of the hatbox and peered

inside. Despite the escape from the palace and the wild ride home, the Peace Hat remained neat and serene, with not a feather out of place.

'All right,' she said in her most determined voice, 'I think we might have to stop a war.'

'If you have grand ambitions like that, Dilly, you really should put some clothes on,' Cook suggested.

Cordelia remembered she was only dressed in her underwear. Goose blushed and examined the paintwork on the ceiling.

Cordelia buttoned up her father's jacket over her dress. It was very roomy and she had to roll up the sleeves several times before her hands appeared, but wearing it made her feel courageous and capable.

Suddenly there was a *BANG, BANG, BANG!* on the front door five floors below.

Goose leaped into Cordelia's arms, his eyes wide with fright. Bootmaker and Hatmaker froze, listening.

'I'll see who it is,' Cook called from downstairs.

For several dreadful seconds Cordelia was afraid the soldiers had realized their mistake. She strained her ears, heard a faint groaning, and then, to her surprise, a giggle.

'Oh, do come down, Dilly,' Cook trilled. 'He's making such a fuss, poor dove.'

Mystified, Cordelia and Goose went down the stairs. Cordelia was glad she had her father's jacket on. She could feel his courage cocooning her, making her braver. She gripped a fire poker like a sword and Goose clutched a candlestick in a vaguely dangerous manner.

Cook, pink-cheeked, hurried them towards the door. Cordelia peered out.

'Sir Hugo?'

The actor was slumped on the doorstep, pounding the ground with his fists and wailing.

'Aye, me!' he howled. 'Aye, me!'

Cordelia opened the door wide and Sir Hugo fell into the shop.

'Ah! The hallowed halls of Hatmaker House!' he crooned, laying his cheek on the floor and stroking the carpet lovingly.

'Can I help you, Sir Hugo?' Cordelia asked loudly, putting down her poker.

'Young Mistress Hatmaker!' Sir Hugo cried, shuffling to her on his tummy and kissing the toe of her boot. 'O nymph of hats! O great creatrix of headwear! I beg your bountiful hands to bestow on mine unworthy head another hat!'

'What?' said Goose, completely confused.

Cook was fanning herself. Cordelia rolled her eyes.

'I am to play Romeo in Shakespeare's greatest love story,' Sir Hugo moaned. 'And I fear that without a hat made by your fine and fair hands —' here Sir Hugo scrabbled to his knees, grabbed Cordelia's hand and kissed it feverishly – 'my performance will not be as loudly applauded as was my Hamlet!'

Cordelia pulled her hand away and wiped it on her dress. She frowned, looking out of the window. The sky was turning pale in the afternoon light.

We must leave within the hour, Your Highness, Lord Witloof had said. The royal coach would already be setting off for the coast. She had to get to the princess somehow!

She turned to tell Sir Hugo that she was not allowed to make him a hat and, anyway, she did not have *time* to help him play dressing-up.

But then she had a better idea.

'If I find you the perfect hat, Sir Hugo,' she said, 'will you do me a very important favour?'

The heavy wooden door to the deepest dungeon in the Tower of London clanked open. Inside, Aunt Ariadne, Uncle Tiberius and Great-aunt Petronella looked up hopefully as a fiery torch flickered in the passage. But their hearts sank when Cordelia was thrown inside by the guards.

The door slammed shut and the iron key rasped in the lock.

Cordelia raised her head – and the Hatmakers realized *it was not Cordelia*!

'Hallo, Uncle!' the stranger who was not Cordelia said brightly. 'Hallo, Aunt and Great-aunt!'

The Hatmakers stared back at her in complete confusion. Then the stranger who was not Cordelia slid her eyes sideways towards the grate in the door, where the dark outline of a guard loomed.

'Ah – *Cordelia!* Hello!' Uncle Tiberius said loudly.

'Cordelia,' Aunt Ariadne whispered. 'You're looking . . . well.'

Great-aunt Petronella watched the stranger with eagle-sharp eyes. The stranger glanced back at the guard's shadow outside the door, before peering at the crusts left over from the Hatmakers' sad supper of dry bread and water.

'Ya gonna eat those?' she asked.

Aunt Ariadne shook her head.

The stranger devoured the crusts in two bites.

'Best get some sleep,' she advised, settling down in a corner. She winked and added, 'Busy day tomorrow.'

Aunt Ariadne and Uncle Tiberius exchanged amazed glances, but when they turned back to the stranger she was asleep and gently snoring.

Great-aunt Petronella smiled.

By moonrise, three black-clad highwaymen were galloping south on the road from London.

They rode three swift dark horses. Silk scarves the colour of midnight disguised their faces, and they wore coal-black capes and tricorn hats. One of them had insisted on adorning his hat with a stylish black ostrich feather.

'It gives an air of mystique and aplomb,' he had explained.

If you had looked carefully, you would have seen that they

By moonrise, three black-clad highwaymen
were galloping south on the road from London.

were not, strictly speaking, three highwaymen. There was one highwayman, one highwaygirl and one highwayboy. And one horse was, technically, a donkey.

That same night, *Le Bateau Fantastique* sailed out from the shore of France on a stiff breeze. The French king sat in the cabin of his royal vessel feeling slightly seasick as the waves buffeted the bow. He wondered if anything Princess Georgina could say the next day would change his mind about her. After all, she had sent him so many unforgivably rude letters.

The princess sat perfectly straight and still in the royal carriage as it trundled through the night. She barely blinked and the glistery crown on her forehead shed a strange light on her face. Opposite her, Lord Witloof checked his glass pocket watch. He smiled as he did sums in his head.

'STAND AND DELIVER!'

The tallest highwayman pointed his pistol, glint-eyed and menacing in the moonlight.

'Stand . . . and deliver?' the highwayboy repeated, somewhat fearfully.

'No, no, no! STAND – it has to come from your belly,
from your guts! STAND AND – go on, you try.'

'STAND AND . . . deliver?' the highwayboy tried
again.

'DELIVER!' The highwayman delivered, as though he
were on stage at the Theatre Royal.

'De-LIVER?' the highwayboy shouted.

'Excellent! Now, *you* have a go.' The highwayman waved
his pistol at the highwaygirl.

'Don't point that at me!' she cried.

'Sorry,' he replied. 'Though it is only a prop.'

The highwaygirl pointed her pistol at the highwayman
and said ferociously, 'STAND AND *DELIVER!*'

'Tremendous!' the highwayman cried. 'We are ready for
the great performance! On we ride!'

They spurred their horses up over the crest of the hill and,
on the silvery road winding below them, they saw a gilt
carriage glinting as it trundled along.

'Only two outriders,' the highwayman muttered. 'This
will be very easy.'

He turned in his saddle to address his comrades.

'Right. Here's the plan,' said the highwaygirl quickly. 'We
stop the coach –'

'I'll do a speech,' the highwayman interrupted.

'All right,' the highwaygirl agreed. 'Then we get the princess out, give her the Peace Hat and then escort the coach all the way to the royal galleon.'

'I shall do some more speeches on the way, if Her Highness would like it,' the highwayman put in.

Before they could answer, he gave a very dramatic 'YAH!' and galloped down the hill. The highwaygirl and highwayboy followed.

They reached the silver road just as the carriage rounded a bend and came rolling towards them. If the driver of the carriage had been keen-eyed, he would have seen the highwayman throw several bangers on the ground as he fired his pistol into the air. But the gunshots cracked and echoed between the hills and the driver only saw the flash of the highwayman's teeth, the mystique of the ostrich feather in his hat and the whites of his rearing horse's eyes.

'STAND AND DELIVER!' the highwayman cried.

'STAND AND *DELIVER*!'

'Stand and de-LIVER?'

Two smaller, slightly less intimidating highwaymen echoed his cry, waving their pistols.

The driver wrenched the carriage to a halt in a cloud of dust. The two outriders on their pure white horses hung back. The tallest highwayman pointed his pistol at them.

'On the ground, lads!' he ordered.

The trembling riders slid off their horses and dropped to

the ground. The highwayman smacked the white horses on their shiny flanks and they bolted off down the road.

'You too!' the highwayman barked at the driver.

He clambered off his seat and lay face down on the ground next to his colleagues.

'Keep your pistol on them. If any of them moves so much as a finger, shoot 'em,' the highwayman snarled to the highwayboy.

The highwayboy pointed his pistol at the three men. If any of them had looked up (which, luckily, none of them dared to do), they would have seen the pistol trembling. They might also have noticed that the pistol was made of wood, painted silver.

The highwayman jumped nimbly off his horse.

'Ho, Sally,' he said, to nobody in particular, though possibly it was to the horse.

He strode round to the side of the carriage and knocked, *rat-a-tat-tat*, on the door.

'Princess,' he pronounced, 'I give you my word as a gentleman of the highway, no harm shall befall you!'

There was silence from inside the carriage. Not even a curtain twitched.

'Do not fear, O Highness!' the highwayman continued, as the highwaygirl dismounted and walked round the carriage, trying to peer inside. 'I would sooner harm a rose in full bloom or a little leaping lambkin than hurt so much as a single royal hair upon your princessly head.'

There was nothing but silence from the carriage, and the highwayman began to look a bit peeved. He was not used to his speeches receiving so little reaction.

In a slightly louder, less chivalrous tone, he added, 'But it really is rude to keep a man waiting for too long.'

The highwaygirl, sensing something was amiss, pulled open the carriage door. She immediately gagged.

'*Zounds!*' the highwayman cried, as stinking air billowed out.

It was the same foul smell that had surged through the Guildhall the night before.

Through watering eyes, the highwaypeople saw a lone woman sitting inside the carriage. She held a silver needle poised in the air and she was surrounded by an ugly mass of pelts from scabby beasts, severed claws and yellow fangs, tarry feathers and a tangle of putrid animal guts. She was in the middle of sewing a live, writhing millipede on to the brim of a cadaverous black hat.

The highwaygirl gaped at the woman.

'You're not the princess!' the highwayman barked, disappointed.

Indeed, it was not the princess. It was —

'Miss Starebottom!' the highwayboy gasped, poking his head between the highwayman and highwaygirl to peek into the carriage. 'What on earth are you doing here?'

'I might ask you the same question, Lucas Bootmaker,'

Miss Starebottom snarled through a dangerously curled lip. Both her eyebrows were at full-menace height.

The highwayboy (Goose) gulped.

'Hatmaker and Bootmaker are still friends, I see!' Miss Starebottom sneered. 'So, the handkerchief didn't work.'

The highwaygirl (Cordelia) gasped.

'It was you!' she cried. '*You* put my handkerchief on Goose's floor after the Bootmakers were robbed!'

The realization set her mind twisting like a Whorlpod. She was dizzy with indignation.

'W-why would you *do* that?' Goose spluttered.

'I lent you that handkerchief when you were sad about your suitor waiting ages to propose . . .' Cordelia muttered.

Everything was beginning to make a horrible sort of sense.

'But he wasn't your suitor, was he – the man in the boat in Hyde Park? It was Lord Witloof! You're working together!'

'If only you were this clever in your lessons,' Miss Starebottom taunted.

'So it was *you* at the Guildhall last night!' Cordelia breathed. 'And all these things – they're from the Guildhall Menacing Cabinet you opened!'

The governess laughed her longest and pointiest laugh as Cordelia stared in horror at the revolting contents of the cabinet. Beneath black spikes of sea urchins and a heap of poison-green toadskins, Cordelia saw –

'Clothes! You're making clothes!'

Miss Starebottom struck like lightning, her cane flashing through the air.

The highwayman shrieked, '*Gad-ZOOKS!*' as the cane slashed in front of his face.

'YAH!' The carriage gave a great jerk and all three highwaypeople leaped backwards as a wheel threatened to roll over their feet.

'*By Iago!*' the highwayman cursed as the carriage lurched away, the driver and outriders clinging to the front bench and whipping the horses into a panicked frenzy.

'Goose!' Cordelia cried. 'You were meant to be guarding the driver!'

'I'm sorry, Cordelia!' Goose said shakily, tearing off his silk handkerchief. 'I wanted to see who was in the carriage!'

'I told you both! Never break character halfway through a scene!' wailed Sir Hugo, throwing his ostrich-feathered hat to the ground.

Cordelia's brain was whirring faster than a wound-up watch. The stink still lingered in the air as the second-best royal carriage disappeared round the bend in a plume of dust.

'They've probably been planning this for ages!' she muttered.

'Planning *what*, exactly?' said Goose.

'Can somebody *please* tell me what in Othello's name is going ON!' Sir Hugo bellowed.

Cordelia checked the Peace Hat. It was snug in the hatbox, which was tucked inside her father's jacket. There was enough room in the voluminous jacket for Cordelia and the hatbox, though the hatbox made her a rather strange shape. She turned to Sir Hugo.

'That woman is working for the enemy,' Cordelia explained. 'She's making clothes for the princess to wear at the peace talks, but they're made out of Menacing ingredients. Things that will fill her with hate.'

'Ah! A villainess! A vile *saboteur*!' Sir Hugo cried.

'What?' said Goose.

'She's going to ruin the peace talks,' Cordelia translated. 'She's making . . . sort of Rage Clothes. They'll make Princess Georgina declare war against France!'

For an awful moment, all Cordelia could see was roiling sea, overrun with battleships and thrashing with cannon fire. Her father would have no hope of surviving it. He would be gone forever beneath the churning waves.

Cordelia! His voice echoed in her head and his arms reached for her desperately, flailing in a violent sea.

'NO!' she shouted.

Goose and Sir Hugo stared at her.

Cordelia stared back. Looking into Goose's frightened eyes, she realized that if war came, it would not only mean that she would never find her father. *Thousands* of children just like her would lose their fathers too.

'We can't let it happen,' she said. 'We have to stop it.'

'How?'

'We have to get our Peace Hat to the princess! If she's wearing it, she won't be able to declare war! It's the only way.'

Sir Hugo snatched up his hat and vaulted back on to his horse. Cordelia and Goose scrambled back on to their steeds and, giving very dramatic *YAH*s, they all galloped down the road after the second-best royal carriage and the villainous governess.

CHAPTER 35

By the time they arrived at the coast, the sun had spilled over the eastern horizon and a pink the colour of Hushdove wings tinged the sky.

They decided to leave the road before they reached the sea, in case the royal guards were lying in wait somewhere. So they rode their steeds (as Sir Hugo insisted on calling their horses) up the green shoulder of a hill. After tying their steeds (Cordelia rolled her eyes) to a stunted thorn tree that had grown hump-backed in the strong wind, they belly-crawled to the wind-whipped edge of the cliff, and peered over.

Far below their snow-white cliff, a magnificent ship floated at anchor in the bay.

'That's the royal galleon!' Goose was awestruck.

'And look!' Cordelia pointed.

On the shore stood two carriages: the best royal carriage

and the second-best royal carriage. Tiny red-uniformed figures scooted back and forth from the second-best royal carriage to a rowing boat floating in the shallows. Miss Starebottom bossed everyone about from the dinghy.

'She must be taking those Rage Clothes over,' Cordelia guessed. 'I suppose the princess is already on board the galleon.'

All around the beach, soldiers glinted with weapons.

'This calls for a costume change,' Sir Hugo announced enthusiastically. 'We are into the final act!'

He tied his highwayman's bandana around his neck and untucked his billowy shirt.

'I really need an eyepatch and a peg leg for this character,' he sighed.

'There's no time, Sir Hugo – look!' Cordelia cried.

The rowing boat with Miss Starebottom and the Rage Clothes was now halfway across the bay to the royal galleon. With the bulky hatbox in her jacket, it proved rather difficult for Cordelia to tie a bandana around her neck, but with Goose's help she managed.

'We've got to get on to the ship!'

Cordelia, Goose and Sir Hugo scrambled down the cliffside and sneaked on to the beach.

The soldiers had returned with the now-empty rowing boat. They pulled it, with a scrunch of pebbles, into the shallows and marched with the rest of the guards up to the royal carriages, eyes trained on the road in case the three criminals they had been ordered to arrest were approaching.

They did not see three figures slink from behind a scrubby bush, dash into the surf and shove the rowing boat out into deeper waters.

The oars were out and the boat was pulling away towards the royal galleon by the time one soldier looked round and raised a shout. Nobody on the big ship heard the cries of the soldiers over the clanking of the anchor as it was hauled from the seabed. Nor did they hear the stutter of muskets firing at the escaping boat.

'Sir Hugo, sit down!'

With a spit and hiss like fat on a hot stove, bullets bit the sea behind the little boat. But they were out of range before the soldiers could reload their weapons.

'She be taking the wind finely this marnin'!' A foot on the prow as it nosed through the water, Sir Hugo watched the royal galleon sail steadily further away.

'We'll – never – catch – up – at – this – rate,' Goose panted, pulling on his oar.

'Can't – you – think – of – some – thing?' Cordelia puffed, between pulls on her oar.

They rowed in silence for several minutes, watching the soldiers on the beach shrink so small they looked like toys. The royal galleon was leaning eagerly towards the open sea, sails as full as white skirts.

'How are we going to catch up?' Cordelia groaned in despair.

Sir Hugo wrapped himself in a canvas sail from the bottom of the boat and leaned against the mast, apparently trying to look mysterious and dramatic against the skyline. Then a crested wave slapped the side of the little boat.

'AAAH! *By Neptune!*' he cursed, falling on Goose.

Goose was swamped by the sail and let go of his oar. Cordelia managed to snatch it before it was caught by a wave and pulled from the rowlock. As she hauled on the oar, she was surprised to see that Goose was smiling.

'I've *got* it!' he said, grinning. 'Just like my boat on the pond in Hyde Park!'

He pulled the sail off Sir Hugo and hoisted it up the short mast. Within a few minutes, they were cutting quickly through the water, oars lying at the bottom of the boat as a generous wind filled their sail. Goose had his hand on the tiller and his eyes were shining.

They were catching up with the royal galleon!

'Let's just hope they don't look back and see us,' Cordelia said. 'Though Jolly Roger over there might be enough of a disguise.'

Sir Hugo, clearly pleased with the new backdrop of the sail, was posing at the front of the boat again. This time he gazed yearningly out to the horizon, shading his eyes against the rays of the rising sun with what he seemed to feel was an expression of noble thirst on his face.

'The first thing we should do,' Cordelia said, 'is find the princess and give her the *real* Peace Hat.'

Goose nodded. 'Then what?'

'Then we ... we get those Rage Clothes from Miss Starebottom and throw them into the sea?' Cordelia suggested.

'Yes,' Goose agreed. 'Good plan.'

The sun was high by the time the royal galleon and *Le Bateau Fantastique* came within hailing distance of each other.

Unseen, a small dinghy slipped behind the bulk of the English galleon. Two industrious sailors lowered the sail and tied their boat to a rope ladder hanging down the side of the huge ship. The third sailor simply watched and growled, 'Arrr, put your backs into it, rapscallions!'

Cordelia peered up. Shouts and whistles came from the deck and they heard the colossal anchor plunge into the sea.

'I think we should climb on board now,' she muttered to Goose. 'We might be able to hide if they're all busy trying to look better than the French.'

'Good idea,' he said.

Sir Hugo whispered, 'Zounds! The hero's quest is nearly at

its peak! The sun reaches his noontime zenith and the game is afoot!' He whipped his sword out of its scabbard and swished it through the air. 'What say you, fair players? Let's whip 'em back to France!'

'No, Sir Hugo – we're not here to whip the French!' Cordelia hissed. 'We're here to help the princess! And to stop Lord Witloof.'

'And Miss Starebottom,' added Goose.

Sir Hugo grinned somewhat blankly and disappeared up the ladder.

'At least he's good with his sword,' Goose muttered as they hurried after him. They found him crouching dramatically behind a barrel and ducked down next to him.

The galleon was a-bustle with activity. Scarlet footmen ran back and forth, arranging flowers and unfurling English flags and putting up flattering portraits of King George (looking exceedingly sensible and most noble). Two velvet-covered thrones faced each other across the deck. One was a lot taller and more impressive than the other.

Across a narrow gully of sea and air, a dozen blue-and-gold French courtiers watched from the deck of the French ship. One, wearing an especially long and curly wig, shouted, 'I 'ope you weel not hexpect our keeeng to eet your Eenglish food.'

Cordelia and Goose peered out from their hiding place.

'Those must be the French Makers,' Goose breathed,

eyeing the most flamboyant people strutting along the deck. 'I heard King Louis has a Perfume-maker and a Wigmaker!'

Cordelia was surveying the English ship.

'The royal cabin will be aft,' Cordelia whispered. 'We need to get below decks.'

She pointed to a door below the poop deck and Goose nodded.

'Argh!' Sir Hugo cried. 'Splinter!' He leaped up, clutching his knee.

A footman screamed and dropped a tray of jam tarts.

Heads turned and everyone froze. Cordelia and Goose crouched as low as they could, not daring to move in case they were spotted too.

'Do not fear!' Sir Hugo announced to all the staring footmen. 'For I come on the noble mission to –'

'What manner of stowaway is this?' a voice boomed.

A man appeared on the poop deck. He wore a royal blue coat with gold buttons, a white wig and a black tricorn hat. He looked very impressive.

'I am no stowaway!' Sir Hugo barked.

'I am captain of the royal galleon,' the figure declared. 'And I know a stowaway when I see one.'

'*I* am Sir Hugo Gushforth,' Sir Hugo cried, slashing his sword in a silver arc. 'And I will not be called a *stowaway* by some strutting jack-a-nape with a splintery ship!'

The captain came down from the poop deck and strode

towards Sir Hugo, who was swishing his sword so fast through the air that it was a silver streak.

'Remember Sir Hugo's duel in the play?' Goose whispered confidently. 'He won easily.'

The captain planted his feet and pulled his own sword from its sheath. In one savage slash, he brought his weapon clean through the silver blur of Sir Hugo's swordplay.

Clang!

'OUCH!'

And Sir Hugo was desperately dodging and ducking as the captain calmly skewered and sliced the air around him.

'Ah,' said Cordelia. 'I think Sir Hugo is only good at fighting when it's pretend and the other person has a wooden sword.'

Goose nodded ruefully, watching Sir Hugo yelp.

Every footman, courtier and sailor on deck was riveted by the fight. Even the French, on their ship, were shouting and whooping as the captain cut the buttons off Sir Hugo's outfit with deft flicks of his weapon.

'Come on!' Cordelia hissed. 'Now's our chance!'

She and Goose scrambled out from behind the barrel and streaked across the deck. They were safely through the door when they heard a loud wolf whistle from a French courtier: with no buttons left to hold them up, Sir Hugo's trousers had fallen down.

CHAPTER 37

It was quiet and everything was gently rocking.

'Which way do we go?' Goose's voice came out of the shadows.

Keep wildness in your wits and magic in your fingertips! Cordelia closed her eyes and opened her nostrils.

The Rage Clothes reeked of evil: a mixture of rotten Firechicken eggs and burned dreams.

'It's that way,' she said, pointing.

'What way?' Goose's voice came back. 'It's too dark to see.'

In the gloom she felt for Goose's hand. Holding tight, she led him down the rolling corridor, following the vile smell wafting through the ship.

A shout rang out and they froze. Cordelia pulled Goose against the wooden wall a second before a crowd of people thundered past, bellowing.

'Intruder on board!'

'Trespasser!'

'Actor!'

Hearts hammering in the dark, Cordelia and Goose froze until the people stampeded away towards the deck. Cordelia breathed a sigh of relief. Then she wrinkled her nose.

'Ugh!'

The stink was stronger than before. She pulled Goose round the next corner and suddenly it was overpowering.

'Phew!' Goose huffed. 'That's horrible!'

Cordelia pushed gently and a door swung open. Bright sunlight flooded the dark and they saw twinkling windows and sparkling waves. A golden crest hung in the entranceway.

The royal cabin!

It was quiet.

'Everyone must be on deck,' Cordelia whispered.

They crept into the cabin and, sure enough, there on the four-poster bed lay —

'The Rage Clothes!'

Goose recoiled. The Rage Clothes were grotesque. Hate came off them in waves.

The cloak was made from the shredded pelt of a scarlet Vampire Squid, dripping with Eelweeds, studded with the angry spikes of sea urchins and — Cordelia squinted —

'Are those *children*'s teeth?'

Goose clapped a hand over his mouth.

The gloves were made of warty toad leather, the knuckles gnarled with knotty barnacles. On the end of each finger were stitched –

'Orcus Fox claws!' Cordelia could hardly believe it.

The boots had rusty nails spiking out of their pointy toes. The laces were twisted from putrid guts and –

'Wrath Ribbons!' Goose gasped.

Peering at the hairy brown watch, Cordelia realized with a jolt of alarm that it was made of a dead tarantula, its legs curled beneath it, finger-thick and bristly.

Goose grabbed her hand.

The hat was a tall black chimney, contorted with iron wires that crackled and sparked, humming with Lightning Strife. Three filthy feathers sagged on it and a single orange whisker curved like a scimitar around the crown, which Cordelia knew could be only one thing:

'The whisker of a Sabre Tiger!'

Most disgusting of all, a thousand live millipedes twisted and wriggled on the brim: the hat was alive with malice.

The children stared in horror. Around them, the ship creaked as though it was straining to contain these terrible secrets.

'Harpy feathers on the hat!' Cordelia exclaimed.

'And Lightning Strife!'

'Goose, these clothes are really dangerous. Even just putting one of these things on could be really bad.'

There was a tiny squeak behind them and Cordelia and Goose whirled round. There, pale as a marble statue, stood –

'Princess Georgina!'

She was so perfectly still that they had not noticed her when they crept in. The glass crown glistered on her head and her eyes were strangely glazed.

Before Cordelia could reach up to remove the crown, the door handle turned. 'Goose, hide!'

She dived behind a carved wooden screen as Goose wrapped himself in the velvet curtains of the four-poster bed. He covered up his feet as Lord Witloof strode into the room.

Cordelia put her eye to a hole in the screen and saw the lord smiling unpleasantly at the princess.

'I have arrested that ridiculous actor,' he said. 'He is being locked in the hold with some bilge rats.'

The princess remained frozen as Lord Witloof continued, 'Delilah suspects there are two stowaway children aboard: a Hatmaker and a Bootmaker. When we find them, we will throw them in a leaky rowing boat and push them out to sea. I am having some holes drilled in a small boat as we speak.'

Cordelia saw the bed curtains quiver.

'Now, Princess, the time has finally come for you to order the cannons!' Lord Witloof's eyes were shining. 'Your father refused to sign this commission. Then you refused. But you *will* sign it now, and my Ironfire Cannon Factory will begin to churn out weapons at a rate nobody has ever seen before!'

Lord Witloof unrolled a scroll of paper on the desk, dipped a waiting quill in ink and grasped the princess's hand. She had no choice but to write her name as his fist guided her fingers. As soon as it was done, Lord Witloof snatched up the paper and pulled his glass pocket watch out of his waistcoat.

'Drat, stopped again,' he muttered, tapping the silent watch.

He carefully unscrewed the lid of the timepiece. Where the beautiful blue butterfly had been, there were now just a few flakes of black ash. Lord Witloof tutted, tipping the ash on to the floor. He took a small wooden box out of his pocket and opened it. Inside were several jewel-bright butterflies, twitching their wings in the sunlight. One ruby-red butterfly took to the air but Lord Witloof caught it by a paper-thin wing.

'You'll do,' he said, as it struggled in his fingers.

He laid the butterfly on the watch, snapping the lid down over it and trapping it behind the glass. It thrashed and fluttered in its prison. Cordelia was sure if she could have heard the butterfly's voice, it would have been screaming.

The watch began to tick again. Cordelia felt sick.

The door swung open and Miss Starebottom slunk into the room.

'Ah! Most punctual, Delilah!' Lord Witloof announced. 'Time for Her Highness to dress for the peace talks.'

Cordelia wondered how she had never noticed how cruel

her governess's twisted mouth was. She looked nastier than a hundred algebra problems as she smiled at the princess and picked up the Rage Cloak. Cordelia shuddered silently as Miss Starebottom slung the rubbery cloak over the princess's shoulders and pinned the tarantula watch at her waist. She tugged the lumpy gloves on to the princess's pale hands and yanked her silver shoes off, then pulled the new boots on to the princess's little feet and tied the slimy laces in knobbly double knots.

Cordelia noticed that Miss Starebottom did not put the Rage Hat on the princess. The glass crown was still holding her in its cold power, like a strong arm holding somebody underwater.

Miss Starebottom stepped back, as if to admire her work. The princess was a sickening spectacle.

Lord Witloof smiled. 'What a *splendid* job. I'm sure the peace talks will go perfectly.'

'She'll declare war, and every Maker will be hanged on the hill,' Miss Starebottom hissed gleefully to Lord Witloof. 'And I will *so* enjoy watching their necks snap!'

It was all Cordelia could do not to cry out in horror.

And then she saw the velvet curtains move.

'STAND AND DELIVER!' Goose's voice shouted, as fiercely as he could, flailing the curtains in outrage.

For a moment, Lord Witloof looked terrified at the prospect of being attacked by vengeful soft furnishings. Then

Goose's round face appeared, ruddy with fury, as he wrestled to free himself from the curtains. He lost the fight, got tangled up, and thudded to the floor in a heap of torn velvet.

'That's the Bootmaker,' Miss Starebottom sneered. 'And the Hatmaker will be close by! Where are you hiding, Cordelia?' she hissed, swatting the remaining curtains with her cane.

'GUARDS!' shouted Lord Witloof.

Three guards came clattering into the room.

'Arrest this child!' Lord Witloof ordered, poking Goose with his foot.

'There's a girl hiding somewhere too. She's trying to sabotage the peace talks!' Miss Starebottom shrieked. 'Find her NOW!'

Cordelia saw a guard lurch towards her hiding place and she was almost discovered when –

'YOU!' Goose bellowed, pointing an accusing finger at Miss Starebottom. 'YOU are the most *twit-faced*, *nose-bogey*, *arse-farting* villainess from hence to *hence*!'

It was such a strange string of insults that everyone in the room turned to stare at Goose. Cordelia took her chance and dived into the one hiding place where nobody would think to look.

All around her chaos unfolded, as the room was torn apart in the search. The wooden screen she had been hiding behind was knocked over and she heard Goose being dragged away, still tangled in the curtains.

It was hot and stuffy. The weight of the Rage Clothes closed around her and she could barely breathe. But Cordelia was safely hidden under the princess's skirts.

She crouched beneath tiers of cloth held by stiff hoops. Her fingers brushed a greasy bootlace, making a tremor of rage quake through her. Feeling the hatbox in her jacket, with the Peace Hat waiting patiently within it, calmed her a little.

'She's definitely not in this room, Lord Witloof!' a guard barked, his feet an inch from Cordelia's hand.

'Search the whole galleon! Find her!'

The guards trooped out. Cordelia felt the floor shaking beneath their boots.

'Princess, follow me,' Lord Witloof ordered. 'It is time to begin!'

CHAPTER 38

It was lucky that royalty was expected to walk in a very slow and stately manner, because crawling along underneath a skirt (no matter how roomy) is quite tricky. Cordelia had to make sure her fingers did not poke out of the front of the princess's dress and that her toes did not poke out of the back. Her legs started to burn as she crept, crab-like, through the ship beneath the princess's dress, trying to avoid the rusty spikes on the toes of the boots and the jagged hem of crow's feathers on the Rage Cloak. Every time she brushed against them she felt a hot jolt of fury.

As the princess mounted the steps to the deck, Cordelia had to hop in time with each stair the princess took. Halfway up, she almost got left behind when the hatbox jolted and she mis-timed the hop. Heart hammering, she scrambled back into the safety of the skirts before her feet could be seen.

The royal party reached the deck with Cordelia still hidden. The brassy tooting of a dozen trumpets greeted them, and someone announced, 'Her Royal Highness the Princess Regent – Georgina!'

The princess stopped, and Cordelia heard a gasp from the awaiting crowd. She could only imagine the expressions on the faces of the courtiers as they saw and smelled the odious clothes the princess was wearing. Uneasy muttering stirred in the wind.

The princess started moving again and Cordelia crawled forward. Suddenly her hands sank into soft carpet and then the skirts shifted around her. She had to press herself flat against the bottom of the throne as the princess sat down upon it.

She carefully peeled up the hem of the underskirts and peered through a fringe of crow's feathers. The two glinting Ws of Lord Witloof's buckles were startlingly close to her face.

Cordelia felt the princess shiver and give a tiny gasp, as if she was coming up for air after a long time underwater. Lord Witloof must have taken the glass crown off her head.

'Now remember, Your Highness,' Lord Witloof murmured, 'King Louis wrote you some very offensive letters *and* he tried to assassinate you.'

The princess jolted as the Rage Hat was placed on her head. Her legs trembled and jerked as though she was trying hard not to dance a very angry jig. Rage was beginning to shudder through her body. Pressed against the side of the throne and with her limbs twisted around the princess's twitching legs, Cordelia was joggled vigorously.

Through the feathers of the hem, she saw a sturdy gangplank from the French ship smack on to the English deck.

'*La Grande Pomme! La Patate Chaude! Le Roi de France – Louis!*' a French courtier crowed as a golden-robed man with long hair and a twirly moustache sauntered across on to the English ship.

King Louis bowed extravagantly to the princess, his hands and hair and elbows all an elegant swirl. He raised a wry eyebrow at the less-impressive throne the English had provided for him, before sitting down on it.

Then came a long procession of brocaded French courtiers, led by a trotting white poodle wearing a gold collar. The poodle, the French Makers and dozens of other courtiers arranged themselves around their king, casting critical eyes over his English rival.

The English courtiers sniffed and shuffled. One had his nose stuck so high in the air he appeared to be staring directly into the noonday sun.

There was not much time left – the peace talks would begin any moment.

What on earth should I do? Cordelia thought desperately. In the Rage Clothes, the princess would never try for peace.

The Makers would be blamed, and they would all be executed as traitors. War would come and the sea would eat her father. He would be gone forever –

No.

She twisted round into the airless folds of the princess's skirts and found herself nose-to-nail with a Rage Boot.

I'll start by getting rid of these, she thought.

She tugged at the slimy laces, and the Wrath Ribbons blistered her fingers. The princess stamped her foot and Cordelia's fingers were crushed under the Rage Boot.

'Ouch!' she yelped.

Luckily at that exact moment, a loud gong was sounded on the deck and her voice was lost in the reverberations.

'Let us commence the peace talks,' Lord Witloof intoned as the sound of the gong died away.

Don't lose your head, Cordelia Hatmaker, she told herself sternly. She grabbed the princess's foot again, trying to loosen the laces on the first Rage Boot.

'Your 'Ighness,' the French king began. He had a chocolate-moussey voice that was rich and smooth.

'You detestable wretch,' the princess spat. 'You dare address me after writing those contemptuous letters?'

There was a shocked silence.

'But *you* are the one who has been writing rude letters, my Preeencess,' the king's chocolatey voice began again. It was the kind of voice used to getting its own way.

'I am not *your* Princess,' the princess snarled. 'I am my *own* Princess. And *you* are a knave of the rudest sort.'

The Rage Boot jerked. The laces resisted Cordelia's fingers, wrapping themselves round her wrist. She tore them off, gritting her teeth as the Wrath Ribbon seared her skin.

'*Knave?*' the French king repeated. 'Would a *knave* have sent you a basket of pineapples?'

Cordelia wrenched off the first Rage Boot and blew on her burning hand.

'*Pine*apples?' the princess snapped.

Cordelia gritted her teeth and started working on the second boot.

'Eet was a gesture of friendship!' the French king replied. 'Zey are very amusing fruits!'

'I never received any pineapples!' Her Highness fumed.

'I sent zem with my finest manservant!' the French king cried. 'Who has never returned! Kidnapper!'

'The only reason you came crawling to these peace talks, you snivelling villain,' the princess hissed, 'is because you are dreadfully afraid of my terrifying army of soldiers and my thousands of new cannons. So you've come creeping over here to pretend you're sorry.'

'I never *creep*!' King Louis burst out.

Cordelia was braced to pull off the second Rage Boot when –

The princess leaped to her feet and sprang across the deck,

leaving Cordelia huddled on the thick red carpet with a fresh sea breeze cooling her face.

But nobody noticed her. They were all enthralled by the wrathful princess. Her face was disfigured with rage and a flaming halo of fury crackled around her. The dripping red tentacles of the Vampire Squid Rage Cloak twisted and writhed, seething with evil. The crooked Rage Hat blasted sparks out of its black wires.

A tentacle from the cloak snaked through the air, wrapping itself around King Louis' shoulders.

'I would *never* be afraid of speaking to you!' the princess hissed. 'You should fear me! I could crush you like a COCKROACH!'

'NO!' Cordelia heard the shout, then realized it was her own voice shouting, 'Princess, STOP!'

But the Rage Cloak did not stop. It twisted up King Louis' throat, winding around his neck, turning his face red. With dreadful strength, it lifted the king off his feet as though he was a rag doll. Everyone on deck was transfixed with horror.

'*Au secours!*'

'Somebody 'elp 'im!'

Cordelia bounded across the deck and launched herself at the princess. She jumped on her back, the rubbery cloak thrashing beneath her, spikes of sea urchins stinging her skin.

'Your Highness!' Cordelia gasped, scrabbling at the glass clasp fastening the Rage Cloak at the princess's throat.

It wouldn't come undone. 'This isn't you! Stop it – *please stop*!'

'GET THAT GIRL!'

A hand yanked Cordelia's hair, trying to pull her off the princess. She kicked out and heard Lord Witloof fall back, cursing.

But something was wrapping itself around her middle. Something stronger than an arm, which wrenched Cordelia away from the princess. Her feet kicked in the air as she struggled in the grip of a Rage Cloak tentacle. King Louis, held at the neck by another tentacle, was turning a royal shade of purple.

Cordelia desperately called to the crowd of courtiers, 'Somebody *help*!'

'Stay back!' Lord Witloof cried, eyes glinting maliciously. 'Nobody move! You might make it worse!'

Cordelia struggled in mid-air as the tentacle squeezed her tight, crushing the breath from her lungs.

The princess's eyes were black with malice. She turned her burning gaze from Cordelia to the king. The tarantula Rage Watch, somehow come alive, was twitching and jerking its way along the tentacle towards the king's terrified face.

'*Princess!*' Cordelia wheezed desperately. She was losing air and hope. She felt the buttons of her father's jacket dig into her chest as she was squeezed.

Those gold buttons . . . They glinted in just the same way hope does.

With the last of her strength, Cordelia kicked. She felt her foot connect with the glass clasp at the princess's neck. It exploded open.

Thud. Thud.

Cordelia and the king slumped to the deck, both gasping for breath.

The cloak slithered, limp, off the princess's shoulders and fell in a stinking heap next to Cordelia. The watch landed beside it, and she slammed a fist on to it. Watch hands and spider legs scattered like matchsticks.

Cordelia rolled over. The princess snarled as the king staggered to his feet.

'Zis is an outrage!' he croaked.

'SILENCE, FOOL!'

One gnarled, craggy Rage Glove smacked him across the face and he went sprawling across the deck.

'THAT is for trying to ASSASSINATE me!' Princess Georgina bawled.

The king groaned, clutching his nose.

'*À l'assaut!*' yelled a Frenchman.

A French Maker dived for the princess, but an English footman tackled him to the ground.

'Come on, lads!' he yelled.

Suddenly around Cordelia, in a great writhing swarm of furious bodies, everyone was fighting.

A pack of French noblemen mobbed an English duke. A posse of English ladies-in-waiting attacked a French Maker. The English captain swung down from the rigging on to a gang of French countesses and quickly disappeared beneath their furious fists.

'One Boot – Watch – Cloak – done!' Cordelia panted, flipping over and scrabbling through a Frenchman's legs towards the princess. 'Now for Gloves – Boot – Hat!'

The princess loomed over the king, her Rage Gloves a whirl around his head.

'You are a VAGABOND! A WRETCH!' she shouted as she hit him.

Cordelia timed it perfectly. She snatched one glove as the princess drew it back to smack the king, and the other glove a moment later. She tossed them both overboard.

Confused, the princess gazed at her bare hands.

'Gloves gone!' Cordelia gasped.

The princess turned, and Cordelia saw a curdled mix of fury and fear in her eyes. The foot wearing the remaining Rage Boot lashed out. Cordelia dived out of the way just in time, sprang back and yanked the boot as hard as she could.

The princess shook her head as though she was trying to rid herself of a buzzing wasp.

The Rage Boot flew off the royal foot.

'YOU!' the princess howled.

She bore down on Cordelia, reaching for her – whether in fury or desperation, Cordelia could not tell. She backed away, tripped, and fell hard on the deck. The princess towered over her.

Cordelia was still clutching the boot. She threw it at the princess's head.

The boot hit its target and the hideous Rage Hat toppled off. A shower of millipedes fell wriggling from the brim and the hat landed in a smash of sparks on the deck.

Cordelia leaped to her feet.

Princess Georgina stood gasping in the middle of the ship, utterly bewildered by the chaos surrounding her. 'Miss Hatmaker?' she whispered. 'What – what have I done?'

'Um, well, you . . . you . . .' Cordelia glanced at the French king, who was cowering behind the throne.

'Your – Your Majesty?' the princess faltered, reaching down and shaking him gently.

He whimpered.

'Louis?' she coaxed.

King Louis peered out from between his fingers.

Princess Georgina peered back at him anxiously.

'King Louis,' she said softly. 'I really would like to talk about having a peace treaty between England and France.'

She held out her hand to help him up. The king scrambled to his feet, ignoring the princess's extended hand.

Around them, French and English courtiers and footmen were still engaged in savage battle.

'HAH!' His Majesty spat, 'You invite me 'ere, on to this ship in the middle of the sea, to have *peace talks*, you say! Pah!'

Princess Georgina nodded uncertainly.

'Zen you insult my PINEAPPLES!' he bellowed. 'And you ambush me with a VILE ATTACK!' The king was wild-eyed with indignation. His wig was askew and his gold cloak was ripped and his carefully curled moustache was frayed like an old rat's whiskers. 'You say you would like PEACE! Zis is not *peace*.'

Cordelia thrust her hand inside her father's jacket and pulled out the hatbox. She ripped off the lid. There, serene (and only slightly dented), was the Peace Hat.

'I hereby declare against England ze most violent and terrible wa–'

Cordelia jumped, lifting the Peace Hat high in the air. She jammed it down on King Louis' head.

'Wa-what a beautiful outfit you are wearing today, Preencess,' he finished.

The Peace Hat glimmered on the king's head. The golden star was at a slightly wonky angle, but it sparkled in the sun. The Sunsugar halo glowed, the feathers danced in the breeze and the Leaping Bean hopped gleefully along the brim. And King Louis smiled at the princess, all trace of fury gone.

'It worked!' whispered Cordelia.

Princess Georgina's dress was smoking slightly, singed by some stray sparks of Lightning Strife, yet she still stood with regal dignity amid the carnage surrounding her.

'Can we agree officially on peace, Your Majesty?' she asked, tentatively stretching her hand out again towards the king.

Cordelia held her breath, as the king took the princess's hand and covered it with kisses.

'Um, does this mean we will have *peace*?' the princess asked, pulling her hand away.

'*Mais, oui!*' the king agreed, beaming like a ray of sunshine. 'Yes, my lovely Princess. Peace shall be ours!'

Cordelia sighed with relief.

And at that moment a cannon fired.

BOOM!

CHAPTER 39

The sound was loud enough to stop the fight in its tracks. The English and the French froze in the middle of battle.

An English duke cowered in a barrel. A French countess stopped assaulting the captain. A gang of English footmen dropped their French foe.

'I will have my WAR!' Lord Witloof bellowed. He was standing on the poop deck next to a smoking cannon.

'*Non!*' a French courtier shouted, pointing at *Le Bateau Fantastique*.

There was a smoking hole in the French ship. In response, a hundred cannons suddenly appeared through gunports in its side: a hundred iron mouths ready to spit fire.

Everyone on the galleon gasped.

'Zey will not attack us!' a French courtier shouted at Lord Witloof. 'Our keeng ees on board!'

Lord Witloof took his cannon by the muzzle, as though it was a dangerous dog, and dragged it round to face the French king.

'He won't be on board for much longer!' he thundered, shoving gunpowder into the black O of the cannon's mouth, and brandishing the long rammer at an advancing English footman. '*Stay back!*'

The crowd retreated, leaving King Louis blinking in the middle of the deck.

'Your Majesty!' Princess Georgina tried to pull him out of the firing line. In response, the king dreamily stroked her hair. '*Louis!*'

Cordelia wove through the horrified crowd and began to climb the rigging.

Lord Witloof grabbed a cannonball and fed it to the cannon.

'*Please* move!' Princess Georgina begged the king.

Cordelia chose her rope carefully.

Lord Witloof struck a match.

Cordelia took aim –

Since King Louis would not move, Princess Georgina stood in front of him. Right between the king and the cannon.

Cordelia pushed back with her legs –

Lord Witloof touched the match to the gunpowder fuse.

– and she jumped!

Wind whirled around her as she sailed in a graceful arc through the air, clinging to the end of the rope.

With a *thud*, Cordelia collided with the triumphant lord.

He staggered backwards, flipped over the wooden railing and disappeared over the side of the ship.

Cordelia hauled the cannon with everything left of her strength as the fuse sizzled down inside the iron fusilage. The cannon kicked like a carthorse, throwing her on to the deck. Smoke and iron blasted out of the metal mouth and seconds later she heard the cannonball splosh into the sea.

'That was close,' Cordelia croaked.

The deck thundered with footsteps as the crowd rushed to the railings to see Lord Witloof floundering in the waves. The cannonball had missed him by inches.

'Oh, bravo!' a French baron cried, then helped the English duke out of the barrel.

Suddenly, all over the royal galleon, French and English courtiers were bashfully dusting each other off, muttering apologies in timid English and hesitant French. An English sailor released a French Maker from a headlock and straightened out his clothes. Lords and courtiers shook hands. Ladies and sailors smiled sheepishly as they disentangled themselves from their opponents.

'Fetch Lord Witloof out of the sea,' the princess ordered.

A looped rope was tossed over the side and Lord Witloof was hauled up, dripping with seawater and fury. He was deposited on the deck at Princess Georgina's feet and

immediately surrounded by a bristling circle of guards, all
levelling their glinting halberds at him.

'Lord Witloof, you are evil,' the princess declared. 'And
you are also defeated. England and France are at peace.'

The lord pulled a wriggling fish out of his wig and flung
it at her. 'I'm not *evil*, I'm a good businessman!' he snarled.
'War creates fear. Fear makes money. It's a very simple
equation.'

He lurched to his feet, water pooling on the deck around
him. His fine clothes were sodden and his wig was plastered
over one side of his face.

'It's an equation your blasted father the king refused to
listen to,' Lord Witloof went on. 'So I got him out of the
way. And that French *blockhead* kept writing you love letters –'

Lord Witloof jabbed a furious finger at King Louis.

'So I burned them,' Lord Witloof leered. 'And forged some
new letters to stir up talk of war.'

'You *burned* zem?' King Louis bleated.

'*Love* letters?' the princess repeated, rolling her eyes.

King Louis blushed and batted his eyelashes.

'My Ironfire Cannon Factory was READY TO BEGIN!'
Lord Witloof roared. 'It would have made me SO MUCH
GOLD!'

His wild eyes lit on Cordelia and he became very still, like
a snake about to strike.

303

'Still, there are other ways to make gold,' he hissed, quiet as poison being poured. 'War is the simplest, but there are greater and more terrible ways to do it.'

He lunged at Cordelia through the circle of glinting halberds. Cordelia twisted out of his hands and, in a heartbeat, five guards had the lord in their grip. His nose was an inch from Cordelia's and she felt his sour breath on her face.

'I will have my *gold*, Miss Hatmaker,' Lord Witloof whispered. 'Gold is *power*. Your father could not stop me and nor shall you.'

'What?' Cordelia gasped. 'What do you mean about my father?'

'Throw this villain in the hold with the bilge rats!' the princess commanded magnificently.

The guards dragged Lord Witloof across the deck.

'If I'm going in the hold, *she*'s COMING WITH ME!' Lord Witloof bawled, pointing at a French lady's maid in the crowd.

All eyes turned to the lady's maid, who was hiding behind a wide fan.

'*Moi?*' she said innocently.

The king's poodle bounded up and snatched the fan out of her hand, revealing –

'Miss Starebottom!' Cordelia cried. She turned to the princess. 'Your Highness, she's working for Lord Witloof!'

'Working for that devil?' Miss Starebottom spat. 'No!'

She swaggered forward, flourishing her cane. 'I have only ever worked for *myself*, Miss Hatmaker.'

With a violent thrust, Miss Starebottom shoved a guard aside with her cane. He fell back, bleeding.

Only when the glinting point of the cane quivered an inch from Cordelia's nose did she see what it truly was:

A swordstick.

CHAPTER 40

At the other end of the swordstick, the narrowed eyes of
Cordelia's governess were slivers of pure hate.

'I don't care about war or peace, or getting rich or having
power,' she spat. 'All I care about is *revenge*.'

'Revenge?' Cordelia repeated. 'For what?'

'Thirty years ago my family was expelled from the
Guildhall,' Miss Starebottom hissed. 'My father was
executed. My mother, brother and I were thrown into a
workhouse. We were shamed and abandoned. Left to die. I
was nine years old.'

Cordelia frowned. She remembered her uncle telling her a
similar story . . .

'But I did not die,' the governess continued savagely. 'I
held my mother and my brother's hands as fever burned the
life from them. But I *survived*!'

Cordelia searched her governess's face, wild with malice and grief.

'I am the last living Canemaker!' Miss Starebottom howled. 'And I want revenge!'

The governess lunged for Cordelia. Cordelia ducked and the swordstick plunged into the mast.

Before Miss Starebottom could pull out the swordstick, strong hands seized her and dragged her back.

'No!' Miss Starebottom cried. '*No!*'

Cordelia looked from the swordstick, still quivering in the mast, to her governess, struggling in the arms of the guards. She felt pity fluttering in her fast-beating heart.

Left to die at nine years old.

'The last living Canemaker?' the princess repeated. 'Is this true?'

'My uncle said they'd all died . . .' Cordelia whispered shakily.

Miss Starebottom jerked, trying to get free. 'Of course all those smug Makers thought everyone was dead. Nobody bothered to find out what happened to us! I was left alone, with no family, no friends. Nobody to take care of me! I was a *child* –'

Miss Starebottom's voice cracked, barely able to contain her fury.

'I grew up in an orphanage, waiting and planning. I took a job with the Hatmakers, and another with the Bootmakers. I spent three years hiding in plain sight, tutoring those ghastly children so we'd be ready to strike! It was I who wound the Summoning Clock to call the Makers to the Guildhall. The Makers have hated each other for years, and I knew if they were gathered together a fight would be inevitable – and it would be impossible for them to make the Peace Clothes successfully. Lord Witloof arranged for the Thieftaker to stage an assassination attempt at the theatre –'

'Don't tell them everything, you fool!' Lord Witloof lashed out.

'*Don't call me a fool!*' Miss Starebottom snarled.

'Take these two traitors away,' Princess Georgina ordered the guards.

'Wait!' Cordelia cried. She was trembling but she had to know the truth.

'Lord Witloof, what do you know about my father?' she demanded. 'What did you mean when you said he couldn't stop you?'

Lord Witloof's lips curled into a sneer.

'Answer her,' Princess Georgina commanded, flashing imperious eyes at the leering lord. 'By order of the Crown.'

A guard poked his halberd into Lord Witloof's side, and he winced. Then he muttered reluctantly, 'The night the Hatmaker ship was due to return, I travelled to the coast and extinguished the torch in the Rivermouth lighthouse. Then I waited until nightfall on the cliff with a lantern. The *Jolly*

Bonnet came sailing over the horizon and, thinking my lantern was the lighthouse, the ship took the wrong course and steered on to the rocks.'

Lord Witloof looked directly at Cordelia and a terrible smile split his face in two.

'The crash was a symphony of destruction. And I saw the captain, standing at the ship's wheel, get swallowed whole by the sea. He went down, tangled in the rigging. I watched Captain Hatmaker drown.'

Cordelia looked into the lord's eyes and knew it to be true. She felt – numb.

'It was a pleasure, seeing my oldest rival die. I've hated him since our days at Cambridge,' Lord Witloof went on. 'After watching the ship disappear beneath the waves, I galloped to Hatmaker House to tell them of the terrible calamity. Their ship had been sunk, and Prospero lost! Oh, what a *tragedy*!'

Cordelia was dizzy with despair as she grasped for the last shred of hope. 'But – Jack, the cabin boy. He knew something . . .'

Lord Witloof clenched his teeth. At a nod from the princess, the guard prodded him with the halberd again.

'Yes, the cabin boy survived,' Lord Witloof sneered. 'As soon as I got wind of it, I made haste to the docks at Wapping and drugged him. I could not risk him revealing the truth about the shipwreck.'

'And when I found out you were meddling, Cordelia, I

nailed him in a crate and put him on a ship to Jamaica!' Miss Starebottom cackled. '*And* I bribed the seadog to lie about it!'

'Take them both away!' The princess turned from them with contempt, and wrapped her arms around Cordelia's shoulders.

Cordelia was stupefied with shock. The truth was sinking in slowly, like a body drifting to the bottom of the sea.

The villains were dragged over to the hatchway that led down to the hold.

'No!' Miss Starebottom whimpered. 'Please! I – I'm afraid of the dark!'

But her wails were ignored by the burly guards. Miss Starebottom and Lord Witloof were booted through the hatch.

Goose and Sir Hugo were freed. Cordelia watched in a daze as Goose bounded towards her.

'You *did* it!' he cried, bowling her over in a great bear hug.

Sir Hugo emerged shakily from the hold, his eyes haunted.

''Twas as black as a hangman's heart down there,' he quavered. 'We have survived many nights without a shred of hope.'

Goose laughed. 'Sir Hugo, we've been in there about forty-five minutes!'

Cordelia smiled, but she felt as though she was drowning.

'You stopped the war, Cordelia!' said Goose in amazement.

She looked over at the princess and the king. His French Majesty was draped over the princess's shoulder, moonily playing with a bow on her sleeve, the Peace Hat still perched on his head.

'I think we can safely agree,' the king crooned, 'zat we are lovers, not fighters. For after all, I have lost my heart to you, Princess. I would surely have lost a war also.'

Everybody around Cordelia cheered, except the princess, who removed the king's arm from around her shoulder.

'I hope I don't have to marry him as part of the peace treaty,' Cordelia heard the princess mutter to herself. 'That would be *such* a bother.'

Cordelia turned her face into the wind and her eyes to the vast ocean. There – far away – was the hard line of the horizon. She had been foolish to think she could have found her father at sea: it was as wide as the sky.

Then something within her stirred. The sea air was brazen on her face and the mewing of the wheeling gulls was suddenly sharp and urgent as she remembered in a rush.

'Goose! We've got to rescue our families!'

CHAPTER 41

At the Tower of London there was already a rescue afoot. Sam Lightfinger surveyed the miserable Hatmakers. Uncle Tiberius, Aunt Ariadne and Great-aunt Petronella all stared back at her. They had spent most of the morning like this, studying each other across the gloomy dungeon. Every so often, Sam glanced at the shadow of the guard at the door.

After a particularly long silence ... 'Lunchtime,' Sam remarked cheerfully.

'How do you know that?' Aunt Ariadne asked.

'Guard's gone.' Sam grinned, jumping to her feet.

AWOOOOOOOOO-AWOOOOOOOOO!

A terrible yowling echoed down the dingy tunnel. Sam peered out of the barred window. In the dungeon opposite, a man with wild hair and a crazed smile was hopping up and down, howling.

'Who the blazes is that?' Sam asked.

'That,' said Aunt Ariadne wearily, 'is the king of England.'

Great-aunt Petronella cackled with dry laughter from her armchair as Sam waved at the king.

' 'Ello, Your Majesty!' she called.

The king paused midway through a howl and blinked at her. Then he licked his hand like a cat and cleaned his ears, purring.

'Right,' Sam announced, getting down to business. 'Let's get outta here, shall we?'

Uncle Tiberius opened his mouth to explain that they were in the deepest dungeon at the end of the darkest tunnel of the Tower of London, and that the damp dripping through the ceiling was the River Thames seeping *downwards* because they were so far below ground. But before he could even begin to explain how hopeless their situation was, Sam Lightfinger whipped a golden hatpin out of her sleeve and twiddled it in the keyhole.

'Is that my hatpin?' Aunt Ariadne spluttered.

Sam grinned over her shoulder. 'Useful little fing, ain't it?'

Click!

'Most sapient!' Great-aunt Petronella cried.

'Who *are* you?' Aunt Ariadne whispered.

'By St Catherine's Holy Cap!' Uncle Tiberius exclaimed as the dungeon door swung open.

Sam put a finger to her lips and poked her head out to check there were no guards prowling. Then she sprang over to the king's dungeon and began twiddling the lock with the hatpin.

Click!

The king was freed. He flapped his arms and crowed.

'Come on, Your Majesty,' Sam said, chuckling.

The king did look rather funny with his wild hair, scarlet jacket, bloomers and purple snakeskin shoes as he scampered out of the cell.

Sam slipped along to the next dungeon and peered in through the door. She saw three glum people slumped on the stone floor.

' 'Ello,' Sam said. They all looked up. 'You must be Goose's family.'

It was indeed Mr and Mrs Bootmaker and Goose's older brother, Ignatius.

'Do you know where my little Lucas is?' Mrs Bootmaker asked in a tremulous voice.

'Not quite sure just at this minute,' Sam replied, wiggling the hatpin in the lock. 'But I fink he's *probably* saving us all from a war.'

Click!

The Bootmakers were amazed. Sam let them out of their cell and they sidled into the tunnel, joining the Hatmakers and the king. Hatmakers and Bootmakers eyed each other suspiciously.

Quickly, and with a series of satisfying clicks, Sam freed

the Glovemakers, the Watchmakers and the Cloakmakers from their dank prison cells.

The last cell of all contained a lone French manservant with a basket of rotten pineapples. The crowd of Makers watched in silence as Sam fiddled the hatpin in the lock. It was easier than trying to make small talk with each other.

Click!

The last lock was picked.

'Here ya go,' Sam said cheerfully, handing the hatpin to the astonished Aunt Ariadne.

A Tower guard appeared at the end of the tunnel. 'What's all this palav– *huh!*'

His mouth fell open when he saw the Makers, Sam, the pineapple-wielding Frenchman and the king standing there.

'Get 'im!' Sam cried.

She snatched a pineapple and threw it at the guard. She had a very good aim. She knocked the guard out cold.

Ten seconds later, Sam, the king, the Makers and the French manservant, armed to the teeth with pineapples, surged up out of the dungeons and into the guardroom. The guards, who were just tucking into their lunch (a rather delicious roast chicken), saw them coming and fled.

The prisoners chased the guards through the wide courtyard, scattering a rabble of ravens, and down to the huge gates in the inner wall. They were almost free! They could see the way out – they just had to get through the archway beneath an ancient tower . . . With a deafening crash, an iron portcullis smashed down in front of them. Ravens wheeled, squawking, in the air.

'*No!*' Sam cried.

On the other side of the portcullis, the guards jeered at them.

'We're stuck in here!' Uncle Tiberius panted, as he brought up the rear, carrying Great-aunt Petronella in her chair.

'RELEASE ME!' the king bellowed magnificently. 'For I am your KING!'

'Nonsense! You ain't the king! You don't look like the bloke on the coins,' one guard sneered.

The king shrugged and cawed at a watching raven.

'We're trapped!' a Glovemaker wailed.

Sam frowned. A raven hopped towards her.

'Only if you fink 'bout it negative,' Sam said, narrowing her eyes at the guards. 'Maybe *they're* the ones who're trapped.'

The raven cocked its head.

Sam dropped her pineapple on to the cobbles and it broke into bright yellow shards. She tossed a bit to the raven. The bird snapped it up and croaked for more.

'Right-oh, 'ere ya go!' Sam grinned. She tossed another bit of pineapple through the iron grille of the portcullis, into the midst of the sneering guards.

Moments later, a black feathery missile with a razor-sharp beak hurtled down on the guards from above. Uttering freakish screams, the other ravens joined in.

The guards shrieked, diving for cover, as the air around them was torn apart by the ferocious birds.

Encouraged, all the Makers copied Sam, throwing bits of pineapple through the portcullis. The ravens gleefully snapped up the food as it landed around the dancing guards.

When they ran out of pineapples, the Makers raided the guardroom lunch table (Sam helped herself to some chicken, too). The guards did not enjoy having their lunch hurled at them. When the roast chicken (and all the trimmings) ran out, the Makers found the supply of dry bread for the prisoners, and kept up the assault. The ravens were not fussy eaters.

'By order of the Crown – cease this rebellion!' a guard yelped.

'Only if ya let us out!' Sam yelled, lobbing a hunk of bread at him.

'Never!' the guard declared, before a raven snatched at his hat, thinking it was a charred crust.

When the royal galleon sailed up the Thames hours later, ready to free the prisoners from the dark dungeons, they found the Tower guards sheltering from a bombardment of food and ravens. Their uniforms were pecked to shreds and covered in bird poo, and they were only too happy to see an end to their torment.

CHAPTER 42

The portcullis was raised and the prisoners charged out. Sam led the way, with the Hatmakers on one side of her and the king on the other. The king was pretending to be a lion.

Cordelia, Goose and Sir Hugo were standing ready to greet them with the princess and all her courtiers. Sam waved wildly at Cordelia, and Cordelia waved back, amazed to see Sam leading dozens of bedraggled Makers.

'Makers!' the princess cried. 'You have been wrongfully imprisoned and for that I am truly sorry! I grant you all your freedom and beg your forgiveness!'

The princess curtseyed low to the amazed crowd. The Makers cheered and clapped. In the excitement, the king spotted a broken pineapple crown lying on the ground and seized it, dancing happily around with it on his head.

When the princess saw her father, the smile slid off her face.

'I see Lord Witloof also lied about sending my father on a trip to the seaside,' she said, tears glistening in her eyes. 'You Makers did all you could, but I fear my dear father is doomed to this silliness forever.'

The king dropped the spiky crown and started hopping from foot to foot, flapping his hands and squealing. The princess shook her head and Sir Hugo gallantly flourished an enormous silk handkerchief for her to dry her tears.

Cordelia, meanwhile, was studying the king.

He still wore the same strange outfit he had been in when the Hatmakers had delivered the Concentration Hat to the palace: puffy bloomers, an unbuttoned scarlet jacket and tightly buckled shoes that were as purple as bruises.

Cordelia frowned at the shoes.

The king had been desperate to take them off, but Lord Witloof had forbidden it.

Why did he forbid it? Cordelia wondered.

There was only one way to find out.

She walked towards the hopping king and knelt down. He stopped hopping and, like a nervous horse, tapped his foot and shifted skittishly as Cordelia started to undo the buckles on his shoes.

One shoe came off, then the other.

The king stood in his socks on the cold cobbles and sighed with relief.

'Finally!' he said. 'Those ghastly shoes are off! Gives a man space in his brain to think properly!'

Everyone stared with open mouths as the king looked round at them all.

'Father?' the princess asked, not quite believing her eyes.

'My dear Georgina!' The king smiled. 'How lovely to see you! I've been in that dungeon a while. Not quite the trip to the seaside I was promised, eh!'

'Addlesnake skin!' Mr Bootmaker exclaimed, picking up one of the purple shoes. 'These shoes are made from Addlesnake skin. They have been causing the king's silliness, I am certain.'

'Too right!' the king barked. 'That rogue Lord Witloof gave them to me as a gift. He knows I have a fondness for shiny shoes. I put them on and, a moment later, I thought I was a kangaroo.'

'But a Bootmaker would never use Addlesnake skin – it's far too menacing!' Mrs Bootmaker blustered. 'Where did he get them from?'

Goose's older brother gave a strangled sort of squawk. All eyes turned to him.

'*That's* where it got to!' he spluttered. 'I – I brought that snakeskin back from the equator months ago!'

Everybody looked shocked. Mrs Bootmaker, for once, was speechless.

'Ignatius,' Mr Bootmaker choked. 'Explain.'

'Oh, uh – yes – well . . .' Ignatius could not meet their eyes as he gabbled, 'I – er – I remember that day . . . I unloaded all the ingredients I'd brought back, but somewhere between the dock and the back door of Bootmaker Mansion, the Addlesnake skin – erm – it disappeared. It – uh – it was in a crate marked DANGEROUS and it – I thought it had fallen off the cart. Went back to look for it but I couldn't find it anywhere. Gosh! Um . . . gosh.'

Cordelia saw Uncle Tiberius grinning delightedly at the Bootmaker's mistake. Even Aunt Ariadne seemed unable to keep her mouth from twitching into a slight smile.

Before Mrs Bootmaker could draw breath to berate Ignatius, Goose piped up, 'I bet it was Miss Starebottom who stole it!'

Hatmakers and Bootmakers all looked confused to hear this familiar name in such strange circumstances.

'Bring her here,' Princess Georgina ordered a guard. 'And we'll ask her.'

'And somebody arrest that lawless Lord Witloof!' His Majesty declared.

'He's already been arrested, Father,' Princess Georgina said proudly. 'Guards, fetch him too!'

Lord Witloof and Miss Starebottom were summoned and hauled before the king. They were both soaked with stinking bilge water.

'Did you steal the snakeskin to make these shoes?' the princess asked the governess.

Miss Starebottom grinned nastily, still green with sea sickness. 'Yes, I stole it from the cart when that stupid Bootmaker's back was turned,' she hissed, pointing at Ignatius, who was determinedly avoiding his mother's eye. 'I made it into shoes using the old Bootmaker workshop in the Guildhall,' she added. 'Not bad for my first pair.'

'I see you stopped hopping long enough to take them off,' Lord Witloof snarled at the king.

'Miss Hatmaker helped me,' King George boomed. 'I am deeply in debt to her for freeing my feet – and, indeed, my entire self – from your villainy.' He looked from the treacherous lord to the governess. 'Who *is* this person?' His Majesty asked.

'That is an excellent question, Father,' Princess Georgina said. Turning to Miss Starebottom, she went on, 'Shall we call you Miss Starebottom? Or do you prefer to be known by your true name: Delilah Canemaker?'

All the grown-up Makers gasped.

'Call me Canemaker,' Miss Starebottom spat, staring daggers at all the Makers. 'You left me to die when I was only a child and you don't deserve to forget it!'

The guards dragged her away, her furious wail echoing off the stone walls of the Tower.

'And this villain deserves a trip to the seaside,' Princess Georgina announced. 'Just like the one he gave you, Father.'

'Take Lord Witloof away!' the king commanded.

Everybody watched as the wicked lord was bundled into the Tower and out of sight.

Silence followed his departure. Cordelia gazed around at the dazed faces of the Makers.

'By Bottom!' Sir Hugo declared. 'Let's see some cheerful spirits! The villains are vanquished and the day is won – this calls for a theatrical celebration!'

Cordelia and Goose looked at each other in alarm.

'More acting?' Goose gasped. 'I thought we were safe!'

Several nights later, the Hatmakers were milling around in the hallway of Hatmaker House, all dressed in fine clothes and fancy hats. Cook and Jones, also dressed in their best, waited by the front door.

Cordelia peeked through the window as a musical jingle sounded outside.

'The royal carriage is here!' she cried.

'Come along, Sam!' Aunt Ariadne called up the stairs. 'We can't be late!'

Sam Lightfinger came thundering downstairs, wearing a pair of shiny new boots and a smart suit. 'Sorry! Took me a while ta do up all the buttons!'

Cordelia thought Sam looked splendid in her new chestnut-brown suit, with her hair braided close round her head. Cook squinted disapprovingly at Sam's trousers.

'Can't think why you refuse to wear a nice dress,' Cook griped. 'Specially on an important occasion like this one.'

'Ya never know when ya might need ta climb a building,' Sam said wisely, adjusting her new waistcoat. 'And climbing anyfing in a dress is a right pain.'

'I agree.' Cordelia nodded fervently, remembering her unhelpfully flapping skirts during their night-time escape from the Guildhall. She squeezed Sam's hand as Uncle Tiberius ushered them outside.

'I can't believe we're going to see Sir Hugo *himself* perform in a play!' Cook squealed. 'And at the palace! Lord love me, I'm all a flutter.'

They piled into the carriage, and four palace footmen hoisted Great-aunt Petronella, and her wheeled chair, in after them. Luckily it was roomy enough to hold everybody, though their knees knocked together as they trundled off into the dusk.

But the royal carriage did not take them to the palace.

A short while later, they rolled to a stop on Bond Street. A footman opened the door and let everybody out on to the street. The Hatmakers found themselves standing at the gloomy mouth of a rather familiar alley. Lanterns glowed along the twisting way, studding the darkness with gold.

'His Highness begs you to join him,' the footman intoned. 'But the carriage can take you no further. Kindly follow the lanterns.'

Aunt Ariadne and Uncle Tiberius's smiles became rather fixed. They knew where the lanterns led.

'The *Guildhall*!' Cordelia whispered.

She began following the chain of lanterns down the dark alley. Cordelia could almost hear her uncle dragging his feet and her aunt's hesitant steps. She supposed that it was difficult for them to return to the Guildhall: they had known it, years ago, as a bright place of friendship. It must be hard to see it now, so sad and abandoned.

Nobody expected the change they found when they got there.

The Guildhall had come alive with lights. The windows twinkled, lit from the inside with a thousand candles. The statue of the man above the entrance (the statue that Cordelia had clung to not long ago) had been cleaned. Somebody had scrubbed the bird poo off his hat and placed a garland of flowers round his neck. The huge oak door stood open in welcome, hung with bunting.

The Guildhall did not look lonely or unloved any more.

Inside, everything was gleaming. The floor was polished, candles flickered from brass sconces on the walls, a merry fire crackled in the fireplace, and new velvet curtains were swagged at the windows.

A palace footman bowed as he ushered everyone through the archway.

The Great Chamber was transformed. The air rang with

music and shimmered with light. Great garlands of flowers festooned the walls. Somebody had released hundreds of Dulcet Fireflies into the dome. They flittered like moving stars above everyone's heads.

'Welcome!'

It was Princess Georgina, eyes shining as she opened her arms to greet the Hatmakers. King George, standing next to his daughter, inclined his head graciously as the Hatmakers bowed to the royals.

'*Blimey*,' Cordelia heard Cook whisper behind her.

'Welcome back to your Guildhall.' Princess Georgina smiled. 'We've spent the last few days making it ready for you!'

There was a long table covered with lace cloths and laden with cakes. An enormous number of pineapples were piled beside them.

'King Louis sent the pineapples,' the princess told Cordelia. 'As a token of his friendship.'

Royal music makers played their instruments on a raised stage and footmen carried silver trays of clinking glasses around.

The Guildhall was full of Makers of every age. The three Watchmakers observed everyone from the edges of the crowd. All the Cloakmakers paced and posed importantly together. The Glovemakers had gathered in a boisterous bunch.

The Great Chamber was transformed.

Cordelia spotted Goose standing in a knot with his family. It was the first time she had seen him since the Tower. He was dressed in a too-tight suit and looked somewhat strangled by his cravat. His mother had his hand clenched tightly in hers. Sam whistled, Goose turned, and Cordelia saw his face light up with a smile as he spotted them. She raised her hand to wave, but Mrs Bootmaker saw and yanked him out of sight behind his father.

'We'll find a way to talk to him,' Sam whispered in Cordelia's ear. 'Come on – let's look around.'

Sam made straight for the table of cakes and Cordelia was about to follow when she caught sight of the Canemaker crest above a workshop door.

Those crossed lightning bolts striking down made her shudder. But beneath her surge of horror, pity fluttered like a baby bird.

Delilah Canemaker had been nine years old when she was left alone, with no family and no friends.

Cordelia walked towards the Canemakers' door. It was the only one left undecorated. Nobody had come to hang flowers and bunting on it: it was bare and abandoned.

She reached for the handle.

'No, miss.' A footman appeared, blocking her way. 'Not allowed in there. It's dangerous.'

Cordelia drew her hand back. 'What's dangerous about it?' she asked.

'Best left well alone, miss,' he said, planting his feet firmly in front of the door.

'MAKERS ALL!' a herald yelled, crashing a pair of brass cymbals. 'Please take your seats! We are proud to present to you a new Theatrical Spectacular! Starring the superlative Sir Hugo Gushforth in a Great Heroic Role as Saviour of the Day! A Tale of Daring and Skulduggery! Of weeping Maidens and dastardly Sailors! Of Courage and Heroism, the like of which has not been seen since Shakespeare himself –'

'Get ON with it!' the king bellowed.

In three seconds, the lamps were out and the play had begun. The Makers shuffled into their seats in the dark as Sir Hugo bounded on to the stage.

The play turned out to be little more than an elaborate sword fight. Five minutes in, after a bit of wailing from a boy dressed as a princess and some unpleasant words growled by a burly sailor, Sir Hugo swept them aside and was plunged into the middle of a heroic brawl. He bravely battled an ugly ship's captain and twelve hulking guards all at once.

Watching Sir Hugo lay waste to his enemies on the stage, Cordelia realized that the actor did not need a hat to help him with stage fright any more. He was doing splendidly on his own.

She turned in her seat and furtively searched the crowd. She saw both pairs of Glovemaker twins wearing expressions of violent delight as they watched Sir Hugo thrashing his adversaries. Three rows in front of them, she spotted Goose. He was wearing an expression of such complete disbelief that Cordelia snorted with laughter.

Goose flicked his eyes over to her. She raised her eyebrows, as if to say: *This isn't quite how I remember Sir Hugo fighting on the ship.*

Goose grinned in reply.

'Have at thee!' Sir Hugo cried. 'Take that! And *that*!'

Sir Hugo cut the buttons off the costume of the actor playing the captain and his trousers fell down, exposing his frilly underwear. The audience roared with laughter and applauded. Sir Hugo took several bows.

The seat next to Cordelia's was empty. Sam Lightfinger had crept away.

I have an idea where she might be, Cordelia thought, slipping off her seat.

Sure enough, when she lifted up the lace tablecloth of the long table, she found Sam underneath. Sam had a cake in each hand and several silver teaspoons stashed down her shirt.

'Mind if I come in?' Cordelia asked.

'Make yerself comfy!' Sam grinned through a mouthful of cake.

Cordelia shuffled under the table, helping herself to a jam tart on the way down. A minute later, the tablecloth was hoicked up as Goose looked in.

'Hello!' he whispered. 'Is there room for me too?'

'Always!' Cordelia whispered back, making space for him. Goose smiled shyly at Sam as he squeezed in beside her.

They spent a happy half hour munching cakes and biscuits, listening to the rumbles of laughter and the applause from Sir Hugo's audience.

'Are you enjoying living at Hatmaker House?' Goose asked Sam.

' 'Sgreat!' Sam said, scoffing a cream bun. 'Cook makes me all the food I want and so far I've only had to have one bath.'

Goose chuckled. 'I hope I'll be allowed to come back and see Hatmaker House again one day,' he said wistfully. 'My mother's still furious with me. She said Bootmakers and Hatmakers have no business being friends with each other.'

He tensed for a second, then peered under the fringe of the tablecloth.

'It's all right – she's watching the play.' He sighed, turning sheepishly back to the others.

Cordelia stifled a laugh.

'But why are you still dressed as a boy, Sam?' Goose asked, ignoring Cordelia's chuckle. 'And why did you do it in the first place?'

Sam twisted her face up and squinted at Goose. Then she glanced sideways through the table legs. Cordelia suspected she was planning an escape route in case things went wrong.

'Truth is, Goose,' Sam said, 'I was a thief. I'm reformed now: good as gold, since Friday. Ain't that right, Cor?' She winked at Cordelia. 'It's a bit easier on the streets if yer a boy,' Sam went on. 'Not lots easier, but a bit. Bad things happen ta boys, but a lot worse can happen ta girls. That's why I disguised meself.'

Goose nodded in understanding.

'Also, I 'ad a bit of a run-in with the Thieftaker, and since he was lookin' for a girl, I made meself into a boy.' Sam grinned. 'And, I gotta say, boys' clothes is a lot comfier than girls'.'

'I agree,' Cordelia muttered, tugging at her sash. 'Maybe I'll try it.'

Sam giggled. 'Cook'd 'ave a tantrum! I'd love ta see that!'

'At least you don't need to worry about the Thieftaker any more,' Cordelia said.

'Why?' Goose asked.

'He was still in the workshop, trussed up in the ribbons, when the Newgate Prison guards came to arrest him for staging the assassination attempt at the theatre!'

Goose grinned, imagining that sight.

'Cordelia Hatmaker! Lucas Bootmaker! Sam Lightfinger!' a voice called.

All three of them jumped and hit their heads on the table.

'Uh oh,' Goose said. 'We're in trouble.'

Sam tried to creep away, but Cordelia held on to her foot.

'Come on, Sam,' she said. 'Let's face the music together.'

They crept out from under the table, wiping crumbs off

their faces. Sam took another slice of cake in case it was the last chance she got.

The princess was standing on the stage, looking splendid in the Peace Hat that Cordelia, Goose, Sam and Cook had made for her. Even though the Peace Hat had been through a lot, the golden spire star still twinkled and the Sunsugar halo glowed and the feathers shimmered and the Leaping Bean hopped. The princess smiled when she saw the children come out from under the table.

'There you are!' she beamed. 'Please come here, Cordelia, Lucas and Sam!'

Feeling very hot and prickly with the eyes of the audience upon them, the three of them shuffled up on to the stage.

'Thank you, with all of my heart,' the princess began. 'This hat you made stopped a war. As a celebration of your immense bravery, I present each of you tonight with the Order of the Golden Heart.'

The princess pinned golden heart-shaped medals on to their chests. Sam immediately bit hers to see if it was real gold (it was). Goose was as red as a Firechicken and Cordelia felt as though a dozen Sicilian Leaping Beans were dancing in her ribcage as the audience cheered them.

Cordelia took a deep breath. She had something she wanted to say. She didn't exactly know the words to use but she knew what she was feeling, and she wanted to give it a voice.

'Makers!' she began.

The crowd fell silent. Every Maker in London stared up at her. She swallowed. Now she had their attention, she had to continue.

'Um . . . We've been Making for centuries, but we always focus on – on the *first* part of our name: Cloak, Glove, Watch, Boot . . . Hat . . .'

She tailed off as she glanced at the closed door of the Canemaker workshop and wondered for a long moment about the nine-year-old girl who for years had burned bitter from the loss of her family.

'Uhm, I mean . . . What I mean to say is: we're all Makers,' Cordelia continued. 'Half of our name is the same. Let's never forget that. Again.'

It was not an elegant speech, nor was it a long one, but it did not need to be. It was exactly how she felt.

There was a small smattering of applause, but in the middle of the Makers, Aunt Ariadne, Uncle Tiberius, Great-aunt Petronella, Cook and Jones clapped loudly and long. Cordelia smiled at them and wished everybody else would stop staring at her.

The king (who had refused all footwear since being freed from the Addlesnake shoes) leaped to his bare feet. 'Now we shall have dancing!' he cried.

The chairs were cleared as Cordelia, Sam and Goose clambered down from the stage on shaky legs. Goose was pulled away by his parents, but Uncle Tiberius leaned down and whispered in Cordelia's ear, 'Your father would be *very* proud of you, little Hatmaker.' Then he flourished his green handkerchief in front of his face and sobbed freely.

Cordelia gazed around at the milling crowd, at all the Makers freed from the Tower, and the king and princess freed from an evil lord. She had stopped a terrible war. Her father would have been tremendously proud of her. That knowledge should have made her glad. But there was only a sad stone in the middle of her stomach because he was gone.

'Cordelia.' It was Aunt Ariadne, looking down at her with serious eyes.

Oh no, Cordelia thought. *She's going to tell me off for making another hat without permission. In front of everybody!*

'I spoke very angry words to you, little Hatmaker,' her aunt murmured. 'I told you, in fury, that you were too young to make a hat. But I was wrong – I am sorry.'

Suddenly Cordelia found she had her own apology to make. In a rush, she gabbled, 'No, Aunt, *I* was wrong! I shouldn't have done that with Sir Hugo's hat – *I'm* sorry!'

But her aunt put her finger to her lips. 'You truly are a Hatmaker now, Cordelia.'

She put her hand in her pocket and pulled out a little velvet-wrapped parcel.

Cordelia took it, feeling the soft material in her palm. She gazed up at her aunt in amazement. 'Is this –'

'Open it.' Aunt Ariadne smiled.

In the folds of velvet lay a beautiful golden hatpin. An aquamarine as big as a blueberry glowed on the end.

'I know you've wanted one for a long time,' Aunt Ariadne said.

'Yes!' Cordelia cried. 'I've wanted one for *ever*.'

'What's that?' Sam asked, poking her nose over Cordelia's shoulder. 'Looks valuable!'

'It *is* valuable, Sam!' Cordelia beamed, sticking the hatpin through her hat. 'It's got special magic in it, like my aunt's, to make me a proper Hatmaker!'

'Oh, Cordelia, my dearest,' her aunt said, laughing. 'The hatpin doesn't have any special magic! Nor does mine!'

'But I felt it,' Cordelia insisted. 'I *felt* the special magic in your hatpin when I put it in my hair. It was like . . . like lots of ideas and energy and excitement all singing through me.'

Aunt Ariadne shook her head and smiled. 'It's just an ordinary hatpin, Dilly! Those ideas and energy and excitement come from *you*.'

And before Cordelia could quite grasp this unexpected fact, the royal music makers began to play a merry polka, and everyone turned to watch the king begin to dance.

A few steps in, His Majesty whirled Sam along with him. Sir Hugo pirouetted impressively and Princess Georgina allowed him to lead her into the dance. All the other Makers hung back. The Bootmakers stared suspiciously at the

Hatmakers, while the Watchmakers eyed the Glovemakers. The Cloakmakers frowned at everyone in general.

Then someone wove through the crowd and grabbed Cordelia's hand. She stumbled as she was pulled through the throng. Cordelia was astonished: it was Goose! He towed her determinedly to the middle of the room.

In front of a hundred people, Goose turned to Cordelia and bowed.

Cordelia grinned and bowed in return. Then Hatmaker and Bootmaker joined hands and embarked on a rather eccentric series of dance steps. Clearly their ex-governess had failed to teach them to move in a dignified manner. They romped rather than danced. Sam whooped as she saw them rollicking past her.

'Why isn't anyone else joining in?' Goose panted.

'When you've been mortal enemies for a long time, I suppose it is quite difficult to just start dancing together,' Cordelia mused, spinning Goose in a circle.

As she twirled Goose under her arm, she saw Mrs Bootmaker scowling at them.

'Your mother's expression could freeze fire!' Cordelia shuddered.

Goose chanced a glance at his mother, tripped over his feet and staggered to a stop. Mrs Bootmaker glowered down at him like an iceberg about to sink a ship.

'Lucas Bootmaker, come here at once,' she growled.

Goose stared at his feet, now frozen to the spot, though they had been dancing a polka only moments ago.

Mrs Bootmaker's lip curled. 'Lucas!' she snapped. 'Here! *Now!*'

The music makers stopped playing their violins, bows sawing the air as they gawped. Goose was still frozen, staring hard at his polished boots. There was a dangerous silence.

Cordelia flicked her eyes from Goose to his mother. She thought she could hear the very air between them sizzling.

Then, in a tiny gesture of defiance, Goose's foot began to tap. He raised his chin and waved a hand at the music makers. They snatched up their instruments again and started playing a fast jig.

And then the whole of Goose was dancing.

He wheeled round and grabbed Cordelia's hand, twirling her wildly. The music was wild and the dance got faster and faster until everything but Goose's face was a blur.

'Aren't you in terrible trouble?' Cordelia gasped as they jigged.

'Just keep dancing!' Goose grimaced, hopping up and down in time with the music and clapping his hands.

He had a slightly panicked look in his eyes and there was sweat glistening on his forehead, but he grinned.

'I'm proud to be your friend, Cordelia Hatmaker.'

CHAPTER 44

Hours later, Cordelia lay in bed, her father's gold-buttoned jacket draped over her and her eyes wide open in the dark. The night had never felt so big and she had never felt so small in it.

After all the excitement of the past few days, she was finally alone. And, at last, Cordelia had to admit one simple fact to herself.

'You're gone, Father,' she whispered. 'You're never coming home. We saved everyone, but . . . I couldn't save you.'

A floor below, in the room that had once been Prospero's, Sam Lightfinger snored gently into her pillow. After two nights spent *under* the bed, tonight Cordelia had managed to persuade Sam to get *into* the bed. And now she was sleeping soundly.

But Cordelia couldn't sleep.

She gently laid the jacket aside, padded over to the window, pulled up the sash and looked out. London was slumbering. The moon was whole in the sky and the rooftops and spires of the city were silver-gilded.

The stars can take you anywhere if you know how to read them. Her father's voice came back to her. *They can take you on a grand adventure and they can lead you home.*

Cordelia searched the sky for Polaris, the North Star. *The star you set your compass by.* For several heart-thudding seconds she could not find it among the rabble of tiny lights.

Then she saw it: the North Star.

It winked in a friendly way.

Cordelia squinted. There was something else in the heavens, making the stars around it flicker and blink.

It was getting closer and closer, flying straight towards her, coming lower over the rooftops, skimming the chimneys.

Cordelia snatched up her father's telescope and pointed it skywards.

It was a bird, with moonlight luminous on its wings. And, as it swooped down over the glinting glasshouse, Cordelia recognized –

'AGATHA!'

The speckled Quest Pigeon cooed softly as she landed on Cordelia's outstretched palm.

'I thought you were never coming back!' Cordelia whispered.

She could feel the bird's heart fluttering, as fast as her own. Agatha bobbed and flurried in her hand, making a strange rattling sound. Cordelia lifted the bird carefully so she could reach the message bottle.

There was no note inside.

But there was something far more important: the seashell painted with her mother's picture.

She had last seen it round her father's neck as he bent to kiss her goodbye before setting off on his next voyage . . .

Now here it was, cupped in her hand.

Remember what you are made of, littlest Hatmaker.

Cordelia fastened the chain round her own neck and the shell rested right over her heart. Feeling it against her skin gave her courage.

'You know what this means, Agatha,' Cordelia whispered, looking up into the wide night sky, full of possibilities. 'Somehow, my father is alive.'

Agatha cooed in an encouraging sort of way. She fluttered to Cordelia's bedside table and blinked a bright eye at the piece of paper lying there. It was the paper that had been hidden in Prospero's telescope.

'It's blank,' Cordelia sighed. 'The ink was washed off in the sea.'

But Agatha cooed again.

The ink.

Like a lightning strike, Cordelia remembered what her father had once told her:

They're special inks! One is invisible, but becomes visible when exposed to the heat of a candle flame. One can only be seen by starlight. One only appears on a Tuesday. They're all good for sending secret messages.

She snatched up the paper and held it close to the candle flame – the paper remained blank.

'What's today, Agatha? Tuesday!' She looked down at the paper. Nothing. 'Only one thing for it!'

Cordelia dashed from the room, Agatha fluttering around her head in a flurry of excited wings. Together they whirled up the rickety ladder and burst out on to the roof.

The world was awash with starlight.

Heart pounding, Cordelia unfurled the blank paper and held it up to the soft dazzle of the stars as Agatha landed on her shoulder.

In front of her eyes, glistering silver lines began to appear on the empty page.

'It's ink that can only be read by starlight!' she whispered.

And suddenly she saw what it was.

Cordelia Hatmaker was holding a map.

Glossary

Here follows a brief but useful list of ingredients most potent and valuable to an Apprentice Hatmaker.

Angelite Enamel – *Ceramica angelicus* – Pale blue and with a pacific, soothing quality, this enamel is often used in conjunction with volatile metals. It also pairs well with wood from the Ardour Tree. Promoting tolerance and equilibrium, Angelite allows the wearer to enjoy the benefits of the metal or wood it is paired with, without suffering the bad behaviour it might otherwise induce.

Angelus Shell – *Concha angelus* – A whorl-shaped shell found in the clear waters of the Paragon Sea. The nymph that sheds this shell leaves an echo of its sea song inside it. Hung

from the brim of a hat, the Angelus Shell creates a chiming sound that comforts and uplifts the soul.

Athenian Owl – *Bubo minervae sapiens* – Only found in the Platonic Forests at the base of Mount Olympus, this extremely wise bird goes to great lengths to avoid humans. A person skilful and subtle enough to locate the owl may win a feather by answering a riddle designed to test their wisdom. The feather can be used for cleverness, concentration, contemplation and other arts of the philosopher.

Benevolence Buttons – *Boutons bienveillants* – A general term referring to any buttons that have been embroidered with a Friendship stitch. Benevolence Buttons decorated with Fellowship Knots are most potent for fostering feelings of goodwill towards humankind.

Braggart Buttons – *Boutons bossets* – Although these buttons are bright gold in colour, they are actually made of brass. Tempered in a fire that must be constantly pumped with bellows and fed with leaves of Radiant Bay, these buttons are useful for promoting self-confidence in the wearer. They should only be worn by a person who is struggling with low self-esteem, otherwise they provoke boastfulness and obnoxious self-congratulation.

Brown Study Spider – *Aranea badia studiosa* – A distinctly hermit-like spider, often found living in the spines of books or between pages of sheet music. Silk from this spider can help the user to stick to their tasks unwaveringly.

Common White Dove – *Columbula alba* – The milk-white feathers from this gentle bird inspire a peaceful frame of mind, encouraging compassion and thoughtfulness.

Concord Moss – *Bryophyta concordia* – An emerald-green moss found in the Forest of Arden. It is made of long strands that extend remarkably quickly, knitting together as they grow. When woven into creations, a strand of this moss inspires diplomacy.

Cordial Blossoms – *Flora benigna affabilis* – Ranging in colour from palest cream to buttercup yellow, these blossoms have a delightful scent and a sparkling pollen that (in ancient Celtic tradition) is said to be a blessing if it falls upon one's head. The blossoms are used to imbue the wearer with a sense of glad-hearted kindness for fellow human beings.

Drowslip – *Primula somnulenta* – Like its cousin the Cowslip, this flower is bell-like and delicate. The flowers are indigo blue and thrive in shady woodland. Silk ribbon is

woven from the soft petals using a special loom, and the weaver hums quiet lullabies while working. These ribbons are used on nightcaps, as they cause a pleasant drowsiness when worn on the head. Only a few inches of ribbon are needed for a nightcap, or a permanent state of sleep may ensue.

Dulcet Fireflies – *Lampyridae he̅dus dulcis* – Small, bright-tailed fireflies from the southern swamps of the North American continent, these sweet-natured insects enjoy flitting into shadows, bringing their hopeful light to dark places.

Dwam Threads – *Droom draad* – Threads twisted with dream strands. They can be made of silk, cotton, trains of thought, wool or copper. Excellent for embroidering nightcaps. Use on a daytime hat causes absent-mindedness and a slumberous mood.

Elysian Eagle – *Aquila elysiana* – The feathers of this majestic bird appear to be plain black, but bright sunlight reveals their rainbow iridescence, containing all visible colours, as well as some invisible ones. A dropped feather from an Elysian Eagle is considered a great blessing: it will encourage the wearer to understand and accept themself fully and courageously.

Fathom Glass – *Speculum cassandrae* – Glass made in a clear-flamed fire out of sand from a well-used hourglass. The glass will help the wearer to answer questions clearly and to have clarity of purpose when contemplating the future.

Flabbercrest – *Avis obstupefio* – A bright scarlet bird, approximately three feet tall, from sub-Saharan Africa. When threatened or trying to attract a mate, a three-foot feather springs from its crest, doubling its height. This crest feather is dropped once the desired effect has been achieved and is used in Hatmaking to most impressive effect. If worn too long, the feather can fill the wearer with quarrelsomeness or insufferable cockiness.

Frenzy Bee – *Apis insania* – This delightful honeybee will fly for miles to find flowers. When a new nectar-rich flower is discovered, a lone Frenzy Bee alerts its colleagues by flying extremely fast in an ecstatic circle, creating a high-pitched sound only detectable by the bees from its own hive. A Maker may capture this sound in a tuning fork and transfer it to a hat with a sharp tap, imbuing the wearer with a sense of vibrant enthusiasm. Honey from the Frenzy Bee is believed to sharpen the senses and was taken by ancient Olympians attempting the discus throw.

Hush Dove – *Columbula tranquilla* – Cousin of the scarlet Shrieking Dove, the Hush Dove, true to its name, is a very quiet bird. Its pale-pink feathers bring calmness to a disordered mind.

Loquacious Lily – *Lilium garrulus* – A dazzling white trumpet-shaped bloom with golden stamens and a heady scent. This flower encourages the wearer to speak their mind and give voice to their innermost thoughts. Used properly, it helps a shy wearer to express themselves with confidence. If the wearer is usually of a talkative disposition, it can open the verbal floodgates and result in gossiping, blathering and tiresome prattling.

Love Beetle – *Scarabaeus inamoratus* – An affable beetle with shiny pink wings, which they shed once a year. Found among the petals of Bulgarian roses, always two insects per bloom. A bite from a Love Beetle provokes feelings ranging from mild fondness to intense adoration. An allergic reaction can cause nausea, dizziness and acute obsession. On hats, the shed wings of the beetles are used to promote feelings of gentle kindness.

Lullwool Sheep – *Scaep lullavellus* – Native to the slopes of Snowdonia, the lambs are born dark blue and grow paler as they age. The oldest Lullwool Sheep are a pale duck-egg

colour. Their wool is used to encourage calm, ruminant consideration.

Mellow Daisy – *Aster melu* – A pale-yellow flower often found growing in the cracks of pavements or on sun-drenched walls. Never choosy about where they decide to flower, these daisies promote a happy-go-lucky attitude and a sunny outlook.

Merrybird – *Avis hilaris felix* – A small, pink-feathered bird with yellow stripes in its tail feathers. Its call is said to imitate the gurgling laughter of a baby. Brings levity and joy when a person's outlook is too serious.

Moonbeam – *Radiatus lunae* – Translucent and fragile, moonbeams create various melodic tones, depending on the timbre of moonlight (and indeed the phase of the moon). Sonorous beams from the full moon are used for fulfilment and plenty. The hopeful tones of beams from the waxing moon encourage optimism, while beams from the waning moon can ring hollow and foster forbearance. All are difficult to see in daylight.

Moonbloom – *Flos lunaris* – Indonesian shrub that blooms only on the full moon. Velvety flowers range from mauve to

indigo. Induces deep and peaceful sleep. Useful for nightcaps. One petal tucked inside a hatband can inspire a soothing daydream.

Moon Cactus – *Cactaceae lunarium* – This small, perfectly round, pale-blue cactus produces yellow flowers with crater-like markings that closely resemble the full moon. Ironically, the Moon Cactus will only flower in full sun.

Moonwing – *Columba luna* – An elegant bird with a black-feathered body and white iridescent wings that form a circle in flight, resembling the full moon. A single wing feather gives the wearer a sense of elegance and lucidity.

Olive – *Olea europaea* – Used since Biblical times as a symbol of peace and renewal, an olive branch can be worn to encourage outreach and friendship.

Pax Palm – *Areca altis paxum* – A tall and graceful palm tree from Palestine. The pale-green leaves can be woven together to make a straw-like hat or used individually to charming effect. Imbues the wearer with a sense of serenity and fraternity.

Paxpearl Shell – *Mollusc tranquillitas* – Found in the shallows of Ease Bay, Paxpearl Shells are cup-shaped with

pearlescent interiors. They help the wearer to hold their peace.

Peace Mountain Crystal – *Quartz pax montana* – A smooth, clear stone that has been tumbled for millennia in the glacier of the Himalayan Peace Mountain. Always cool to the touch, it is most often droplet-shaped. Instantly calms the temper and refreshes jaded spirits.

Peacock – *Aves phasianidae* – The tail feathers encourage poise and showy flamboyance. Can also promote a sharp-eyed perceptive streak when used sparingly. Overuse in hat decoration results in egomania and dangerous self-confidence.

Politic Cord – *Rudens diplomaticus* – This cord is made by spinning tactful arguments together with strands of hemp or silk. Hemp is used when a robust attitude is required from the wearer, while silk is reserved for more delicate persuasions.

Pyrite – *Ferrum scintilla* – This bright gold mineral is a form of iron and is sometimes called Fool's Gold. Although it can amplify foolish qualities already innate in the wearer, this effect can be tempered by using it in conjunction with something that brings soothing and wise qualities (such as

Angelite Enamel). In this harmonious state, Pyrite will stimulate the flow of ideas and bring confidence and clear-sightedness to the wearer.

Risible Mushrooms – *Fungi ridiculosa* – The most exuberant of all mushrooms. Small and pale grey with bright violet gills, they enjoy hiding in plain sight to pop up and surprise their fellow fungi. Used on a hat, they will help a bashful person surprise themselves with their own spirit and sense of playfulness.

Rosemary – *Salvia rosmarinus* – An evergreen aromatic shrub, useful for aiding memory and boosting the power of the brain. Worn on a hat, it can be invigorating and help to activate the memory and focus the mind.

Sage Ribbon – *Ligamentum philologus* – A Sage Ribbon is made by weaving hairs from the head of one or more scholar, philosopher or learned person. If hairs from more than one individual are used in the same ribbon, it is wise to ensure that the viewpoints of the individuals are more or less in harmony, lest the ribbon cause confusion and wild swings in opinion. Head hair is recommended, though beard hairs may be used by more experienced Makers. It is, of course, strongly recommended that the Maker seeks

permission from the donor before they attempt to pluck the hairs.

Saturn Cactus – *Cactaceae saturnus* – With a prickly temperament, this cactus has a ring of thorns round its middle but is otherwise completely smooth. A thorn used as a hatpin can give confidence, particularly when speaking in public.

Siberian Ice Spider – *Aranea siberica* – A spider from the northern icefields of Russia, which freezes its web as it spins. Useful for cooling hot-headedness. Overuse can cause an uncanny tingling sensation down the back of the neck.

Sicilian Leaping Bean – *Legumen siciliano exulto* – A long-podded speckled bean from the Mediterranean isle of Sicily. Famous for bouncing exuberantly, these beans give the wearer a sense of levity and gladness of heart. There are several wild colonies of beans on the isle. When ripe, they spring forth from their pods with a popping sound. Once they have got their bearings, they are notoriously difficult to catch.

Silverglass – *Vitrum argentum* – Made by mixing Venetian mirror-dust with molten glass, Silverglass reflects glamour on the wearer, accentuating their finest features. Once the

hat is removed, the effect wears off, which can result in a disappointed paramour if Silverglass has been used too liberally.

Singing Sapphire – *Sapphirus sonorus* – A precious blue stone found growing, like a pearl in an oyster, inside the egg of a nightingale. Once the bird is hatched, the stone can be collected and used to inspire vocal confidence. If worn for too long, a Singing Sapphire may provoke a loud, tuneless whistling inside the wearer's head, causing them to shout in order to hear themself over it, thus becoming a nuisance to those around them.

Sooth Crystal – *Crystallum psychicum* – A clear crystal formed in underground caves where fresh water runs. These precious stones bring clarity and truthfulness, helping the user connect to their intuition. Worn on a hat, a Sooth Crystal will help the wearer to follow their instincts.

St Aegis Vine – *Vitis aegiea* – A climbing plant originally from the Levant. The golden-yellow flower promises a positive outlook, while the fruits can be used to make a cordial, which, if imbibed, instils a sense of quiet confidence. Wine made from the fruits can cause bombast if drunk to excess.

Starlight – *Lux stellaria* – When strained through glass into a silver bowl, starlight is used to give hope and guidance to lost souls. Sprinkled on a hat, it fills the mind with sparkling ideas for adventures that promise to renew the spirit.

Thunder Rain – *Pluvium fragorum* – Raindrops shaken by a thunderclap. If caught in a strong enough bowl or jar, the water can be used to infuse dyes and ribbons. An excellent strengthening solution, it can also allow the wearer to express emotions in a healthy way. Particularly good for unleashing bottled-up anger or sadness. Most potent when the essence of a lightning bolt is also caught.

Timor Fern – *Embryophyte timiditum* – A very shy evergreen fern from the Amazon basin, often found hiding beneath the leaves of larger ferns. Wearing the fronds encourages gentle conversation. A sensitive wearer may even feel the need to whisper.

Upstart Crow – *Corvus corax cachinnans* – An oft-misunderstood avian with a distinctive caw. Regarded by some as a nuisance and a pest, and by others as a bird with vocal talents to rival the nightingale. The plumage of the Upstart Crow is showy, bestowing on the wearer a sense of self-confidence, which mean-spirited onlookers may describe as vainglorious.

Vapour of Valour – *Nebula valoris* – A pale-purple mist made by gathering the breath from the roar of a lion at dawn. Used to infuse a hat with spirit and courage, the roar reverberates even after the sound and vapour have gone, fortifying the heart.

Vesuvian Stone – *Pumice magmae* – A rock taken from the crater of Mount Vesuvius in Italy. If exposed to sunlight or excessive heat, the rock will ooze lava. Useful for Alchemists and practitioners of the Making arts for forging metals and melting glass.

Waltz Moth – *Eacles tanzen* – True to its name, this mauve moth performs an elegant wing-dance in triple time. Particularly attracted to light from Alchemic fires, its wingbeats stir rhythm into the Maker's work. A hat favoured with the wingbeats of a Waltz Moth has amplified power. The wearer may find themself skipping on every third step.

Warble Ribbon – *Ligamentum melodium* – A ribbon made from Song Moth silk, which is sewn on to the costume of an opera singer. Ideally, the ribbon will be worn for several performances before being used by the Maker, giving ample opportunity for it to absorb the powerful vibrations of the singer's voice. Ribbons from a soprano are most potent and

should be used sparingly. Warble Ribbons help the wearer to fearlessly express and celebrate deep emotions, although overuse can result in melodramatic wailing that may eventually prove tiresome.

Whorlpod – *Legumen vortexis* – The high-climbing Whorlvine can reach the top of a tall tree in a matter of days. When it has grown as high as it can, the vine puts all its energy into growing a cluster of spiral-shaped pods. These pods burst from the vine and corkscrew through the air, making a high-pitched whistling sound as they go. Whorlpods are used in Making to decorate hats for dancing. They are especially popular in Scotland, where they are known as 'Birly Bonnets'.

A Note on
Menacing Ingredients

No good can come of telling the reader how to breed a Firechicken or indicating in which forest one might find the Orcus Fox.

We shall not disclose the whereabouts of the Sabre Tiger nor reveal the name of the sea that the Vampire Squid frequents.

We have no advice to communicate on the cultivation of Eelweeds.

We do not intend to make public any knowledge on the creation of Wrath Ribbons, nor shall we divulge the ways and wherefores of gathering Lightning Strife.

No word shall be written on the ethics of collecting Harpy feathers.

Of the Croakstone we shall say only this: avoid on pain of death.

~ NOLI NOCERE ~

New Ingredients Discovered by the Proprietor of this Book

Acknowledgements

Much like making a magical hat, it takes a lot of love and dedication from many people to create a book. I have so many people to thank for helping to bring *The Hatmakers* to life.

Firstly, my parents, for bringing me and my siblings up in a house full of books, for reading us bedtime stories when we were small and teaching us to care about literature as much as you do. Thank you, Mum and Dad, for always encouraging me to write.

My sister, Kate (aka Big-Little), for going on adventures with me across the garden and across the globe, for helping me with my Latin and being my absolute favourite person to be a mischief-maker with.

My family and friends around the world who have patiently listened as I philosophized about magical hats: you've encouraged me through the hard times and lavishly celebrated the victories, and I love you all.

ACKNOWLEDGEMENTS

My truly brilliant agent, Claire Wilson: you have worked your extraordinary magic on me and on *The Hatmakers*, and I am so tremendously glad. Thank you for *everything*.

My utterly wonderful editor Nat Doherty, for believing in *The Hatmakers*, for guiding me with such kindness and vision to transform this story into the best version of itself. It has been such glorious fun making this book with you!

Thank you to all the fantastic Makers of Books at Puffin: Wendy Shakespeare, for your brilliance and for making the book better with every suggestion; Daphne Tagg, for your amazing eye for detail; Emily Smyth, for your gorgeous vision for the design of Cordelia's world.

To the wonderful Jane Griffiths, Naomi Green, Roz Hutchinson and Alesha Bonser.

To the brilliant Sarah Roscoe, Geraldine McBride, Kat Baker, Toni Budden, Rozzie Todd, Becki Wells and Karin Burnik. And to the marvellous Zosia Knopp, Anne Bowman, Maeve Banham, Susanne Evans and Lena Petzke.

Thank you to Paola Escobar, for bringing the Hatmakers' world to life with the most beautiful illustrations and cover I have ever seen.

To the American team at NYR, especially Simon Boughton and Kristin Allard, an enormous thank you for introducing the Hatmakers to America!

ACKNOWLEDGEMENTS

To Jonathan Barnes, Teacher of Classics: *kleos* to you for ensuring the wild imaginings of the Glossary make grammatical sense!

To Anna James and Catherine Doyle, for your wildly kind and generous words – it is an honour to have quotes from two such wonderful writers on the cover.

To Jonathan Smith, for running the afternoon creative writing club at school and for your friendship ever since. I can draw a line as straight as the string of a kite from the work we did on those afternoons directly to the pages of this book. And to Dr Jo Seldon, who was a wondrous teacher. To Isabella, for sharing so much wisdom about the creative cycle and helping me to find my own.

To the V&A Archives, for the treasures you preserve and lay out on tissue paper for people to study. I have never, before or since, seen such an illustrious bicorn.

And finally to Barney: this book wouldn't exist without you. Thank you for your immense heart and humour and support all through the adventure of telling this story. Thank you for all the love and laughter you bring to my life. And thank you for when I woke you up at 4.30 a.m. one January morning jabbering about a family of magical Hatmakers – thank you for encouraging me to write down my dream.

Tamzin Merchant has been an actor since the age of seventeen. Her acting work has taken her around the world and on a journey through time. She has been a Tudor, a Victorian, a Jacobean and a Georgian. She survived the Blitz in 1940 and succumbed to pneumonia in Edwardian times. She's been an alien, a witch, a doomed queen, a feisty Scottish warrior and a rebellious high-society runaway.

The Hatmakers is Tamzin's first book.

Follow Tamzin on Twitter and Instagram
@tamzinmerchant
#TheHatmakers

Where will the map
lead Cordelia?

Find out as her adventure continues in

THE
MAPMAKERS

SPRING 2022